TO MAKE
THE BITTER
SWEET

DISTRIBUTED BY
CHOICE BOOKS
SALUNGA, PA.17538
WE WELCOME YOUR RESPONSE

TO MAKE THE BITTER SWEET

The Sequel to BEYOND THE DISTANT SHADOWS

PATRICIA DUNAWAY

BETHANY HOUSE PUBLISHERS

MINNEAPOLIS, MINNESOTA 55438

A Division of Bethany Fellowship, Inc.

Published by Bethany House Publishers
A Division of Bethany Fellowship, Inc.
6820 Auto Club Road, Minneapolis, Minnesota 55438

Printed in the United States of America

Library of Congress Cataloging-in-Publication Data

Dunaway, Patricia, 1936–
   To make the bitter sweet.

    I. Title.
PS3554.U4633T6   1986   813'.54   86–18865
ISBN 0–87123–864–0 (pbk.)

THE AUTHOR

PATRICIA DUNAWAY attended Baylor University and South-western Seminary. She has taught fiction writing at Central Oregon Community College for two years. She is married, the mother of three children and they make their home in Bend, Oregon.

CONTENTS

CHAPTER 1

But woe unto you, Pharisees! for ye tithe mint and rue and all manner of herbs, and pass over judgment and the love of God: these ought ye to have done, and not to leave the other undone.
Luke 11:42

"Dr. Jarrett, it has come to my attention that your, um, discontentment with conditions here at Indian Camp hospital is causing some of the others, staff and patients alike, to be, um . . . discontented as well."

Adam Jarrett stared at the portly man who sat across from him. As chairman of the board, Jason Bledsoe was an important man. Adam knew that if he didn't say just the right things, his position at the hospital would be in jeopardy. But he could no more have stifled his reply than he could have stopped breathing. "Mr. Bledsoe, the word *discontented* is much too mild. Conditions here are intolerable."

"Intolerable for you as a doctor, you mean!" Mr. Bledsoe stated matter-of-factly, lowering his bushy brows in disapproval. He was almost bald, with a long, luxuriant brown beard reaching midchest.

"I can't deny working conditions here are the worst I've ever experienced, but that's not what I'm referring to—and you know it." Adam's black eyes probed, daring the man behind the massive dark oak desk to deny his statement.

Mr. Bledsoe couldn't deny it. He scowled and responded strongly, "We're doing the best we can with the funds available, and you should realize that, sir!"

Adam knew from the deepened tone of Mr. Bledsoe's voice that he was getting angry, but he continued. "Your best is pit-

9

ifully lacking. More than that, it's inhuman to treat sick people the way they're treated here."

"You were aware that this facility had certain . . . um, inadequacies when you decided to come here, Dr. Jarrett—"

"Mr. Bledsoe," he interrupted, "the population has grown from the original seven who arrived here in 1898 to sixty-two in the five years since, and there is no room for another bed anywhere. Two, sometimes three patients, are crowded into a tiny room not big enough for one. And to compound the problem, the incipient, advanced, and terminal cases are indiscriminately mingled together." Adam burst out of his maroon, velvet chair and placed both hands flat on the chairman's desk. He leaned forward slightly, trying to keep the anger he felt under control. "Those miserable slave huts in which patients are housed are hardly protection from the summer sun, much less winter cold. The roofs leak and there are cracks in the walls large enough for creatures of the wild to crawl through."

"Are you quite finished, Doctor?"

"No, as a matter-of-fact, I'm not. Has anyone told you about the hideous burns some patients suffered last winter? How some with the anesthetic form of Hansen's disease huddled so close to their small stoves they were burned and weren't even aware of it?"

"No one is saying leprosy isn't a horrible disease," Mr. Bledsoe said, attempting to defuse the powder keg before him. "But these things take time, and we—"

"My patients don't *have* time! Some of them are dying now, and they need better care than I'm allowed to give them."

Possibly feeling at a disadvantage because he was sitting down, Bledsoe pushed back his chair and stood. Unfortunately, he was a good five inches short of Adam's six feet. Nevertheless, he drew himself up to his full stature. "Sir, you force me to tell you that my colleagues on the board also question whether you are the man we need in this hospital."

"Really. Well, I wonder if your esteemed colleagues have any idea how far short this facility falls from living up to the name, hospital?" Adam asked, his face grim. "There is no adequate water supply, and often what we do have is abominably tainted. The so-called kitchen is a disgrace. There are no tubs for medicated baths, medical supplies are grossly insufficient, and I have no equipment to carry on the research that is vital if we intend to beat this disease." He paused, recalling his own laboratory at Greenlea, all the supplies and books that had burned in the senseless fire those prejudiced maniacs had set. "Mr. Bledsoe, we don't even have surgical instruments!"

"Equipment like that is not easily come by," Mr. Bledsoe defended, his bushy brows lowered as though he felt they were a defense against Adam's onslaught.

"But do you have plans to supply us adequately?"

The blunt question had to be faced. "Dr. Jarrett, we are doing the best we can! Why, think of the generous contributions made last year—"

"As best as I can calculate, those 'contributions' consisted of mixed nuts, baseballs, cigars, rocking chairs, sofa pillows, harmonicas, firecrackers, a billiard table, guava preserves, garden seeds, and a subscription to the *Pittsburgh Star*."

"Now wait a minute! Those are all useful things, given by people who care about these poor lepers—"

"I'll not deny that they were nice things, but what we really need are medical supplies, capable nurses and doctors who want to change the deplorable conditions of those confined here!"

Mr. Bledsoe took a deep breath. "Dr. Jarrett, I have been given authority to terminate your position by the board if—"

"You mean fire me? Won't that be a little difficult, considering the fact that I volunteer my services?"

Mr. Bledsoe rubbed a hand over his perspiring head. "I feel, that is, we all agreed if you and I could not reach an amicable agreement—"

"Not likely."

"—that it would be best for all concerned if you were to cease to offer your services here," finished Bledsoe in a rush, as though he knew he must say the words quickly or they might not come out at all. His expression was tinged with apprehension as Adam stepped against the desk which divided the two men.

"And how do you propose to replace me?" Adam's words were dangerously quiet. "Hollis Freman is a fine doctor, but he is young and his practice in Planquemine is flourishing. You'll pardon me if I don't believe it will be easy to find a reputable physician willing to come to this godforsaken place."

"Almost anyone would be better than you," muttered Bledsoe as he edged toward the door. Whether he intended to show

Adam out or merely wanted some distance between them was a tossup. "You have constantly stirred up the patients—"

"Who should be aware of their rights—or their lack of them. Here, they have none, and they're made to suffer the most inhumane medical treatment—if you can grace it with that term."

"The sisters do a fine job," stated Mr. Bledsoe with conviction.

"That's right, they work very hard. I never meant to imply they don't, but it's not enough!"

"You don't have the slightest notion about the processes involved in administering a facility of this kind, Dr. Jarrett." The chairman opened the big double doors and escaped into the foyer, his relief comically obvious.

"It's you," Adam said, following him into the hall, "who don't have the slightest notion of what it takes to run a hospital for the benefit of the patients—you and that board, wielding its almighty power like a club." Fists clenched at his sides, black brows low over his black, piercing eyes, Adam stared hard at the man. "You might stand correct on one point: maybe I'm not the best man for the job."

"A colossal understatement," agreed Mr. Bledsoe under his breath. A great deal more loudly he added, "At any rate, as of the first of August—that's tomorrow—" he said pointedly, "we will no longer require your services."

Adam bit back the angry retort that rushed to his lips when he saw three sisters standing nearby, their heads turned in great interest at the conversation between him and Mr. Bledsoe. Without another word, he walked out of the stately old mansion, glad to be in the open air no matter how hot and moisture-laden it was. They'd had rain several times that week already, and the gray afternoon sky promised more.

Adam Jarrett walked slowly, almost aimlessly down the brick walkway, unaware of the heavy, sweet scent of magnolia and the lighter overtones of honeysuckle. He felt so alone, so far from his native New York. When he came to the low hedge intended to separate the "pure, untainted" likes of Mr. Bledsoe from *them*, he stopped, fists clenched, the terrible injustice of it all filling him again with anger.

The very hedge at his feet was a symbol of that injustice. The bushes that were now low would grow and grow, broadening the miserable distance between those with the dreaded disease and those without. He agonized at the thought of telling the patients who trusted him that he must leave. Another feeling crowded in, one that was unfamiliar to the self-assured, close-to-arrogant Adam Jarrett—regret. Regret that he had not kept his feelings in check with Mr. Bledsoe, that he had caused his association here at Indian Camp to be severed.

"Dr. Adam?"

Startled, he looked around and saw Rose, her pale-blue eyes wide and anxious. "Rose, what are you doing here?"

"I was watching for you to come out. I . . . we all knew you were talking to Mr. Bledsoe. You seemed so angry just now; did something happen?"

Adam stared down at her plain face, as yet unmarked by the disease that had brought them all to this godless place. Even now he balked at calling it leprosy. He had embarked on a personal crusade to educate people to call it Hansen's disease, after the man who first isolated the hateful bacillus. "Yes, Rose," he said gently, "something happened. Depending on how you look at it, I was fired, or I quit."

As he'd anticipated, Rose's face paled even more as she gasped, "But why?"

"Mr. Bledsoe and his hospital board feel I'm not suited to Indian Camp."

"Who is?" she asked bitterly.

"Be that as it may, he told me my services are no longer wanted as of the first of the month—tomorrow." He gazed at the tall pecan trees, their towering branches draped by gray moss. Beyond them he could see the marshy meadow, and nearby was the Mississippi River, invisible because of the high levee.

"But you can't leave us!"

"It seems I have no choice. The board has decided I don't belong here, that I'm not the kind of doctor they want tending you."

"But it isn't true! Don't they know what you did for me, for Anson and Jimmy and the others? What you've done since we came here?"

Adam knew she was referring to his constant protests against the inadequate medical supplies, the unsanitary food preparations and living conditions. "What I do doesn't matter,

Rose; it's what I am and what I say that offends them."

"They just don't know you." Rose stopped in the middle of the brick pathway that led to where she knew he kept his buggy. "Dr. Adam, isn't there some way you can change their minds? What will we do without you?" Tears streamed down her face as she twisted her hands as if they were in pain.

Her words echoed in his mind. *Ah, Rose, the question is, what will I do without all of you?* The patients with whom he'd come to Indian Camp had taken up his thoughts, his very life, for so long, he already felt the gnawing emptiness of an existence without them. With heavy heart he declared, "I'm afraid it's settled."

"But if you . . . apologized, if you—"

"No, I can't do that. They're wrong about a lot of things, but perhaps they're right about believing I'm not the man for this job."

"How can you say that?" she whispered.

"Because in the fourteen months I've been here I've not accomplished one thing—except stir up trouble." He started walking again, and she caught his arm.

"That's not so, Dr. Adam. You gave us hope, you made us believe . . ."

He stared down at her anxious face, at the plain brown hair tied back severely at the nape of her neck, the drab dress. Hope. She said he had given them hope. How could that be, when he had none himself? Clasping her hand with his, he said, "Rose, you must never give up hope. Dr. Freman and Landra will be here, and I'll keep in touch. Maybe I'll be able to come back in time." He knew deep inside it was an empty promise.

"Oh, Dr. Adam, I hope so!"

He nodded. "And now I must go and tell Landra and Hollis . . . and Carrie."

Carrie. As Adam said goodbye to Rose and promised to look in on Jimmy before he left, it was Carrie Chaumont, his son Rob's nurse, who was foremost in his mind. It had been only six months since he'd sent for them, and as he harnessed his horse, it was not difficult to imagine what she would say; he was certain she would be upset and frightened.

Late that afternoon he sat in the tiny front room of the house he'd rented for Carrie and Rob, holding his son and listening in surprise as she calmly said, "Maybe it's for the best that it happened, Adam. I know how the place upsets you." Her confident face carefully disguised the tumultuous feelings within. "What are your plans?"

"I hadn't thought much beyond the fact that there is certainly no work for me around here."

"That's true. And if I'm not mistaken, the money is very low." Her voice was steady, but her eyes betrayed her outer calm. "You certainly don't have to worry about paying me, but I understand that you must find employment, and soon. It won't take long to pack Rob's and my things—"

"Now hold on, Carrie," Adam interrupted. "You're right, the money is low. But there's enough to keep you and Rob here until I find a suitable place to settle."

"We won't stay behind this time, Adam, so don't even consider it!" The color in her cheeks rose as it always did when her emotions ran high.

"I don't have the faintest idea of where I'll be going, and we both know that for you to travel alone with me would be bad for your—"

"Reputation?" she supplied when he stopped. "Adam, you of all people should remember I didn't have much of a reputation when you first met me." She glanced at Rob, who was dozing against his father's chest. "Surely you can see how much being near you has done for him." *And for me,* her heart silently cried.

"But to drag him along from place to place is not the best way to raise a child," objected Adam.

"To be with you, his father, is what's best for him." Her blue eyes challenged his. "Can you manage with Rob by yourself?"

"You know I need someone to take care of him while I work."

"I won't keep him here for you, Adam. You've got to take your son with you."

"Which means I take you as well." His words were slow, measured; his black brows were drawn low in a near scowl.

"That's right." Carrie's chin was high, but the uncertainty she felt was in her voice as she whispered, "Is that such a terrible prospect?"

"Of course not!" he answered gruffly. "It's just that my future is so uncertain. I will not go back to New Orleans, or even to New York."

"Then let's go west," Carrie quietly suggested.

"West?" For the first time since he'd come there was a look

of something—not quite hope, but almost—on his face. Slowly he said, "How many men running from something have done just that, set their sights west."

"Do you have a better idea?"

"No," he admitted, looking as though his head hurt, "I don't."

"When do you want to leave?" she asked as she rose.

"Early tomorrow morning. Can you get packed and ready on such short notice? There's not much point in staying here."

A brief smile lit Carrie's face. "Of course, Adam!"

He stared up at her for a moment, then stood, the sleeping Rob cradled in his arms. "I'll put him down and let him sleep while you work." When he returned from the boy's room and started to leave, Carrie caught his arm.

"Adam, I promise you'll never regret taking me with you." She tried to keep the yearning she felt in her heart, not at all certain she'd succeeded. She wanted desperately for him to say he needed . . . no, wanted her with him as badly as she wanted it.

"This isn't fair to you, we both know that."

"Rob needs you, and . . . he needs me, too. I'm the only mother he's ever known." She realized it was risky to bring up Rob's natural mother, Bethany. Carrie knew the ghost of Bethany Jarrett stood between her and the man she'd loved since he'd first come and asked if she would care for his newborn son. Until he let go of his dead wife's memory, he would never be free to love her. But Carrie Chaumont was determined to win this hurting man's love.

Adam went to the window and stared out, his shoulders slumped in such dejection that Carrie was touched to her core. With a calm strength that surprised her, she affirmed, "From now on I'm going with you, wherever you go, Adam."

He turned to face her. "It doesn't seem right."

"But it will be, you'll see." She looked up pleadingly into his eyes, exercising every shred of willpower she possessed to keep herself from putting her arms around him, drawing him close and comforting him as she did Rob. "You'd best be going. I'm sure you want to speak with Dr. Freman and Landra."

"Yes, of course," he replied slowly; "that's exactly what I have to do, and I'm not looking forward to it."

"I'll be ready in the morning," Carrie said softly, for he was already moving toward the door.

"I'll come by at seven," he said. "I don't know the train schedule, but we should probably be there before eight."

"I'll be waiting." Carrie stood in the doorway and waved to him as he drove away, a fierce, determined hope filling her. *He'll love me, he will! I'll make him love me.*

When Adam pulled up at the little bungalow on the other side of the village where Landra and Hollis Freman had set up housekeeping after they were married, he felt warmed at the sight of light spilling from their windows. Being with Landra, Bethany's sister, helped him remember Bethany before her illness. The aroma of some rich stew came drifting out as Landra answered his knock and cried delightedly, "Adam! You're just in time for supper!"

"I didn't come to eat," he protested.

Hollis, as pleased to see him as Landra, joined in, "Dr. Jarrett, of course you'll eat with us. Unless you've eaten already?"

"No, I haven't. But I came to tell you something."

"Then tell us over supper," insisted Landra as she drew him toward the attractively set little table, her green eyes alight with justifiable pride at the domestic scene she'd set with such care. "Hollis says I've become quite a good cook," she said as she went to get another plate.

Hollis enthusiastically agreed. "That she has, Dr. Jarrett. Sit down, and tell us your news."

As Adam sat down, Landra returned and began dishing up her savory meal. "The news can wait," Adam decided. "Let's eat first." The conversation as they ate centered mainly on the patients at the leper home. Hollis added some brighter notes about the patients who'd begun to come in increasing numbers to the office he'd set up in the village.

Landra laughed. "He certainly keeps me busy. So busy that . . ." She trailed off and got an almost shy look on her face, which was unusual for Landra. "That I don't know what I'll do when the baby comes."

"You're going to have a child?" asked Adam softly as she nodded. "Landra, I'm so glad!" He hesitated, then added, "I regret very much that I won't be around when the baby is born."

"You're leaving?" asked Hollis, his look on Adam keen. "Is this your news?"

"Why, Adam? Why would you want to leave?" cried Landra.

Briefly he told them of the afternoon's conversation with Mr. Bledsoe. "You can't make me believe you haven't seen it coming."

Hollis didn't deny it, but obviously he couldn't allow Adam's efforts to go unremarked, either. "You've worked unceasingly, and for no financial remuneration whatever. I've half a mind to go to the board and protest—"

"No, Hollis," interrupted Adam, shaking his head wearily. "At all costs you have to maintain your association with the board that operates at Indian Camp. The patients need you desperately, Rose and Jimmy in particular. I went to tell Jimmy goodbye this afternoon, and he was quite bitter. But then, he's bitter about everything these days, isn't he?"

"We'll be here for them, Adam. But they need you, too," said Landra passionately.

"I'm not so sure anymore." Not even trying to hide the heavy discouragement he felt, Adam rubbed the spot between his eyes. "Maybe it's for the best that I leave."

"You can't believe that," challenged Hollis. He scowled and asked, "Just where do you plan to go?"

"West," answered Adam simply. "Beyond that, I don't yet know."

"You're bound and determined to do this?" asked Landra. At his slow nod she said, "We'll look after Rob and Carrie, won't we, Hollis?"

Before Hollis could voice his agreement Adam said, "She insists on going with me."

"And you agreed?" It was clear that Hollis was surprised.

"When I say *insists*, I mean just that. She refuses to be left behind this time." Adam stood up and looked at the two of them. "Thank you for that good meal, Landra. I'll always remember this special time with you two."

"Oh, Adam, won't you reconsider?" his sister-in-law begged.

He shook his head. "I'll write when we get settled somewhere, and you must let me know immediately when the baby is born. Hollis, I don't want to impose, but would you please drive us to the train station early tomorrow morning?"

"Of course." Both he and Landra, who was obviously fighting tears, followed Adam to the door.

Adam smiled a little as he brushed a tear from her cheek.

"A sure sign you're pregnant. The Landra I know doesn't cry so easily."

"Easily? Adam, how can you say that? I'll miss you terribly, and I'll miss Rob . . ." She choked a little. "It's not goodbye forever, is it?"

Gruffly he answered, "Of course not." He allowed himself one light kiss on her forehead and a hard handshake to Hollis.

"God go with you," she called as he walked to his buggy and climbed in.

To himself he muttered, "I don't think so. God turned his back on me a long time ago . . ." He gave the horse a smart slap with the reins and the buggy moved into the darkness, away from the brightly lit house, away from everything that meant anything to Adam Jarrett.

CHAPTER 2

Is there no balm in Gilead; is there no physician there? why then is not the health of the daughter of my people recovered?
Jeremiah 8:22

The first thing Adam Jarrett noticed when he, Carrie, and Rob stepped off the train at the Beaumont, Texas, station the next day was a still, white-faced woman lying on the muddy planks of the platform. Although there was a milling crowd of people, no one paid any attention to her or to the young woman with bright red hair kneeling beside her.

Just then the red-haired woman looked up and scanned the crowd. "The doctor . . . is he coming yet? Does anyone see him?" Her voice, low and controlled, was edged with anxiety.

Adam, bag in hand, stepped forward. "I'm a doctor, miss."

Carrie's hand immediately reached for his arm. "Adam, maybe it would be better if we don't get involved. After all, it looks like she's expecting another doctor, and I don't think it's good for Rob to see this." The little boy was peeking curiously from behind her skirts.

"I can't just let her go without care," declared Adam.

"But she looks like a—" Carrie halted, but her meaning was clear.

Adam's expression showed he couldn't agree with her more. The pale-faced woman was obviously a "lady of the evening," with her bold crimson dress and heavy makeup. But that didn't keep him from crossing the distance between them in a couple of strides. He knelt beside the unconscious girl. "What happened?"

The red haired woman wore a dress the color of coffee and her eyes, large and as dark a brown as her dress, met Adam's.

"I expect she was trying to get away from her . . . her manager, and he smacked her harder than he intended. She must have hit her head when she fell," she said, glancing up toward a tough-looking man standing nearby.

Adam was examining the ugly, gaping wound on the girl's cheekbone from which a trickle of blood flowed. He gave the man a glaring look that, after a couple of seconds, made him turn and stalk away.

"This certainly will require stitches. Did you say a doctor is on the way?" he asked the young woman still hovering over the girl.

"Maybe, maybe not."

"I'm afraid I don't understand."

"Dr. Melrose is a drinking man, sure as the world," the young woman said in her low, faintly Irish brogue. "Now, he's a good enough doctor when he's sober. But when he's not, well . . ." She shrugged her shoulders. "It might be better if you do what has to be done, if you've a mind to, that is."

"Here?" Adam's reluctance showed as he looked around. The sound of curses split the air from time to time, adding to the general confusion as mule skinners "encouraged" their teams. With the long whips singing a grim song on their backs, the animals labored to pull heavy wagons laden with oil-well supplies through the deep mud of the narrow street that ran beside the train station.

"Well," she decided, "I suppose it would be all right if we took the girl to the hotel, for as long as it takes to patch her up. Mum will pitch a fit if we mess up her kitchen, though."

"Her kitchen?"

At Adam's questioning frown she said, "She's the cook at the Crosby Hotel. It's supposed to be the best in town, so no rude remarks when you see it." Her brown eyes twinkled a little. "By the way, my name's Jeannie Gallagher."

"Adam Jarrett." He was about to introduce Carrie, but Jeannie Gallagher had turned back to the injured girl, who murmured and tried to sit up, then fell back. "Careful, now. The doctor will have you right again in two shakes of a lamb's tail."

Between the two of them, Adam and Jeannie carefully helped the injured girl across the muddy street, dodging riders on horseback and mule-drawn wagons. Carrie followed, her face set, with Rob in tow. At not quite three the child was obviously fascinated by the noisy, chaotic scene, his bright eyes taking it all in.

If the Crosby Hotel is the best in town, I'd hate to see the others, thought Adam as they approached the frame structure that had a second story added on behind. A wide gallery, partitioned into narrow stall-like places, ran around the entrance. Each stall was occupied by men who seemed to be selling something, for money was changing hands at an amazing rate. The excitement in the place was high, and Adam thought he'd never seen so much money.

"What in the world is going on?" he asked as they stepped inside.

"You mean you don't know about the Spindletop oil boom?" asked Jeannie in surprise. "Why, it's been like this since Lucas brought in his first well two years ago, out in Gladys City."

Remembering a half-listened-to conversation on the train, Adam nodded. "Where can we lay her down?"

"Like I said, the kitchen's the best, if Mum doesn't catch us." Once again her dark eyes twinkled, and her mouth quirked in a smile.

"Adam?" Carrie's voice was hesitant as she caught up to them.

He saw the look of uncertain anxiety on her face. Gently he said, "You and Rob should probably wait here, Carrie."

Drawing the child even closer, she glanced around. A blue haze of cigar, pipe, and cigarette smoke hung over the noisy throng of humanity swirling around them. "If we could get a room, I believe that would be best for Rob."

"None to be had, here or most anywhere in town," Jeannie replied with a shake of her head. "I'll be happy to let you and your wife have my room, Dr. Jarrett. Doctors are in short supply around here, and long in need."

"Miss Chaumont and I are not married," said Adam, his black eyes unreadable. "She cares for my son Rob." At the mention of his name, Rob peeked around Carrie's skirts at Jeannie, who smiled, then winked at him. He grinned back, then ducked his head again.

"Well, Miss Chaumont, maybe you'd not be minding sharing my room with me, and we'll try and find a spot for Dr. Jarrett. Though as you can see, even the chairs in the lobby here are rented twenty-four hours a day. Why, I've even heard them tell of buying a ticket on the train so they can sleep on the coach overnight, then getting a ticket back to Beaumont the next morning!"

Carrie soon realized there was no other avenue open to her. For some reason she also felt the need to be wary of the warm, red-haired Jeannie Gallagher. "Thank you, Miss Gallagher, but we don't want to put you out."

"I don't mind a'tall. My room's the last door on the left," she said, pointing down the hallway. A little moan from the painted doll of a woman who sagged between her and Adam took her attention then.

Carrie, having had experience with Adam's single-mindedness, said, "Come along, Rob, we'll find a place where you can take a nap."

"No nap!" was his wailing reply. After a pleading glance at his father, who shook his head, he allowed Carrie to take his hand, and followed as she made her way down the hall.

In the spacious kitchen, Adam set to work immediately on the girl's wound, cleansing it, then swiftly stitching it before she regained full consciousness. Fortunately, the lighting was good, and Jeannie anticipated his needs with amazing efficiency. As he was carefully tying off the last stitch, two things happened almost simultaneously. The girl awoke, and Reba Gallagher returned to her kitchen.

"What's all this?" a voice boomed. "What are you doing in my kitchen? Jeannie, if I've told you once, I've told you a million times, I don't want you messing up my kitchen!" A small, red-haired woman stood in the doorway, her face screwed up into a fierce scowl, hands on her ample hips. But as she came near to the girl who lay on the long oak table she used to prepare the mammoth meals three times a day, her expression softened in spite of herself. "Girl, you ought to be with your mother instead of in a mess like this!"

The girl, dizzy but recovering fast, swung her shapely legs over the side of the table. Once on her unsteady feet, she was obviously determined to leave on her own. "Thanks, Doc. Don't have no money, but Jake will pay you." She touched her cheek cautiously. "I shoulda knowed better than to try to run off like that."

"You can't mean you intend to go back to him?"

"Where else have I got to go?" She glanced back at Mrs. Gallagher. "My mama sure wouldn't have me. Wait here, Doc. I'll get your money from Jake."

None of the three made a move to stop her as she headed out the door. Within a couple of minutes she was back with the money.

"Thanks again, Doc. Hope I don't need you again. Guess I shore learned my lesson." Her young-old eyes flickered over Jeannie's concerned face and that of her scowling mother, then came to rest on Adam's. "By the way, the name's Ginger. Maybe I'll see you around, hmm?"

After she had left, Adam said, "Are there many like her here in Beaumont?"

"More than you can count," Jeannie said quietly. "And their managers, and gamblers and saloonkeepers on every corner and thousands of oil-crazed men bent on making their fortunes. They say it's worse than the gold-rush towns."

Mrs. Gallagher, proceeding to wash down the table added, "And isn't that the very reason we came, Jeannie, to make a little money? We're not all that different from the others, I guess. How about you, Doctor? Did you come to Beaumont to make your fortune?"

Adam met her bright, inquisitive eyes for a moment, then looked away. "Ah . . . no, Mrs. Gallagher, I . . . we were just on our way to . . ."

"Who's we? Your missus?" she asked cheerfully when he paused. "By the way, I'm Reba Gallagher."

"Not his missus, Mum." Jeannie, intuitively sensing Adam's reluctance to reveal any personal details, said. "It's his little boy's nanny, Miss Chaumont. She and his boy are going to share my room."

"A little boy you say? Now isn't that nice." A fond smile lit the older woman's features. "Your wife will be coming on later, then?" Her curiosity didn't have a malicious edge, but to Adam it seemed relentless.

"My wife is . . . is no longer with us." Adam cursed himself inwardly for wording it that way, for it was an extremely ambiguous answer and could be taken in more ways than one. He was about to add something further to the effect that they would not be staying long when Jeannie spoke up.

"We need to find a place to put a cot up for the doctor, Mum. It's a good thing you've come, Dr. Jarrett, for the need here is truly great." She stopped, her brown eyes studying him. "Would you go with me to meet Dr. Melrose? I've got a notion he never left his office."

"I . . ." Somehow Adam could no more break away from her steady gaze than he could voice his earlier decision, made a few moments after they'd stepped off the train, to leave Beaumont immediately.

"Please?"

"I guess it wouldn't hurt to talk with him," said Adam slowly, wondering why he agreed to go. "But I should tell Carrie first."

"Good. I'll arrange for a hack. You haven't lived 'til you've seen a boom town close up!" Jeannie Gallagher kissed her mother on the cheek and was gone, leaving the room somehow less bright; her very presence seemed to generate energy.

Adam nodded to Mrs. Gallagher, and was off to find Carrie and Rob.

He took very little time glancing around the room to which Jeannie Gallagher had directed Carrie. It was neat, but sparsely furnished with a bed, a washstand, and a small rocker. Carrie sat in the rocker, holding a sleepy Rob close. His legs almost reached the floor, Adam noticed with a pang; he was going to be tall. It wasn't right to drag him around like this . . .

With the strain of the past twenty-four hours in her voice, Carrie asked softly, "Adam, are we going to stay here?"

He took a deep breath. "I'm not sure. There does seem to be plenty of work, and we're short of money. I'm sorry about all this, Carrie. You and Rob shouldn't have to be uprooted and subjected to all this."

"It doesn't matter, if we're together." She kissed Rob, who looked up and smiled sleepily at his father; then his eyes fluttered shut again.

Adam nodded. "I'm going to meet this Dr. Melrose that Miss Gallagher talked about. Maybe I can work with him until we get enough saved to move on." He didn't say there was no place to go; they both knew that. They also both knew that the heartbreak they'd left behind at Indian Camp would follow them no matter where they went, but he didn't say that, either.

"You'll be back soon?"

The appeal tugging at him made him feel guilty about leaving her, but he forced himself to gently say, "As soon as I can. Don't worry. I have the feeling you're safe with the Gallaghers." He laid a hand on Rob's head for an instant. "When he wakes up I'm sure Miss Gallagher's mother will be glad to give you some lunch. Robbie, no doubt will be hungry."

"Is she . . . will Miss Gallagher be here?"

"No, she's going along to introduce me to Dr. Melrose."

"I see." Her hand touched Adam's, light as a butterfly, then silently withdrew. "I . . . we'll be waiting for you, Adam."

"Don't worry, Carrie. We'll work it all out," he said gruffly. Then, because he could not bear the subtle pleading in her eyes any longer, he kissed the sleeping child's head and left.

Jeannie Gallagher was waiting in the hall. "Well, Doctor, are you ready for your introduction to the great boom town of Beaumont?"

Adam didn't return her smile. Something deep within him, something vague but very strong, made him resist its warmth. "Miss Gallagher—"

"You must call me Jeannie," she interrupted, "if I'm going to help you find a job."

She started in the direction of the lobby and Adam followed, carrying his bag. "I haven't decided to stay."

She glanced back at him as they came once again into the hotel lobby, then out to the makeshift gallery beyond. "I think you will have a much better chance to make your fortune than all those fellas."

"I suppose," was all he could say. Intense excitement filled the air. Adam had to admit that in his quiet, secluded life as a research scientist, he'd never seen so much money. The blue-prints of the Spindletop oil fields plastering the walls made a vivid contrast to the seemingly endless stacks of greenbacks.

Well-dressed businessmen stood shoulder to shoulder with slicker-suited drillers and oil-grimed roughnecks, while the men operating the stalls, working as fast as they could, ex-changed oil leases for greenbacks. The noise of the furious trad-ing, of higher pitched women's voices plying their trade, of curses expelled for one reason or another, made the air thick with more than smoke—with feverish humanity.

Outside, the steadily falling rain was a welcome. "There's our hack," said Jeannie. "Uncle Jude, Mum's brother, is the driver, but it's not his favorite occupation."

Adam tried to wipe the mist from his face, then decided it was wasted effort. "What would he rather be doing?" he asked politely.

"He'd rather be back home in the Thicket. Uncle Jude works just enough to live, and I've never known him to let work get in the way of pleasure. That means hunting, fishing, walking trails that most people can't even see," she finished cheerfully.

"Doesn't sound too ambitious," murmured Adam.

"Ambitious?" Jeannie laughed. "Why, he radiates unambition, if there is such a thing! And right now he's sick and tired of big city life and wants to go home."

She waved to the tall, cadaver-lean driver of a hack that had seen better days. It was hitched to a couple of muckledy-dun horses standing hock deep in the Texas gumbo mud, appearing less than enthusiastic about another run. "Uncle Jude!" she called, grasping Adam's arm and pulling him along the plank sidewalk, "here we are!" He waved back at her with a wicked-looking whip.

For a small woman she has surprisingly strong fingers, thought Adam as he helped her up into the hack, then took his seat, with Jeannie between him and the grinning, tobacco-chewing driver who spat into the street and said, "Howdy. The name's Jude, Jude Chapman."

"Adam Jarrett."

"Dr. Jarrett," amended Jeannie. "Uncle Jude, would you please take us to Gladys City to see Dr. Melrose?"

"Shore, honey-gal." Jude leaned forward and cracked his whip just above the bony backs of the hopeless-looking horses. All three passengers fell back onto the lumpy, sagging seat whose springs had died long ago when the startled animals lunged forward.

As he threaded his way among the throng of other hacks and muddy-footed pedestrians, Jude said, "Been in Beaumont long, Doc?" Before Adam could frame an answer, the man shot another brown stream of tobacco juice into the mud and went on. "Ain't this a pistol? Beats anything I ever saw. It was the Lucas gusher two years ago what started this whole blooming mess. Come in with a galloping roar—on January 10, 1901, to be exact."

He stopped his recital for a few seconds as he navigated a turn. Adam glanced at Jeannie, whose little smile told him she'd heard all this before. Interested, Adam responded, "This is all new to me; go on, Mr. Chapman."

"I was planning to, and call me Jude. Well, anyhow, that there oil gushed out, shot up into the sky and floated on the wind, it did. People come from everywhere to see it." He grinned. "Folks in Beaumont wasn't so pleased about having to have all their houses repainted."

"Just how far did the oil go?" asked Adam.

"Well, I dunno 'zactly how fur, but it was the sulphur gas what tarnished the house paint. Made a right proper mess, it did." He cracked his whip at the nags, and the hack moved almost briskly down the magnolia-lined street. Jude grinned again. "I don't never touch 'em, but they don't know I'm not gonna."

Occasionally the horses misstepped into one of the deep holes made by the wagons carrying heavy machinery and pipe to the oil fields. The old hack lurched back and forth like an old boat on a storm-tossed sea. Adam gathered that it didn't seem to bother the red-haired girl at his side nor the driver, and they were soon out of Beaumont proper. Once out of town, he noticed that there was nothing but flat, dreary-looking salt-grass prairie land with only an occasional scrubby tree to break the monotony.

As the first oil derrick came into view, Jude obviously felt it was his duty to inform Adam of its history, the name of each member of the company who owned it, even the driller's name. Adam found his attention wandering. He wanted to know about Dr. Melrose, what kind of office he had, and whether or not his practice was large enough to accommodate two doctors. When Jude brought the horses to a halt in front of a broken-down building, Adam thought he'd made a mistake until he saw a rough, four-inch board nailed to the door with Dr. Melrose's name crudely painted on it. The sign was the only distinguishing difference between the doctor's "office" and the other dreary, unkempt buildings on the makeshift street.

"I'll wait for you, honey-gal," said Jude as Adam helped her out of the hack. She nodded, and the two of them walked up the broken steps and entered a curtained-off place that obviously served as a waiting room. There was only one dirty little window, but several cracks in the wide board walls let in the weak afternoon light. A man who looked to be around fifty stepped out from behind the curtain.

"Dr. Melrose," said Jeannie, "do you remember me?"

" 'Course I do, girl," he acknowledged, his heavy, puffy eyes on Adam. "You're the one who delivered that breech baby over at Batson. Did a good job of it, too. Who's this you got with you, a patient for me?" His tired face bore signs of years of dissipation, and when he came closer, Adam could smell stale whiskey on his breath, the food-spotted vest, the soiled linen.

He reached out his hand to Dr. Melrose. "I'm Adam Jarrett."

"Dr. Jarrett," put in Jeannie, who stood back a little as the two men eyed each other.

"Is that a fact," muttered Melrose, unintentionally ignoring the outstretched hand. "Doctor, I do believe you may be just what the doctor ordered," he said, a liquor-laced bark of laughter making Adam draw back slightly. "Tell me about yourself, where you trained, your experience."

Wanting to refuse, to turn around and walk out, Adam felt compelled to do as the man said. "I was trained and served my internship in New York City."

"And since then?"

Adam hesitated, not wanting to disclose the nature of his research, or the death of Bethany and Anson and the awful events which had led to his fleeing Greenlea. And he most certainly did not want to mention that he had been dismissed at the leper hospital at Indian Camp. So he merely said, "I've been engaged in research at Tulane University in New Orleans for the past few years. Why do you ask?" Counter a question with another question, he'd been taught.

The tobacco-stained mustache which covered a sizable portion of Dr. Melrose's pock-marked face twitched. "Because I believe you are just the man I've been looking for."

"How so?" queried Adam, glancing at Jeannie, whose usually mobile face was now still.

"I've been needing to go on a rootin'-tootin' tear of a drunk and I need a bona-fide doctor to take over here." Melrose went to the rack by the door, took down a dusty black derby hat, and jammed it on his head.

"But I haven't done much practicing of medicine for a long while—"

"You can trust him, Dr. Melrose," interrupted Jeannie smoothly. "Why, I watched him stitch up a girl's face this morning and do a fine job." She cast a sideways glance at Adam, warning him to keep silent.

"Glad to hear it." One hand on the doorknob, one raised in farewell, Dr. Melrose added, "Don't know when I'll be back. Might take a while to rid myself of this raging thirst." With a jaunty wave he was gone, leaving Adam staring at the closed door.

"I don't believe this is happening," he said slowly.

"Believe it," said Jeannie, her smile radiant. "Now don't be getting me wrong, I like Dr. Melrose and all. But he started on this drunk several days ago no matter what he was saying. I'm sure that's why he never came to the train station. A drinking doctor is sometimes worse than none a'tall." She eyed Adam keenly. "Sir, are *you* a drinking man?" Adam, still frowning in disbelief at Melrose's defection shook his head, and Jeannie said, "I believe with all my heart that it is God himself who has brought you to us."

"Miss Gallagher, you could say He drove me here and be nearer the truth."

"You're to call me Jeannie, remember?" she said, obviously choosing to ignore whatever had prompted the cold, angry words. She went and peeked behind the curtain and came back, shaking her head. "We've got a lot to attend to."

"To what end, if I may ask?"

"Why, to make this a place where you can work, Dr. Jarrett. Surely you wouldn't be wanting to leave it like this?" With a broad sweep of her arm she indicated the dirty, shabby room.

"I haven't said I intend to work here."

"Ah, but you will." She smiled, opened the door, and was halfway out as she said, "Be back in a minute."

"Where do you think you're going?"

"To tell Jude to come back for us in a couple of hours. It'll take longer, but we can get started."

Before Adam could protest she was gone, shutting the door quietly behind her, leaving him alone in the grimy little room. The muffled shouts of mule skinners filtered in as Adam turned to inspect the room. Lifting the curtain to the inner office, he walked over to a wooden box in the corner and fingered through the outdated, stained instruments within. He couldn't believe his eyes as he surveyed the room. An ancient operating table stood beneath the one rain-streaked, fly-specked window. On the floor all around the table were dried-up, blood-stained cotton swabs, and nearby a few instruments lying on a rough plank shelf. A half-empty bottle proved to be alcohol; Adam wondered if it had been for surgical procedures or for the doctor's internal use.

The thought uppermost in Adam's mind was the irony of the situation. How often he had bemoaned the inadequacies of Greenlea, and recently his dismissal from Indian Camp due to his persistent protests concerning its inadequate facility. The word "inadequate" was a joke here. This place wasn't fit to treat animals! Yet, on the other hand, he was sure many humans in dire need had been successfully treated here since the boom began.

What had that young woman said? *God brought you to us . . .* His smile was bitter and grim as he thought, *Well, if God has brought me here, it's for a punishment.* Hearing Jeannie Gallagher's light footsteps behind him, he turned, ready to tell her he was sorry, but this arrangement wouldn't suit him at all.

She was already rolling up her sleeves. "Let's get to work, Dr. Adam," she stated, smiling broadly. "I've a notion 'twon't be long a'tall before a bloody mess walks through that door, needing a doctor."

Adam had no idea why he conceded. "All right," he said, setting his bag down, "I'll tend to the instruments first—such as they are." With that the two of them set to work.

CHAPTER 3

. . . and the fruit thereof shall be for meat, and the leaf thereof
for medicine.   *Ezekiel 47:12*

The cleanup operation had scarcely begun when the office
door flew open and two rough-looking, excited men carrying a
third between them entered the office.

"Sure is a good thing you cleaned up the instruments first,
Doctor," said Jeannie as she stood aside to let them pass.

They'd obviously been in the office before, for they went
directly to the inner room and laid the man on the operating
table. "Where's Doc Melrose?" the taller one asked Adam.
"Yancy here got his leg tore open out in the field."

"Dr. Melrose isn't here, he's—"

The other man snorted. "On a drunk, huh?"

"He left me in charge," said Adam, already moving to the
table to examine the man, who had the glazed-eyed look of
shock. His khakis had been ripped to the knee of his left leg,
revealing a gory mess below the red bandanna they'd used to
stop the bleeding.

"Hey, hold on here! Who are you, anyhow?" asked the first
man.

Adam shook off his restraining hand. "I'm Dr. Adam Jarrett,
and I'm going to tend your friend." Before the man could protest
further, Adam had untied the blood-soaked handkerchief. "Severed artery," he murmured as the blood spurted like a small
geyser. Neither of the two offered to interfere further as Adam
stopped the hemorrhage, sewed up the cut, cleaned up the whole
leg, then from his own bag produced a clean bandage to cover
the wound.

The injured man's friends eyed each other, then the taller

32

one said, "You did that a heap sight better'n Melrose could if he was cold sober. Right, Bo?"

His companion nodded. "That's for sure. You practicin' in these parts, Doc?"

Adam glanced at Jeannie, who remained silent now as she had throughout the entire operation. But he saw the challenge in her eyes and found himself saying, "Yes. I'll be working here for a time, at least."

Bo stuck an oil-grimed hand into the pocket of his overalls and drew out a twenty-dollar bill. "Thanks, Doc. We appreciate what you did for Yancy, there. All three of us work over at the Hogg-Swayze tract. You'll come around and check on him?"

It was difficult to suppress the surprise Adam felt as he put the bill away; twenty dollars was far more than he'd expected to receive for an office visit. He kept his expression and voice neutral as he said, "Yes, of course." Thoughtfully, he watched as they picked up the injured man and carried him out the same way they'd carried him in. In the quiet which followed, Adam said slowly, "It would seem I've made a decision."

Jeannie Gallagher's eyes were bright as she said, "One you won't regret, Dr. Adam."

Her use of the name that Rose and Jimmy and the others used made him squeeze his eyes shut for a brief second; thinking of them brought a sudden pain. "That remains to be seen, doesn't it."

She ignored the harsh sound of his words. "Make no mistake, they'll soon circulate the story all around town of how neat you sewed up Yancy."

Adam thought back to the time when he'd been shot, the day the news broke about the plans for a hospital for lepers at Elkhorn, across the river from New Orleans. There'd been grave doubts then that the damaged nerves in his arm would heal, or that he could ever function as a practicing doctor again. Aloud he said simply, "I'm glad I was able to help the man."

"Sure, and for certain. And now, let's finish getting this place in order before someone else comes." Even as she spoke she was in motion, picking up the bloodied handkerchief that had served as a tourniquet and the instruments Adam had used.

For the better part of an hour, the two worked steadily at the formidable task, not speaking much. They stopped only when the door burst open and a boy, no more than ten or eleven years old, spoke breathlessly. "Is the doctor here? My mom sent me. My little sister's not so good!"

Adam nodded, and while he repacked his bag, Jeannie tried to make sense of the boy's garbled recital of his sister's ills, as well as his directions to where he lived.

When they arrived a short while later, Adam was shocked to find the family living in a tent almost surrounded by water and the ever-present mud. A few pieces of half-submerged plank kept the three from sinking up to their ankles in the mire. Inside the tent, two more pale children were huddled together on a makeshift bed placed directly on the dirt floor. The baby, Adam's patient, lay in a large dry-goods box on the kitchen table. Odors of a recent meal lingered in the air, but overriding this was a wretched smell of something dead or dying. Adam glanced at Jeannie and saw the same revulsion in her eyes that he felt.

The mother's anxious blue eyes were dulled by the poverty which surrounded her, but when she picked up the baby girl there was tenderness in her touch, caring love on her face. "Can you help our Susie, Doctor? Seems like she's just wasting away since we got here. And today she won't eat nothing a'tall. I'm . . . I'm afraid for her, or I wouldn't never have bothered you."

The baby, a thin, yellow-faced mite, had a well-developed case of rickets, and he informed the woman of this after a brief examination. The child's poorly bound arm concerned him even more, however; it hadn't taken long to decide that was where the nauseating smell was coming from.

She nodded, obviously not comprehending. "But what can I *do* for her? She just lays there, so still, not hardly moving, even." She hesitated, then said slowly, "I wouldn't have sent for you, only . . . only I got scared she was dying."

The steady beat of the rain outside made Adam reluctant to say, "I can prescribe a tonic, but what she needs is plenty of sunshine. Are you giving her milk?"

"Milk? Sunshine?" The words were close to a sigh. "I'm doing the best I can, Doctor, but my man's got oil fever."

Adam drew a deep breath. "Madam, tell me about the wound on her arm."

"Oh, she fell against the stove," she answered. "I try to keep it covered up and clean, but it's so hard here."

When Adam unwound the soiled rag, he couldn't keep from gasping at the ugliness of the ulcerous wound.

Jeannie saw his reaction and came to stand beside him. She shook her head. "Not good," she murmured, speaking so softly only Adam could hear.

"How long ago did this happen?" he asked the haggard mother.

Vaguely she answered, "Oh, it was before we come here, a month or more, I reckon."

Adam grimaced. To Jeannie he said, his voice low, "I'm afraid she doesn't have much of a chance if we can't get this healed up."

"What are you going to use on it, Dr. Adam?"

"I . . ." Suddenly there was a burst of activity outside the tent and a loud question as to the doctor's whereabouts.

"Here, let me have the wee one," Jeannie quickly said. She took the little girl as a man lifted up the tent flap and peered in.

"Doc, can you come right away? There's a man hurt bad! They told us you were in here—"

Jeannie, holding the thin, sad-faced child close, said, "You go ahead, Dr. Adam. I'll take care of things here and make sure Mrs. Chandler understands what to do for the baby." Adam nodded, then hesitated. "Now don't worry yourself over me getting home," she urged. "I'm used to taking care of myself."

She looked so calm, so certain, so much in control of things that he had no trouble moving toward the flap of the tent to join the man. "I may be late getting back to Crosby Hotel, Miss Gallagher."

"That's likely. Come to the kitchen and someone will have a bite for you and a place for you to rest." She gave him a smile. "Now go on with you. There's no telling what you might find. These men do themselves some terrible harm at times."

He left hurriedly with the man. When they arrived at the accident scene, he was reminded of her parting words. The man lying on the derrick floor not only had a badly fractured leg, but was also bleeding from the head in a couple of places. It was not merely his lack of clinical experience that made Adam reluctant to treat the man; the shamefully unsanitary conditions made it dangerous to do anything for him there. But the inescapable truth was, the man was hurt far too seriously to move without some treatment. His eyes were shut, and Adam wasn't even sure he was conscious as he checked to see the extent of his injuries.

"Pretty bad, huh, Doc?" The boss of the rig broke the silence as he leaned against the wooden upright.

"I certainly can't deny that," admitted Adam as he rummaged in his bag. Though he kept some bandages and a few medicines such as calomel, quinine, and bismuth in it, there wasn't nearly what he needed for the situation facing him. "This man should have an anaesthetic."

For the first time since Adam arrived, the suffering man spoke. "Just give me a big slug of that whiskey Jeb has and go ahead, Doc." Before Adam could respond, one of the drillers handed over an almost-full bottle of whiskey. The man took it in his bloody hand and tipped it up; when he stopped drinking, it was because the bottle was empty. In a short while his words slurred, both from pain and booze, he groaned, "Get it over with, Doc."

With nothing more than some hot water from the boiler and the meager supplies in his bag, Adam set to work on the man, who proved to be a good patient with admirable fortitude. Blood still oozed from his forehead, and while he worked to stop that, Adam instructed the man the driller had left with him to find some pieces of board to use as temporary splints for the broken leg.

The job was far from easy, but when Adam had done all he could and the man had been sent to the hospital on a makeshift stretcher, the boss called out, "Good job, Doc. You're new around here, aren't you?" Adam looked up as he rewrapped his suturing needles in their case and nodded. "Ever seen an oil field up close before?"

"No, as a matter-of-fact, I haven't."

"Then come on, and I'll give you a look-see at this one."

Feeling a curiosity that surprised him, Adam followed the man. The derricks they passed were built very close together, sometimes touching or overlapping each other. Intense excitement filled the air, closely linked to what Adam had observed at the Crosby Hotel earlier. The men, cursing and lashing at the stubborn mules and the teams of unruly oxen, jockeyed impatiently to unload their pipes or machinery.

The man leading Adam through this semiorganized chaos remarked, "They're fixing to bring in a well any minute over on the Keith-Ward tract. I heard the driller say he's just about to the level where they will strike the oil. Been watching close, and I got faith in his judgment. He says the gas pressure is strong, and they should get a gusher. That's something to see—"

He broke off as they neared the derrick of which he spoke; the men working around it were in a frenzy of activity. One of them yelled, "She's coming! Look out, boys!"

Adam heard a bubbling, hissing noise; then the six-inch stream of oil suddenly spouted, with a blowing, roaring sound, into the air several hundred feet above them. The stiff south wind caught it, spraying the oil northward. The fountain covered buildings, tanks and nearby derricks as the crew worked furiously to direct it into a shallow earthen tank off to the side of the rig. Everyone else had obviously seen it many times before and was intent only on doing his job, but Adam found the scene thrilling. He watched in fascination until the boss who'd brought him said, "You'll get used to such sights as this, Doc. Happens all the time."

With an effort Adam broke the trancelike state into which he'd fallen, and nodded. "I should be getting back. If you'll point me toward town, I'd best get started."

"Hey, you ain't intending to walk, are you?"

"Well, I need some time to—" He broke off, reluctant to voice the need he felt to sort out his feelings, to try to make some sense of the turn things had take since they'd gotten off the train in Beaumont that morning. "If I change my mind I can get a ride."

"That's so," said the man, eyeing Adam's black bag. "Like as not we'll be seeing more of you. We try to be careful, but it's a dangerous job, that's for sure. Thanks again, Doc." He was moving away as he spoke, in response to a shout from one of his men.

Adam soon found himself in the general vicinity of his inherited office, and not far from it he spied a pharmacy. Wanting to be prepared for the next emergency, he decided to purchase some supplies and introduce himself to the druggist. As he entered he saw several roughnecks and drillers, and suspected from the way they stopped talking that he might have been the subject of their conversation.

"Hey, Doc, I heard about how good you sewed old Yancy up." He gave a raucous laugh. "Aw, old Melrose did the best he could, but you wouldn't have to be real good to be better. The boys say you are plenty good."

Adam nodded at the tribute, then introduced himself to the

druggist, who must have been feeling the effects of the steady rain outside. His long narrow face didn't lighten much even when Adam gave him a long list of supplies. He was fairly well stocked, and when Adam left a little while later he felt more than ready to meet any emergencies that might come.

He walked aimlessly down the street, the signs assaulting his eyes as the sound of countless voices reached his ears. Barbershops, promising a haircut for 25¢; shaves, 15¢; hair singe for 30¢; the saloons proclaiming, "Boys, if you are not 21, DO NOT COME IN!" "Pabst on tap." "Please!!! Do Not Spit on the Floor." "Free Lunch." Throngs of people were pushing and shoving to take advantage of the multitude of opportunities to spend their money.

None of the gambling houses, or stores, or saloons had doors. Adam concluded it was probably because they were open around the clock. Not having ever been a gambling man, he nonetheless found himself walking into one of the gambling houses. With a curious sense of detachment, he watched the professional gamblers, the pimps, drillers and businessmen standing side by side with the gunmen at the bar. Their filthy stories and arguments and the curses accompanying the heavy drinking mingled with the higher voices of painted women hovering almost at the elbow of every man. After being accosted by a couple of women, one who Adam was sure had been past her prime when he was in knee pants, he made his way out into the night air again, marveling at the mixture of fascination and revulsion that stirred within him.

He walked on, feeling detached, as though nothing he saw really affected him. But on a deeper, almost subconscious level he sensed that this place, with all its chaos, offered something he needed, something he had not had at the leper hospital. He could lose himself here, lose the man he'd become—and hated. There was work enough here to absorb him completely.

By the time Adam got back to the Crosby Hotel, it was almost ten o'clock. Realizing he hadn't eaten anything since his midmorning lunch, he remembered Jeannie's words, *Come to the kitchen*—and did just that. He was surprised to see her there, and grateful for the aroma of ham sizzling on the great iron stove.

"I thought you'd be coming soon," she said as he entered the room. "Come, sit down, and we'll have a bite. Been busy, have you?"

He nodded, and did as she said. Once seated, his weary body reminded him just how long the day had been. Somehow the sight of Jeannie Gallagher, still working, still fresh-looking, irked him. "What are you doing up at this hour? Don't you ever get tired?"

She slid the ham onto a plate and skillfully broke three eggs into the skillet with one hand. "You'd need a stronger word than tired to tell how I feel, Dr. Adam. I've been with a woman who needed a bit of help with her birthing. Took almost a day and half for that wee one to come, and they didn't call me 'til both mother and babe were almost gone."

Once again Adam felt that vague stirring which he couldn't wholly name; it was a combination of grudging admiration and disbelief that anyone could be as good as this young woman seemed to be. Bethany had been, a little voice in his mind whispered. Angrily he shoved the memory of his dead wife to the back of his mind. "I take it they both made it?"

"Yes, praise God for that."

Adam thought more credit was probably due to Jeannie Gallagher than God, but he didn't say so. "It wasn't necessary for you to wait up and cook for me."

Ignoring the brusqueness in his tone, she carefully placed two of the eggs on his plate, the third one on hers. "I was hungry myself." Then sitting opposite from him, she bowed her head for a few seconds, and began to eat.

Because he was very hungry, he downed his food quickly, and had to admit he was grateful she'd gone to the trouble. A bit grudgingly he told her so, then added, "Are you often called to attend births? You seem young for such responsibility."

With a faint smile she said, "I'm twenty-four, Doctor, and I've been bringing babies into the world over half my life."

"You started when you were *twelve*?"

"About that age. I used to go with Grannie Annie, the midwife who delivered me." Jeannie nibbled at the last of her thick slice of homemade bread, eyes full of remembrance. "By the time I was ten I was begging to go along with her. Mum let me, and Grannie Annie discovered I had good hands."

"Good hands?" In spite of himself Adam found he wanted to hear more.

She nodded, her small hands held up, their slender fingers bare of any rings. "I can't explain it any other way except to say that God gifted me. Women in the throes of labor, no matter how difficult, respond to me, to my hands."

Taken without her obvious humility, the words would have been boastful; and as much as Adam wanted not to, he couldn't help but be impressed by them. "I see. So you attend a great many of the women in the area."

"That I do. Of course, I've not had the formal training you've had, Dr. Adam."

He would have preferred that she was arrogant; he had no defense against her humility. It made him unaccountably resentful, and before he could stop himself he declared, "Well, now that I'm about to set up practice here, they'll no doubt seek the services of a real physician."

"Maybe so," she replied with a faint smile.

Then, feeling slightly guilty for his arrogance, Adam said slowly, "I should go back to the Chandlers' first thing in the morning. That child's arm is bad, as bad as I've ever seen."

"Yes, it certainly is." Jeannie took a sip of her milk, then said, "I hope you don't mind; I started a course of treatment."

Curiosity warred with the faint aggravation in Adam's mind. And because he hadn't been at all sure what he intended to do himself, he said, "What kind of treatment, if I may ask?"

"Poultices of comfrey. When you mash the leaves together, a sort of sticky stuff comes out. It's like okra, gluey."

"You mean mucilaginous."

Jeannie shrugged. "I reckon. Anyway, you put it on a cloth, and spread it on the sore. I've seen it cure things lots worse than little Susie's arm if you keep at it."

"I'm not sure I approve of that sort of thing." Even as he spoke the words, he remembered the many remedies he, as well as his colleagues, had tried against Hansen's disease. But he was aware he couldn't bring that up.

"You mean doctoring with herbs?" At his nod she put both arms on the table and leaned forward, her expression earnest, her brown eyes alight with enthusiasm. "Look at it this way, Dr. Adam; we could be kind of like partners."

"Partners," he repeated, resisting her words, her very presence.

"Yes," she said, softly now. "I saw how you were with Susie, and with Ginger. You care, you really care."

"Of course I care." His words were gruff. "Any doctor cares—"

"That's where you're wrong," she broke in gravely. "I've

been around enough doctors to know you're not all alike. You're one of the good ones, and you want these people to have the same thing I do."

In spite of himself, Adam was caught by her intensity. "And just what is that?"

"Health," she answered simply. "I want their eyes to sparkle, I want their skin clear, their hair shiny, for them to be strong, like God intended!"

Adam stared, thinking she could be speaking of herself; her brown eyes glowed, her cheeks were flushed with the passion she felt, and that amazingly curly hair was aflame beneath the lamplight. "Yes," he said finally. "I want that for people, too."

"Well, Dr. Adam, God gave us everything we need."

Wishing she'd leave God out of the conversation but deciding not to say so, Adam asked, "Such as?"

"Simple. He gave us plants to eat for food and plants to heal us. Of course," she added with a smile, "we have to add one thing."

"Which is?"

"Faith. Faith in Him and His love, in ourselves as His creatures."

It was on the tip of his tongue to say faith didn't always work when she murmured something about cleaning up. She reached across the table to pick up his plate and inadvertently her hand brushed Adam's in the process. Her eyes met his, and neither looked away for a long moment.

"I thought I heard your voice," said Carrie as she entered the room. "Oh, Adam, I'm so glad you're back!"

Both Adam and Jeannie drew away quickly, and Jeannie barely avoided knocking over a glass tumbler as she finished gathering up the dishes. As she carried them over to the sink, Jeannie said, "I'll have these done in a jiff; then it's off to bed for me. Been a long day, and tomorrow will be just as busy, I'm sure."

Frowning, Adam said, "Carrie, why aren't you sleeping? Is something wrong with Rob?"

"No, Adam, he's fine," Carrie assured him. She stole a glance at Jeannie. "I told Miss Gallagher that she should keep her own bed, but she insisted Rob and I take it."

"Mum made a place for me with her, and we found a cot for you, Dr. Adam. It's set up in the storage room over there," she indicated with her head as she washed the last of the dishes and set them to dry. "Well, a good night to you both."

Before either Adam or Carrie could reply, she was gone. The stillness that followed was distinctly uncomfortable. Finally Adam said, "It's late, we should both get some sleep."

"Yes, it's very late," she agreed, hugging her shawl about her tightly. "Adam, can we . . . shouldn't we look for another place to stay tomorrow?"

"We aren't likely to do better for a while, Carrie," he said. "And I plan to move the cot they've set up in the storeroom down to my office."

"Your office? What are you talking about?"

"I committed myself to taking a doctor's place while he . . . takes a leave of absence."

"Without talking it over with me?" Her voice held equal amounts of dismay and shock.

"It happened, Carrie, it just happened, and it seemed right. This place may be what I need now."

Carrie felt desperate, trapped; instinctively she knew it wasn't the situation she feared so much as Jeannie Gallagher. But she was wise enough to say nothing of her fears. Slowly she conceded, "I . . . I suppose. There certainly seems to be plenty of work for you here."

"That's right, if today and tonight were any indication. I've been busy since we stepped off the train." He rubbed his eyes.

Smitten by the weariness she saw on his face and in the slump of his shoulders, Carrie moved close and laid a hand on his arm. "Whatever you think is best, Adam. I . . . we, Rob and I, we trust you."

"I can't tell you how much that means to me, Carrie. If you'll just be patient . . ." He trailed off as though he weren't quite sure what he wanted her to be patient about.

Her hand stole up to his cheek, felt the rough stubble of his dark beard. *I'll be patient, Adam, forever . . . however long it takes for you to know you love me the way I love you.* "You're tired. I shouldn't be keeping you up—"

His hand caught hers and held it tightly as he interrupted her. "I'm sure you're tired, too. We should both go to bed."

"Yes, Adam," Carrie whispered, "whatever you say." With an effort she slowly turned from him and left the room, not wanting to leave but knowing she must at all costs avoid crowding Adam.

He watched her go, troubled but not sure why. Then he

sighed deeply and went to find the storage room which Jeannie Gallagher had spoken of.

His dreams that night as he lay on the narrow cot were a jumble of thin, yellow-faced babies; sad mothers; broken, bleeding men; and an occasional glimpse of a young woman with bright-red hair and capable slender fingers.

CHAPTER 4

*Another parable put he forth unto them, saying, The kingdom
of heaven is like to a grain of mustard seed, which a man took,
and sowed in his field: which indeed is the least of all seeds: but
when it is grown, it is the greatest among herbs, and becometh
a tree, so that the birds of the air come and lodge in the branches
thereof.* Matthew 13:31–32

Considering the lateness of the hour when she'd finally gone
to sleep, Jeannie Gallagher woke quite early. Even so, her
mother was not beside her in the bed. Her eyes took in the
shabby room. Her mother's shapeless, faded flannel nightgown
hung from an iron hook on the back of the door, the mismatched
bowl and pitcher sat on the battered chest with her mother's
brush and comb beside it; there was nothing more.

She sat up and stretched, thinking (not for the first time,
by any means) how temporary everything was. Longing for her
own little house in the Thicket, for her own things, she rose
and stepped to the grimy window. *No time to clean it, no time
for any of the things I love and miss so much.* The day was still
dim and barely born as she watched the gray light creep over
the building across the street.

"Dear God, I'm lonely for my home . . ." She was quiet for a
few moments then, listening to a voice that had often spoken
to her when she was in the Thicket, but, it seemed, less often
here. In her heart an answer formed. *I know . . . I know it's not
forever, Lord. Help me to make today count for you.* After a few
more moments she turned and went to where she'd left her
clothes the night before. Wrinkling her nose at their soiled
condition, she realized she needed to get some fresh things from
her room.

Reluctant to bother Carrie Chaumont but even more reluctant to begin the day without fresh clothing, she went down the hall and stood irresolutely in front of the door of her room. Something about the young woman bothered her, and she suspected it had to do with Dr. Adam Jarrett. Jeannie hadn't had many suitors, simply because she'd always made it clear she wasn't interested in the least. But inexperienced as she was in the ways of men and women and romance, she had the distinct feeling that Carrie Chaumont felt threatened by her, was actually even jealous. Somehow she'd have to reassure Carrie that she didn't have the slightest interest in the man except as a doctor.

Though she carefully, quietly pushed open the door, Rob's wide black eyes flew open and his smile flashed as she placed a warning finger to her lips, then went to get her clean clothing from the large, upright wardrobe.

He slid off the bed and came to stand beside her, his expression much the same as his father's often was—quite solemn. Jeannie smiled at him, wondering what Adam Jarrett would look like if he smiled; he hadn't come close in the short time she'd known him. "Good morning, Rob," she whispered. "Did you sleep well?"

He nodded, one hand wadding up his little blue nightshirt systematically, then letting it fall and repeating the whole process again. "But she cried lots."

Jeannie glanced at Carrie's still form, lying turned toward the wall. "Well, maybe it was because she was in a strange place and was a bit frightened. Were you frightened, too?" She knelt beside him and placed a gentle finger on his rosy cheek. Once again he nodded and stuck his thumb into his mouth. Jeannie laughed softly. "I see you've brought your friend along."

Out came the thumb. "Where?"

With a grin Jeannie tapped the puckered white thumb. "Right there. Has your father tried to make you stop sucking your thumb?"

Shyly he ducked his head. "We don't tell him," he said, sneaking a quick look at Carrie. "Mama says not to."

"I see," said Jeannie thoughtfully. "Your mama—"

"Not my real mama, but I love her."

"I'm sure you do." She was about to leave when Carrie

stirred and discovered Rob was not beside her.

"Rob?" She sat up, her black hair tumbling down her back, the white lawn nightgown she wore modest but not totally disguising the lush beauty of her body.

"I'm sorry to have wakened you, Miss Chaumont," Jeannie apologized, "but there were some things I needed."

Clutching the sheet to her as she reached for her wrapper, Carrie replied, "That's quite all right. After all, this is your room. Rob, are your feet cold? Here, get back into bed until I can get you dressed."

He shook his head. "I'm hungry." As though he knew who could do what for him, Rob slipped his hand into Jeannie's.

Laughing, she said, "Get dressed, Robbie-boy, and I'll take you to your breakfast. Where are your clothes? I'll help you with them."

"You don't need to bother," said Carrie, unable to keep the stiffness from her tone. "Rob is my responsibility."

"I . . . I didn't mean to interfere," assured Jeannie, her smile fading.

"I want to go now!" insisted Rob, spying his clothes laid over a chair. Before Carrie could protest he'd gotten them and placed them in Jeannie's hand.

She cast a troubled look at Carrie. "I only wanted to help."

"I . . . thank you." Carrie bit her lip; Jeannie's sincerity was obvious.

Jeannie smiled, then quickly dressed Rob, marveling at how fine looking a child he was. From his mop of straight black hair, his square, black-eyed face, to his sturdy little body, he was an extraordinarily handsome child. "He looks like his father, doesn't he? You come on when you're ready. Mum will be happy to see the boy." Dragged by the dancing child, she left the room, closing the door softly behind her.

Carrie stared at the door as highly conflicting emotions rocked her mind. How could anyone be as kind, as helpful as Jeannie Gallagher . . . and stir such antagonism within her? Finding no answer, she quickly dressed, taking pains to arrange her hair as attractively as she could.

The early batch of boarders had eaten and gone, and the first thing Carrie saw as she entered the big, warm kitchen was an enthralled Rob, his mouth moving slowly as he ate the mush that Jude was spooning in. It was Jude's story that kept him entranced, not the mush; Carrie knew he hated it.

She addressed Jude, "I'll finish feeding him. Thank you for taking the time—"

But Rob's protesting wail was loud and efficient. "I want Jude!"

Mrs. Gallagher, her face flushed from the heat of the stove, turned around. "Let Jude finish the tale, and maybe the mush will be finished by then as well." Her eyes were bright with interest as she added, "Set down, girl, and I'll get you some coffee."

Though she still looked doubtful, Carrie watched as Jude resumed the story and Rob resumed eating. "Thank you, Mrs. Gallagher."

"You're entirely and completely welcome," said Mrs. Gallagher, placing a steaming cup before Carrie. "Have you worked for the doctor long?"

"I've cared for his son since he was born," she said quietly.

"I see. His mother died birthing little Rob, then?" With long, practiced strokes she wiped the smooth surface of the oak table.

"I . . . no. She was . . . very ill and unable to care for the infant."

"Is that a fact. Child-bed fever, was it? Jeannie's lost a couple of mothers to that, I believe. It's a terrible thing."

Carrie's face bore a slightly desperate look now; for the past three years she'd been sheltered from this kind of questioning and was at a loss as to know just how to respond. She couldn't very well say, "Rob's mother was a leper, and infants and young children are very susceptible to the hateful germ that causes it, so Adam took him away as soon as he was born . . ."

No, she couldn't say that, even if it was the truth. She was saved from her dilemma by Jeannie, who'd come in a moment before and stood listening at the door.

"Mum, don't be asking so many questions. It's too early in the morning for such." She swept into the room, her plain, rust-colored dress setting off her hair.

Carrie was resentful and grateful at the same time for Jeannie's interference. "Could I have some cream and sugar, please?" Carrie asked as she smelled the strong coffee set before her.

Mrs. Gallagher laughed, a nice hearty sound in the big room. "You sure can! Lot's of folks think I make it too strong.

But my late husband Sean Gallagher—God rest his soul—liked it that way. Always said most folks camped too close to the creek to make good coffee!"

"It isn't that at all," said Carrie. "I'm from Louisiana, and coffee doesn't get stronger than my family makes—" Too late, she saw the gleam of interest in the woman's eyes.

"Your family lives in Louisiana, then?" she said as she beat batter for hotcakes. "And I suppose Dr. Adam's does, too."

"Does what?" asked Adam from the doorway. He looked from one woman to the other; none of the three spoke. But Rob clambered down from his chair and ran to his father.

"Papa, Jude tells good stories!"

Adam took a napkin and wiped the boy's mouth. "You should call him Mr. Chapman, son."

Jude shook his head. "Nope, I told him to call me Jude, like everybody else, Doc."

Mrs. Gallagher smiled as she expertly poured great rounds of batter onto the hot griddle. "Neither Jude or my own dear husband Sean ever stood on ceremony." Looking heavenward for a moment, she added, "Sean died when Jeannie was not quite sixteen. Sure, and a good Irishman he was, even if he did drink too much. Now then, Doctor, set down and I'll give you some of the best flapjacks in the state of Texas!" She flipped them skillfully; they were approximately the size of dinner plates.

"One will probably do," murmured Adam, awed at their size.

"Don't be silly. You need a good breakfast. From what Jeannie tells me, you're a good hand at doctoring, and you're likely to be busy from now on." She set the plate of hotcakes before him, shoved the butter and syrup down the table, and by her look dared him not to finish off the whole thing.

Surprising himself, he was doing just that when a knock sounded at the back door. Jeannie went to answer it and found Ginger, the young woman whose cheek Adam had stitched the day before.

"Oh, you've got to come right away!" Her face, heavily made up some time the evening before, was streaked with tears.

Jeannie's calm hand rested on her arm. "Now, Ginger, tell me what the problem is."

"It's Floralee, she's . . . she . . . it's horrible!" Her eyes went around the room, taking in the sedately dressed Carrie, the wide-eyed Rob, Mrs. Gallagher—whose face bore its usual look of interest—Jude, and Dr. Jarrett. "You've got to come, now!"

"Wait here while I get my things."

Ginger shook her head, the bleached curls bouncing on her shoulders. "I'll go on and meet you at the Lady Slipper." Then she was gone, as though she thought Jeannie might refuse to come to the saloon even in broad daylight.

Jeannie, her heels tapping smartly on the linoleum floor as she crossed the room, said, "Dr. Adam, I'd be grateful if you'd not mind coming along."

He didn't answer, for she'd disappeared into the hallway. But when she returned he was ready, bag in hand. The look on Carrie's face was unfathomable as they left; she'd gone to Rob and was holding him tightly. " 'Bye, Papa," he managed to squeak out; "bring me a baby wildcat like Jude told about in the story!"

"Hush, Rob," murmured Carrie, "hush."

Outside the day was brighter than the previous one had been, but even the welcome sunshine did little for the muddy streets. By the time they reached the saloon where Ginger worked, they both had to do a great deal of shuffling to remove the clinging mud from their shoes. Ginger was waiting for them just inside the swinging doors of the Lady Slipper and beckoned for them to follow her up the stairs.

Though it was not yet eight in the morning, several men were drinking, and others were playing cards in one corner of the large room. Jake, Ginger's "manager," was one of the card players, and his sullen, suspicious eyes followed the three of them as they went up. The stale air gave an oppressive feeling to the place, and upstairs it was even worse. As she halted before one of the closed doors, Ginger spoke softly, her eyes huge and anxious, "She's in there . . . I told her you were coming."

Adam saw the apprehensive look Ginger gave him. "Perhaps you'd like for me to wait out here."

Ginger shook her head. "Floralee's going to need all the help she can get, if it's not too late already."

Her hand on the white porcelain doorknob, Jeannie made Ginger meet her eyes. "You've not said what it is we'll be facing, and it will surely help if we know."

The words were gentle and quiet, but there was a steel edging that made Ginger utter in a strangled whisper, "A knitting needle, she used a knitting needle."

"Oh, dear Lord." Jeannie's long lashes brushed her cheek as she shut her eyes briefly. "How long ago?"

"Last night, some time last night, I guess. I found her this morning . . ." Her words trailed off, the horror she'd obviously felt infusing her face even now.

"And how far along was she?"

"Maybe a couple of months," answered Ginger, her eyes downcast. "If you don't need me, I'll go on downstairs." She turned and fled.

Adam, his tone harsh, growled, "We'd better see what that woman has done to herself. What fools women can be."

When he made a move to go in ahead of her, Jeannie stopped him, her arm barring the door. "You'd best make a choice right here and now, Doctor."

He frowned. "What choice?"

"Either you leave that attitude here in the hall, or stay yourself here. I mean it."

"Speaking of attitude, yours is rather high and mighty. I am the doctor, after all," he said slowly.

Her brown eyes glowed, her cheeks flamed with color. "And I'm the one Ginger came to. You can come in, you can help, but I won't let you condemn the woman, no matter what she's done."

Adam glared at her. "Miss Gallagher, you're impertinent."

"Maybe. If you'll excuse me, we've wasted enough time." She opened the door and slipped inside.

Stifling the anger he felt, he pushed open the door and followed her. The scene that met his eyes was one he wouldn't forget soon. Jeannie Gallagher was bent over the girl, who lay quite still on the messy, tumbled bed. When she turned around the look on her face was one of compassion mingled with such horror that he found himself saying, "It's bad, isn't it?"

"As bad as I've ever seen," she whispered. "She's been bleeding for a very long time, and I'm afraid she's done for."

Adam crossed the room and took the girl's limp wrist. "Hardly any pulse."

"She's so pale." Jeannie drew the faded rose-satin coverlet up over Floralee, but not before Adam saw the carnage beneath.

"That's because she's dying, Miss Gallagher, because almost every drop of blood in her has drained away," said Adam savagely. "How could she be so stupid—"

"Hush!" commanded Jeannie. "She's trying to speak . . ." She knelt by the bed, one hand taking the girl's wrist from Adam, the other placed tenderly on the pale cheek. "I'm listening, Floralee, I'm listening."

"Didn't mean to . . . didn't want to die. I'm so sorry, so sorry. Will God forgive me for my wasted life?" The last agonized question was only a whisper.

"God loves you, Floralee," Jeannie said warmly.

Floralee's eyes fluttered shut. Silent for a few seconds, she then spoke, "When I was a little girl . . . used to go to Sunday school . . . was baptized . . . I do love Him!"

"And He loves you," assured Jeannie again.

"Even after what I did . . ." She trailed off and was so still that Jeannie reached for her pulse, which was weaker than before.

"Yes, even after that."

The drawn, pained look slowly drained from her white young face, and a slight smile touched her mouth. Then her breathing ceased, and she did not move again.

Jeannie's eyes were tightly shut, and Adam took a couple of steps back. They had been in the room only three, four minutes, maybe less. But it felt like an eternity. Jeannie opened her eyes and pulled the soiled pink coverlet over Floralee's quiet, peaceful face. "This should not have happened," Adam said, his voice low and controlled, but filled with anger.

"Ah, Doctor, but it did; you can't deny it did—" She broke off as Ginger knocked, then peeked hesitantly in. "She's gone, Ginger. There was nothing we could do. You must call me sooner next time."

"Next time!" Adam's words were a small explosion. "You can't mean this happens often?" When Jeannie merely shrugged he went on, "But why did she do it? Surely she must have had some idea of how dangerous it was!"

Ginger spoke now, her face grim. "Doc, have you got any idea what Jake would do if he knew one of us was caught with child? It was awful how Floralee died, but there's worse ways." She touched her cheek, where the stitching Adam had done the day before, and continued. "You ever been stomped, Doc? I bet not. Well, I sure ain't going to stick around. When Jake finds out what Floralee done, he'll be madder'n . . . I'll be back after I think he's had time to cool off." She shut the door firmly behind her.

It was a moment before Adam said, "Let me get this straight. This girl's boss is going to be angry that she killed herself?"

"Bluntly put," stated Jeannie as she walked toward the door, "but true. After all, Floralee was real pretty, and he'll lose money until he replaces her."

Adam followed her. "You seem rather coldblooded about this matter. I'd have thought a religious woman like you would feel—"

She whirled to face him. "I'm not coldblooded a'tall, Doctor! Just realistic, and you'd best learn the difference between the two. And while you're about it, there's a fair amount of difference between being 'religious' and being like Jesus, and I hope I keep trying for the last and never am the first!"

He stared angrily down into her brown eyes. She never looked away, never gave an inch. Adam Jarrett had always been able to intimidate others, sometimes unwittingly, sometimes with clear purpose, but not this time.

"Floralee was one of God's creatures and He loved her, just as I told her He did. She just got off on the wrong path," she said softly, yet firmly.

"That's undeniable," muttered Adam, as he looked away. "I think we'd better leave. There's certainly nothing more we can do here."

"Well, you're right about that, Doctor," said Jeannie. Her inflection implied he was not right about everything. "But keep a hold on your temper. We do have one more thing to do, and that's tell Jake that Floralee is lost to him."

Whether it was her remark about his temper, or the fact that if he lost it he might do Jake serious harm, Adam stood tight-lipped throughout Jake's tirade. Amazingly, Jake accepted absolutely no blame in the situation. He kept saying Ginger should have gone for help sooner, that Floralee shouldn't have been so stupid as to get herself caught, or to inflict such horrible wounds on herself.

Once outside Jeannie shook her head. "So young, to end her life in an awful place like that. Away from home and loved ones—"

"The way she lived her life was her own choice, Miss Gallagher."

"How do you know that? You don't know the circumstances that led her to this day!"

"I know that in spite of what you told her, she was in no way prepared to meet God," he retorted. "After the life she'd led?"

"Who appointed you judge and jury, Doctor?" Jeannie flared, then bit her lip. "I'm sorry. Sometimes I've got a sharp tongue. But I didn't tell her anything that wasn't true. God does love her, and she had faith in that love. You may think her faith wasn't much, but the truth is, the most important thing is how great God is, not how great her faith was."

Adam's face remained stony. She sighed, and pressed close to the building to avoid stepping on a large brown mess that looked like chewing tobacco. "No matter how often things like this happen," she said, "it never fails to touch me. These women must not think much of themselves to begin with, or they wouldn't get started in such a life. Women ought to be cherished and valued, not . . . not used and degraded!"

For the rest of the block the two walked in silence; Adam could think of nothing he wanted to say aloud. He had cherished and valued Bethany beyond measure, but Bethany had been a pure and fine woman, far different than these poor creatures, Ginger and Floralee. Jeannie Gallagher seemed to think God loved them just as He would a woman like Bethany, or herself.

In spite of himself he glanced at her—at the clean lines of her profile, the high forehead from which her hair curled and waved back. The small, straight nose turned up just a bit impudently over the firm chin. She was nothing like Bethany. This young woman defied him, felt no such awe for him as Bethany had.

And yet she valued his professional skill. That was all he really wanted, he told himself—proper respect for him as a doctor, nothing else. The remainder of the walk back to the hotel seemed interminable to him. Jeannie Gallagher either knew everyone in Beaumont, or they knew her, and she kept stopping to chat. Finally he said, "I'm going to have the cot I used last night moved to Melrose's office, if that's agreeable with your mother."

If he thought his decision might disturb her, he was mistaken. "A good idea, Dr. Adam. I'll check to see how you're getting on later." Then she turned back to the matron who'd just hailed her, and listened intently as the woman launched into a long, involved tale about her daughter's first pregnancy.

Feeling as though he'd been dismissed, Adam left, not allowing himself to say anything further, not allowing himself to wonder why he had such conflicting feelings toward Jeannie Gallagher.

CHAPTER 5

For one believeth that he may eat all things: another, who is weak, eateth herbs. Let not him that eateth despise him that eateth not; and let not him which eateth not judge him that eateth: for God hath received him.   Romans 14:2–3

Though he didn't like being away from Rob so much, Adam had to admit he enjoyed the solitude that living in his office provided. After almost a month he—and Jeannie Gallagher—had it looking fairly decent inside and out. Jeannie had cheerfully confessed one day last week that she'd often wanted to do as much for Dr. Melrose, who had told her repeatedly it wasn't necessary and usually had sent her off on some errand instead. And while Melrose had, from all reports, had plenty of patients, Adam was drawing far more. Every day the outer office was crowded with waiting sufferers of all kinds; sometimes they even overflowed onto the porch outside. It hadn't taken long for Adam's reputation to spread.

What intrigued Adam most about his new situation was Jeannie Gallagher's reputation. As he listened to the accident-battered roughnecks, the pathetic sickly mothers and children, the hordes of prostitutes with their amazing variety of ailments (mostly job-related), Adam got an ever-clearer picture of the red-haired young woman's range of abilities. She had an amazing knowledge of the multitude of medicinal plants in the area, and the faith most of the people showed in her was phenomenal.

"Miss Jeannie can cure a fever in jig time," enthused one gaunt woman. "If I'm not mistook, she makes up a tea of cayenne, ginger root, lemon, and honey. It don't even taste too awful bad."

"Miss Jeannie can get a young'un through croup like no-

55

body's business. Uses horehound, I think. Works ever time."

"Miss Jeannie's got a bag of simples that'll get rid of anything what ails you."

"Miss Jeannie can deal a blow to malaria, sure as shootin'. . ." and on and on, until Adam wondered if they were being altogether truthful. He was tempted to challenge some of the more extravagant tales, but several things stopped him. In the first place, he certainly didn't want to discredit her. Secondly, there were enough indications of her real skill to make him realize that every glowing word they spoke of her was quite possibly true. For instance, he'd seen Susie Chandler himself, and her arm was almost completely healed. "It was all because of Jeannie's comfrey treatment," declared the child's mother. She'd also confided to Adam that Jeannie managed to bring them food . . . and milk, at least three times a week. When Adam had replied, a trifle resentfully, that maybe Jeannie Gallagher was also responsible for the welcome sunshine they'd been having, Mrs. Chandler agreed that might be true.

However, it was Miss Jeannie's hands, her unerring ability to handle even the most difficult of birthings, that brought the most glowing reports. The praise of her skills was so lavish that Adam decided privately (he lacked the courage and had the good sense not to dispute it aloud to any of those singing her praises) that though she might be good, no one could possibly be *that* good. However, Bridey Malone and her firstborn changed his mind forever.

As is so often the case, it was well after midnight when Mr. Malone rapped at the door of the office, and even though it was late Adam had been in bed less than an hour. It took several knocks to wake him. He got dressed, then stumbled groggily to the door, groaning to himself; he knew that more than likely it was a maternity call. Sure enough, the man who stood before him, hat in his nervously twisting hands, said, "My missus needs you bad, Doc. I'm afraid something's not quite right, and it's her first baby and all."

Motioning for the man to follow him back to the inner room so he could pack his bag, Adam asked, "How long has she been in labor?"

"Quite a spell. Let's see, maybe since noon or so?"

Over twelve hours already. "Why didn't you come sooner, man?"

Mr. Malone scowled at the anger in Adam's tone. "The womenfolk in my family never had no trouble birthin' babies." The words were said with a swagger, but the young man's underlying anxiety was obvious.

Adam snapped his bag shut and headed for the door, grateful that he'd rented a small hack and horse. Both were now readily available in the shed behind his office. As they drove through the darkness, Mr. Malone's defensiveness fled in the face of his worry for his young wife. "I guess I shouldn't have brought her with me, her being with child and all. Things is pretty rough in a situation like this. But she begged to come, said she didn't want to stay home without me."

When Adam reined up in front of the place Malone indicated, he silently agreed on two counts: it was too rough for a woman, and Malone should have left her at home. Malone's "home" here in the oil fields was much like the Chandler's. A twelve-foot square tent-shack sat on a floor made of planks laid flat on the ground. It was boarded up four feet high with rough boards and covered with tarpaulin. Obviously the simple structure was used for sleeping, dining, living and cooking. As Adam entered the poorly lit makeshift home, he noticed in a corner an unpainted iron bed. Upon it lay a pale, wide-eyed young woman, holding the great mound of her belly on both sides by her clutching hands. Though she uttered no sound, Adam could tell she was having a strong contraction.

Bending over her, Adam placed his hands alongside hers. Minutes went by before the contraction subsided. The girl's eyes closed and a faint whimper of relief escaped her lips. As he felt for her pulse, which was fast but regular, Adam saw that she was younger even than he'd first thought, perhaps seventeen or so.

"Your husband tells me this is your first child, Mrs. Malone. I'm Dr. Jarrett."

Her breathing was quick and shallow but she nodded weakly. "Oh, Doctor, I don't know what, but something's wrong."

"Don't worry, we'll see that you and your baby are fine. Mr. Malone, would you mind stepping outside while I examine your wife?"

For a moment Malone looked as though he minded very much leaving his pretty young wife alone with another man, doctor or not, but he nodded and moved to the flap of the tent. "I'll just get some more wood from the Browns next door, and stoke the fire."

Adam knew he was saying, "I'm not going far, and I'll be back soon." Time was precious for the young woman on the bed; a quick examination showed him just how precious. She was almost totally exhausted and with good reason; what should have been a normal, relatively easy birth had turned into a nightmare. The baby had done its best to be born, but it was almost certainly, as nearly as he could ascertain, in a transverse position . . . literally crossways to the birth canal.

Despite the clamminess of the night air, Adam felt a trickle of sweat run between his shoulder blades. For although the neck of Mrs. Malone's cervix was almost completely open, no part of her baby presented itself; the child was lying horizontally across the uterus. Proper procedure would call for forceps, Adam knew that. But he had no such specialized instruments, and would have been uncertain as to how to use them if he had. Just then a small, animal-like cry erupted from the girl's lips.

"Oh! Oh, I'm sorry!" She had blond, soft-looking hair that undoubtedly was very lovely when it wasn't soaked with perspiration as it was now. Her large, cornflower-blue eyes were wide with pain and pleading; the contraction was obviously a very strong one. "My baby . . . am I going to lose my baby?"

"Of course not." Adam spoke with a great deal more assurance than he felt; his helplessness was not easy to handle. "Breathe deeply and try to relax."

"But I'm so tired, and it hurts awful. I don't mean to complain Doctor, but I'm scared, I'm really scared!"

Adam patted her hand awkwardly. "Perfectly understandable, Mrs. Malone. Is the contraction almost over?"

She nodded, then said, "I'm called Bridey." Her eyes closed, as though she was grateful for the respite.

"Bridey, then." Adam had reached a decision, and he put all the confidence he could muster in his tone as he said, "I'm going to try to turn your baby around, and you'll have to help me."

"Turn him around? *Why?*"

"Because it's necessary. Calm yourself," commanded Adam, scanning the dim room, which was lit only by a kerosene lamp with a carbon-smudged chimney. He spied a basin and pitcher and washed his hands as thoroughly as possible. Then he began the complicated, delicate procedure of stroking and pushing the tiny head (he hoped that's what it was, and cursed his lack of experience) downward between the next two contractions, which were coming now with scarcely a couple of minutes between them.

"That's very good, Bridey, very good," soothed Adam, who hoped desperately that what he felt was the baby's head close to the girl's pelvis. But then the next contraction came and peaked far more rapidly than the preceding ones. He'd not been lying, Bridey had been doing very well. But now, she arched her back suddenly, her head thrust into the pillow, and her scream pierced the air. When Adam checked, he found to his intense disappointment that whatever progress he'd made was lost. The baby had slipped back to the transverse position.

Bridey lay still, her eyes squeezed shut, her face glistening with perspiration. Even in the dim light afforded by the kerosene lamp, he could see that her last reserves of strength were ebbing fast, and he didn't have the faintest idea as to how to help her. He knew it was possible to turn the baby internally, but when he looked down at his large, square hands he also knew it was beyond his capability. With a feeling of painful helplessness, he was about to begin the external manipulation once again, but Mr. Malone burst through the flap of the tent.

"Bridey! Are you all right? I heard you clear over at the Browns'—" He went straight to the bed and took her limp hand in his. "Oh, darlin', if anything happens to you, after your mama warned me not to bring you—"

Adam clenched his jaws a couple of times, then finally ground out, "Perhaps you should call Jeannie Gallagher."

"The midwife?" Malone turned to face Adam, his expression bleak. "Doc, I went to her place before I came to yours. She was out."

"I see." Though he was ashamed of it, for a couple of seconds Adam's dismay at the man's having gone to Jeannie first took precedent over his disappointment that she was not to be found. "Mr. Malone, I must tell you, your wife is in danger of her life if we cannot deliver the child."

"Then do it!" was the low, savage reply. Just then Bridey Malone's eyes flew open, and she cried out, her hands clutched at the mound of her belly. Mr. Malone dropped to his knees on the dirty plank floor. "Doc, *do something!*"

Though the medical circumstances couldn't have been more different, Adam's feeling at that moment was very near to what he'd experienced when Anson dePaul lay dying for want of air that night at Greenlea ... it seemed so long ago. Adam's wounded arm had made it impossible for him to perform the tracheotomy that would allow the life-giving air into Anson's tortured, deprived lungs. And now, his lack of knowledge and experience . . . and his large hands, all combined to make it just as impossible to help this suffering girl. He was about to ask the husband—with his dark, accusing eyes—to leave so he could try external manipulation once more when suddenly he heard voices outside and that low, almost musical voice saying, "Is this Malones'?"

Seconds later Jeannie Gallagher slipped through the flap of the tent and her eyes went from the girl on the bed to the distraught young husband who scrambled to his feet, to Adam's tense face. "Ah, now, Mr. Malone, is it?" He nodded, not speaking, but hope flared in his eyes when she said, "I'm Jeannie Gallagher. I heard you were looking for me. Now, outside with you, sir, and we'll see what orders Dr. Jarrett has for me." Even as she spoke she gave the poor man a gentle nudge, and moved toward the bed. Her hand smoothed the damp, tangled hair from Bridey Malone's forehead and she murmured, "There, girl, we'll soon have you right." She glanced at Adam questioningly.

"Transverse position," he disclosed in a low voice. Her quick, troubled frown mirrored his deep concern. "I've tried external manipulation to no avail."

She nodded. "And your hands are too large for internal manipulation with such a slip of a girl as our Bridey is. How long have you been in labor, lass?" she asked as she laid her slim fingers on the girl's wrist.

"Since yesterday noon, or a little before—" Bridey sighed, then convulsed suddenly as a particularly strong contraction hit her.

"Too long." Jeannie's murmured words were lost as Bridey clung to her hand throughout the contraction, then, when it was over at last, lay back white and spent. "Dr. Jarrett, would you like for me to help you move Bridey?"

"*What?*"

Jeannie's brown eyes looked almost black as she stared directly into his. "I know you'll want her on her hands and knees."

He started to protest that what she was saying was ridiculous, but several things stayed his tongue. First of all, he remembered that the girl was almost totally exhausted, that the child and mother were in serious danger, and . . . that he hadn't the faintest notion as to what to do for either one of them. "Of course, Miss Gallagher."

"I'll just help her onto her side," said Jeannie calmly, managing to direct him with her eyes.

Adam followed her amazing, wordless instructions and they almost had Bridey shifted onto her hands and knees when the girl whimpered, "Oh, let me alone, I can't stand it anymore!"

Once again Jeannie brushed the soft, tangled blond hair from the girl's face and her voice came low but laced with command, "Bridey, you're going to do exactly what Dr. Jarrett says. And he says you have to help us get you onto your elbows and knees. You *have* to."

Bridey, responding with what must have been her last shred of strength, did as she was told. Jeannie allowed her to rest for a few moments, her fingers moving gently and rhythmically on the girl's back.

"I . . . I do feel a little better," said Bridey, who sounded surprised.

"Of course you do. That fine big baby isn't mashing the daylights out of your backbone anymore! And soon that little rascal is going to—"

Suddenly, Bridey gasped. "Oh, what's happening? My baby, it's like he's tumbling around inside me!"

Adam moved quickly to prevent Bridey from falling. "The baby!" he exclaimed; "it's shifting!"

And so it was. A quick examination showed that the child's head was presenting itself in the proper position for a normal delivery. They quickly helped Bridey onto her back again, and Adam, after a wordless nod from Jeannie, assisted the girl as she birthed a healthy, large baby boy.

Quickly, efficiently, Jeannie took the infant, who let out a couple of indignant squeaks, and cleaned the creamy vernix from his nose and mouth. Then she laid the baby on Bridey's abdomen.

"Is he . . . is my baby all right?" she whispered, her hand wandering over him, the exhaustion on her face now mingled with hope.

"Yes, and he's a fine boy," said Adam, his throat tight with unexpected emotion.

"Oh, Doctor, how can I thank you?"

"But, Bridey, it wasn't—" he began.

Jeannie broke in smoothly. "We're sure lucky Dr. Adam decided to stop in Beaumont, aren't we, Bridey? Doctor, would you like to tell Mr. Malone that he has a son? I'll clean things up here, and get this fine man-child ready for company."

Adam stared hard at her, but she smiled and turned away. He stood for a few moments, but could think of no way to make the situation right short of contradicting her, which he was unwilling to do. "Yes, that's a good idea, Miss Gallagher. You get things squared away in here, and I'll go and tell Malone the good news. We'll need to discuss this case at length later, you realize."

"Yes, Doctor," she answered almost meekly. "It's an interesting one, to be sure. Mrs. Malone has been a fine patient, has she not?"

Still looking as though there was much he wanted to say, he turned to go. Adam felt as though he'd been completely, skillfully outmaneuvered and manipulated as surely as Jeannie Gallagher had manipulated that baby into a proper birth position.

Later, as he drove her back to the hotel, he said, "There's something I want to know."

She glanced over at him. The carriage wasn't large, and they sat fairly close together. The sun had not risen, but there was the hint of its coming in the air, which seemed fresher because of the promise of a new day. "You're wondering where I learned that little trick, how I knew putting Bridey on her hands and knees would cause the child to turn within her, right?"

"Well, yes, I did wonder about that. But—"

Before he could phrase what was really on his mind, she responded with a smile on her lips and in her voice as well. "Grannie Annie taught me. Now mind you, it doesn't happen that you'd need to use it often, but you've got to admit it's a nifty trick."

He nodded. "I've never, not in all my years of study, read of anything like it."

Her laughter was quick and low. "Sure, and it's too simple for your fine and complicated medical books. It's just an old midwifery method, one among many that we use. We're not allowed the use of the forceps all of you doctors seem so fond of, not that I would if I could. There are times when doctors, learned as they are, simply do not think of the patient first, but of their own learning and skill and the cost of their fine instruments, which they feel they must use." She cast him a wise, knowing look. "Sometimes the simplest things, even if they are old-fashioned, are the best."

"For a young woman, you seem rather wise," Adam said thoughtfully.

"I'm not so young as all that, Dr. Adam. I'm twenty-four years of age, I'll have you know!"

With a smile on his face, and a gleam in his eyes, Dr. Adam could not help the gently needling comment that fell from his lips now. "*That* old and still not married? Why, you're practically middle-aged." Thinking she would bristle and fire back, her delayed reply surprised him.

When she did speak, the words were obviously from her heart. "Dr. Adam, it will sound awfully uppity, I imagine, but the truth is I have never found a man I could love, one who would be—"

"Worthy of your love?" interrupted Adam.

Her head was turned slightly from him as she continued. "He has to be a man I can admire, one I can look up to, whose leadership I can follow, who is strong and loves God—"

"Sounds as though you're talking about God's little brother instead of a real flesh-and-blood man."

"There's no need to be sacrilegious," Jeannie retorted. "At any rate, the man I marry . . . will be a special man indeed."

"You're not likely to find him in this wild place." Adam gave the horse a light slap with the reins. "Now, as to the other matter I wanted to discuss with you."

"What matter is that, Doctor?" asked Jeannie coolly, professionally, her tone quite different now from the way she had spoken only a moment before.

"Why did you allow that girl and her husband to think it was I who saved her life and that of her baby?"

"You sound angry."

He scowled. "I suppose I am, a little. It made me uneasy."

"Surely you aren't angry because I saved Bridey's life. Could it be because I gave you credit for it?"

The calm, logical question illogically made him even angrier. "Miss Gallagher, you are an exasperating young woman. What are your motives?"

Her lips twitched, but she did not smile. "*Middle-aged* young woman. And as to my motives, I've no need to build a reputation." The quiet, matter-of-fact statement implied that had been done already, that people knew Jeannie Gallagher and what she could do. "My concern was that the girl birth her baby safely, and that she and her husband have confidence in you, as the doctor in charge, the one they called to help them."

Unwillingly he admitted, "Mr. Malone went to the hotel to

look for you before he came to me."

"That's only natural. I've been here longer."

In the time that followed as he drove the few remaining blocks to the Crosby Hotel, neither spoke, not even when he reined up and stepped down to help her from the carriage. She gave him her hand as he proffered his, and then stood beside him on the plank sidewalk for a long moment, staring up at his face in the beginning glow of morning.

Finally he said gruffly, "I feel I owe you an apology."

"For what, Dr. Adam?"

"For my . . ." He trailed off, unwilling to say, *My resentment, my anger that you are capable and honest . . . and attractive.* So he said, "Thank you for your help this night. I don't have to tell you how important it was. And thank you for allowing them to think it was my skill, not yours, that saved the day, or, as the case may be, the night."

"You're very welcome, Doctor." Slowly, she pulled her hand from his. "As I've said before, if we're to work together, we must try and understand each other."

Adam gazed down at her face, at the tendrils of curly hair straying from the large bun on the back of her head. She'd spoken of understanding, and yet he knew he was far from understanding the feelings in his own heart at that moment. He only knew that he didn't want to understand, to feel. "Good night, Miss Gallagher." He turned and got into the carriage so abruptly that the horse was startled, and almost shied as Adam snapped the whip smartly and set off down the deserted street.

CHAPTER 6

*Better is a dinner of herbs where love is, than a stalled ox and
hatred therewith.*   *Proverbs 15:17*

Jeannie watched until Adam turned the corner, still driving
too fast, and disappeared from view. Even then she didn't move.
The feelings that warred within her were too numerous, too
unsettling. No one could deny that Dr. Adam Jarrett was a
fascinating man, even if he was hardheaded and abrupt on oc-
casion. Tonight she'd seen a different side. He'd been totally
helpless in the face of that girl's dilemma, and he'd known it.
But hard as it had been for him to admit his helplessness, he
had accepted Jeannie's help. She knew not every doctor would
have. Some were so impressed with themselves they'd have let
the girl die before admitting they were useless in the situation.

Breathing deeply of the soft, predawn air, Jeannie stretched
her hands high over her head and surveyed the quiet street that
would, very soon, be bustling with activity. There were times
when she longed for the quiet comfort of the Thicket—so much
so that it was like a physical pain. Now was one of those times.
She needed the deep, secret beauty of the woods, the real alone-
ness they provided, especially when she was confronted with a
situation that puzzled her. It was Adam Jarrett, or more to the
point, her feelings about him, that were the source of her confusion now.

Just the thought of his black, fathomless eyes, his ever-sad,
haunted face, made her shiver. She hugged her body tightly,
assuring herself he was not the kind of man she'd always
dreamed of, that he had painful, inescapable memories dogging
his every step. And there were Rob . . . and Carrie.

She sighed deeply and, as she did often, shut her eyes and spoke to God within herself. *Oh, Lord, you know my heart . . . You know what I need. But I feel so . . . so drawn to Adam Jarrett. Did you really lead him here? Is there something you would have me do or say? Dear Father, I love you, and I know you love me . . .*

Suddenly the air was rent by the shouting curses of a mule skinner whose early morning delivery was going to be a little late; his lead mule was floundering in a particularly deep hole down the street. With another sigh, Jeannie turned to go inside the hotel, wishing she was at home in her own little cabin.

Just as she walked through the door she caught sight of Carrie standing at the front window. Something told her that Carrie had been watching when Adam brought her home. Her first words confirmed that suspicion.

"I was watching you with Adam."

Had it not been that Carrie was extremely pretty, even at this time of morning, she would have looked pitiful. Her hands nervously clutched the pale-blue satin wrapper about her, and unshed tears glistened in her eyes. A little shocked at the implication she heard, Jeannie said, "Carrie, you sound as though you think there's . . . that something's going on between Dr. Adam and me—"

"Can you deny you're attracted to him?"

"Why . . . I . . . of course I'm not, not the way you mean!"

"There's only one way that a woman is attracted to a man, Miss Gallagher. Only one that counts, anyway."

"Please believe me, there's nothing like that between us. We work together—"

"Were you working together all night?"

"I . . . no, not all night." No matter how much Jeannie told herself she had nothing to hide from this young woman, the fact came back to mock her that only moments before she'd admitted her attraction to Adam Jarrett to herself, even prayed about it.

"It's morning," Carrie challenged, "and Adam just brought you home."

Stricken, unwilling to defend herself but knowing she must, Jeannie pointed out, "We were both called, at different times, on a difficult delivery. He was there when I arrived, and it seemed the thing for him to do was to bring me home when we were through."

"The thing to do." Carrie stared up at Jeannie for a long while, her blue eyes wide and troubled. Then she said slowly, "The thing for you to do is to stay away from my fianceé, Miss Gallagher."

"Your fianceé?" echoed Jeannie. "You're engaged?"

A look of uncertainty flickered over Carrie's face; then she lifted her chin. "I . . . no. But we will be, soon. He's still in mourning for his wife . . ."

She faltered, and Jeannie felt a stab of compassion. "It's difficult for you, I know. His wife must have been a fine woman."

"He's still grieving for her, even though it's been over two years since she died."

"How did it happen?"

"Pneumonia, but it was really because of that terrible—" She stopped, then said almost angrily, "You ask too many questions."

"I'm sorry. I only asked because I care."

"You just care about Adam, not me!"

"Oh, that's not true," said Jeannie, troubled. There was something about his wife's death that both Adam and Carrie wanted left hidden, something that was either fearful or shameful. She quelled her curiosity and placed a gentle hand on Carrie's shoulder. "I want to help you, I really do."

Carrie shook off her hand and took a step back. For a long moment she planned exactly what she wanted to say. Then, taking a deep breath, she explained. "His wife was very ill when Rob was born, and he was only hours old when Adam brought him to me to care for. I'm the only mother he's ever known, and the three of us belong together. Do you understand?"

"Please believe me, I have no desire to take Dr. Adam away from you."

Carrie, her expression anxious but her voice determined, declared, "I plan to marry him. So work with him if you have to, but always keep in mind that he belongs to me."

"I think I understand," Jeannie assured. "And I promise, Carrie, to respect your feelings."

The triumph that Carrie felt showed in her eyes. "I have to check on Rob."

Jeannie nodded, and watched as she walked through the

lobby, ignoring the approving glances some of the wakening men gave her. Suddenly the fact that she hadn't slept in almost twenty-four hours combined with the confused, helpless feeling about the situation that cluttered her life made Jeannie feel purely exhausted. She made her way wearily to her mother's room, hoping that she was up already and in the kitchen. At that moment all she wanted was sleep, and a few moments later, it was hers.

Carrie found that Rob was up early and in his favorite place—Mrs. Gallagher's kitchen. Jude took his meals there even though he had a room elsewhere and was telling yet another story to the child, who spooned oatmeal into his mouth as though he were hypnotized.

Jude looked up as Carrie entered, and winked at her, never missing a word of his tale. "Yup, boy, I tell you a feller's dog is mighty important. Why, there's lots of panthers in the Thicket, terrible fierce critters. They say that one ol' cur dog saved a lady and her baby from one."

"How?" asked Rob through a mouth full of mush.

"Don't talk with your mouth full," murmured Carrie automatically as she accepted a cup of coffee from Mrs. Gallagher, who eyed the pretty blue wrapper.

Jude sipped his own coffee delicately past his mustache and continued with a grin. "Oh, she was taking a jug of milk to a neighbor, and set off through the woods with her little girl child under one arm, the jug under the other. Took the dog, Sam, too."

"What color was Sam?" asked Rob.

"Yaller. He was a tough ol' dog, and a good thing, too. T'wasn't long afore a big panther got wind of 'em, and started follering real close. That Sam, he'd go back and fight that cat, and the poor little gal just kep' a'running, hoping she could outrun him. She dropped her bonnet once, and the panther tore it all up."

"Tore it up?" Rob's eyes were wider than ever.

"Yup. Only thing what saved her, 'cept ol' Sam, a'course, was the jug of milk. She dropped it and that cat he jumped on it and rolled it round like it was alive. And when she got to the neighbor's, she was panting like a workhorse from all that running. The men went back and killed the cat howsomever."

"And ol' Sam? Was he hurt?"

"Boy, they had to take a sewing needle and stitch that poor dog's innards back in, he was tore up so terrible."

"Jude!" admonished Mrs. Gallagher. "He's just a baby." She glanced over at Carrie, wondering why she'd allowed Jude to tell the child such a wild tale. But Carrie's preoccupied look told her the young woman had other things on her mind.

When Carrie spoke she was sure of it. "Jude, I'll pay you if you will take me somewhere in your hack."

"You name the place, little lady," he said genially.

"I'd like to go to Adam's—Dr. Jarrett's office."

Mrs. Gallagher turned the sizzling sidemeat she was frying; the rich aroma of well-cured pork filled the air. "Jeannie tells me she and Dr. Adam have got it looking fine as frog's fur. Took 'em quite a while, I gather, in between all them calls they make." She cast a sideways glance at Carrie. If she'd expected a reaction to the reference that her daughter and Adam Jarrett spent a lot of time together for one reason or another, she wasn't disappointed.

"I know that your daughter has helped Adam a lot, and I . . . we're grateful for that help." She sounded angry instead of grateful, however. Realizing that too late, she took great pains to make her next words calm and gentle. "I'll be ready about nine, Jude. Will that be all right?"

"You bet. We going to take my swamper, here?" He tousled Rob's hair.

Carrie hesitated, knowing that she wanted to speak to Adam alone.

Mrs. Gallagher came to her rescue. "Leave the little feller here with me if you want, and we'll make ginger cookies. Would you like that, boy?" She smiled as Rob enthusiastically shouted, "Yes!"

Carrie nodded, even though she preferred not to be obligated to anyone in the family any more than she already was. "Thank you, Mrs. Gallagher, if you're sure it won't be too much trouble?"

"None a'tall. I like that young'un," the woman said cheerfully. "Now you go on, and leave him to me. What he ought to be doing is playing outside, chasing a cur dog like old Sam."

"I want a cur dog!" Rob shouted, running around the table.

Feeling weak but wanting to escape, Carrie tried to calm him, then went to dress at Mrs. Gallagher's suggestion. It was almost an hour later when she met Jude outside the hotel. The ride through the busy, muddy streets of Beaumont was an eye-opener. "I can't get over how many people there are here. It's so confusing."

"I know what you mean. There's times I really get to hankering for the Thicket. The peace a man can find there just don't exist in this mad place. A man can hear hisself think in the quietness of nature. Then there's the birds. My do we get them in the Thicket! Guess my favorites are the singing birds, though, specially the mockingbirds and warblers."

Carrie nodded; she'd grown up in Noirville and had known the peace as well as the problems of a small town. "Jude, look at that man! He looks drunk."

The man of whom she spoke was staggering as he made his way across the street in front of them. Jude snickered. "Probably is drunk." Suddenly, Jude reined up sharply, for traffic had come to a standstill in front of them. The sounds of shouts mingled with angry screams permeated the air. "Why are we stopping?" Carrie asked.

"There's a fight ahead of us, and I guess everbody wants to watch," he said amiably.

"But . . . they're women!" was Carrie's low, shocked observation.

By this time there was quite an enthusiastic crowd watching two flimsily dressed girls. One was a tall, blowzy blond who looked as though she might be able to fight and beat off that panther in Jude's story. The other combatant, a slight dark-skinned girl, seemed intent on making her opponent bald instead of blond.

"Sure. That's the best kind of fight," Jude stated with a grin. "Why, people pay money to see them girls fight sometimes."

"That's . . . it's terrible," whispered Carrie, horrified, thinking that if it wasn't for Adam and his child, she might be in a similar, scandalous situation. The very thought made her urgently say, "Can't you get through the crowd somehow?"

Jude shrugged reluctantly. "I reckon I can try." In a short time he'd skillfully manuevered the hack around the bystanders and was able to get to Adam's office a little later. "When do you want me to pick you up?"

"Would an hour be all right?"

"Right as rain," he answered, grinning. "Tell the Doc I said howdy, and that he missed a good cat fight."

Choosing to ignore Jude's last remark, Carrie hastily entered Adam's office to discover that he was very busy. The outer room was almost full of waiting patients, and though he didn't see her, she could watch him through the space in the curtain as he stitched up the hand of a very important looking man. The man's voice carried easily, and he'd obviously been trying to explain the oil business to Adam.

"And, Doc," he was saying, "even though under common law the man who owns a piece of property owns the minerals under it, this oil boom has made some brand new legal problems."

"How's that, Mr. Chadwick?" asked Adam, intent on meticulous, even stitches.

"Well, as long as the minerals are solid and stay in one place, no problems there, right? But oil and gas migrate, Doc, from areas of high pressure to areas of low pressure. You understand what I mean?" He was a large, florid-faced man, and his checked suit looked expensive. Adam's apologetic little shrug gave Mr. Chadwick the encouragement he needed. "It's like this. When we drill a well into an oil-bearing formation, it creates a low pressure spot at the bottom, and the gas pressure brings oil from the surrounding area."

"I'm beginning to get the picture," agreed Adam. "The oil could come from a neighbor, who wouldn't take kindly to losing it, I'd imagine."

"Right. So, the legal question becomes, who owns the oil?" Mr. Chadwick watched as Adam clipped the suture thread and applied a bandage. "What the Supreme Court of Pennsylvania did was to find a common law that governs the capture of wild game."

Adam, cleaning up the clutter he'd created during Mr. Chadwick's treatment, said, "I'm afraid you've lost me now. What does a wild game law have to do with oil?"

Mr. Chadwick stood up, a little smile on his round face. "Well, you see, it's like wild deer that wander wherever they want. Any man who shoots one, no matter whose property it's on, it belongs to him. This court decided oil is of a feral nature and should be governed by the same rule."

At this interesting interpretation of the law, Adam stopped his cleanup operation. "Fascinating. So the oil belongs to whoever captures it on his own land."

"Exactly! But as you can probably deduce, it causes an awful lot of drilling. If, say, Mr. Jones drills and makes a gusher, Mr. Smith, his neighbor, gets right on it and drills quick, too, so he gets what's on his property before Jones gets it all. That's why a lot of the real estate men are making a killing, too. They're selling land in sixty-fourth-of-an-acre plots, you know."

"Let me guess," said Adam. "That's the size of a derrick floor, right?"

"Right, Doc." He flexed his hand carefully. "You did a good job on this paw. I'll pass the word on. What do I owe you?"

Without hesitation Adam answered, "Twenty dollars, Mr. Chadwick." It never ceased to amaze him how the money flowed as easily as the oil here.

Mr. Chadwick peeled out three tens and shook his head before Adam could protest it was too much. As he replaced his wallet he made one last comment. "The main problem with all this is still coming. With all the competition between land owners, not to mention the oil companies that are springing up like mushrooms, it won't be long before this field will be drilled out. I've heard tell that they're drilling over at Batson and Saratoga now. A smart man would look in that direction, I'd say."

Adam, thinking that Saratoga was where Jude and the Gallaghers came from, nodded. "Is that so?"

"Yessiree, Doc." Mr. Chadwick winked. "And this town'll go back to being . . . let's see, what have I heard 'em call it?"

"Queen of the Neches?" supplied Adam as he walked the man to the door. His eyes widened a little in surprise when he saw Carrie waiting with all the others in the little room. When Mr. Chadwick went out he said, quite formally, "You can come back, Miss Chaumont."

Supposing it was because he didn't want his patients to think he was conducting personal business during office hours, Carrie waited until they were behind the curtain, which she pulled tighter, then said in a low, confidential voice, "Adam, I need to talk to you."

He finished clearing away the instruments he'd used to suture Mr. Chadwick's hand before he asked, "Does it have to be now, Carrie?"

"Yes, I think it does." She went to stand quite close to him, her back to the curtain, her voice lower than ever and pleading. "We have to leave this place; we have to!"

He stared down at her. "Carrie, do you realize that Mr. Chadwick, the man who just left, paid me thirty dollars to sew up a cut on his hand, that I've got a room full of patients almost all the time and that most of them have the money to pay me like Mr. Chadwick did?"

"You never used to think of money so much," she whispered.

"That was when I had plenty." Though he spoke no more loudly than she, his tone was harsh. "And it's not just the money. I like working hard."

"Do you like working all night?" Even though his brows lowered in that familiar scowl, she rushed on. "I spoke to Miss Gallagher after you brought her home this morning."

"And?"

"And I felt she . . . that you and she . . . oh, Adam." Carrie searched for the right words. "I don't know what I'd do if I lost you!"

The scowl left his face and he looked down at her for a long while before he said gently, "There's no need for you to be jealous of Jeannie Gallagher, no need at all."

"Are you so sure? I saw . . . I thought you and she—"

"Quite sure. And whatever you thought, it isn't true." He touched her cheek gently with the back of his hand. "We can't leave just yet, Carrie. Can't you see, this is my chance to catch up, to regain at least a little of what we lost at Greenlea. My dear Carrie," he sighed, "what can I do to reassure you?"

"You could tell me you love me." The words were no more than a thought quietly expressed.

He drew a deep breath. "Of course I love you, Carrie. How could I help but love the woman who loves my son, who's been so faithful to us both?"

"I love you, too, Adam." Her smile was tremulous and hopeful. With all her heart she willed him to go on, to say they would be married.

His face was turned slightly away from her as he murmured, "This is not the place to talk about it. I have patients waiting."

She felt the smile on her face stiffen, but she was determined not to let it fade. "Of course, Adam, I understand. Can we talk about it later?"

He faced her now, and said in a louder voice as though he were talking to a patient, "Yes, we'll discuss it again, Miss

Chaumont. Thank you for consulting me." Taking her arm, he walked with her to the curtain, and called out, "Next, please?"

Carrie left the office in a sort of daze. She'd come to persuade Adam to leave Beaumont, and failed miserably in that. He'd said he loved her, yet she felt no less anxious and disturbed. Still convinced that leaving was the only answer for them, she went outside to wait until Jude returned. Waiting for Jude, no matter how long it took, was easy; it was infinitely harder waiting for Adam to realize they belonged together, to agree that they had to leave this place or they would never be happy.

CHAPTER 7

*He causeth the grass to grow for the cattle, and herb for the
service of man: that he may bring forth food out of the earth.*
                                                    Psalm 104:14

Adam's dreams were rarely good. They were often
haunted—by the memory of Anson dePaul, his ruined face cradled in Landra's lap as he lay dying; by Rose's quiet, despairing
pain; by Jimmy's raging frustration, his sightless, staring eyes
still begging for help. Adam would struggle to be free from the
snares of sleep; the horrible helplessness lying like a heavy
weight on his soul.

On the night of September 11, 1902, however, his sleep was
deep and dreamless. But when the light invaded the small back
room and the shouts of confusion filtered through his deep slumber, he thought he'd begun to dream. It was the sound of pistol
shots and curses that made him cry out, "No, don't shoot him!
He's a man. Anson dePaul is a man, not a monster!"

He jerked upright, his eyes staring at the flickering firelight
that lit the sky outside. Dressing hurriedly, he went out, only
to be knocked about by the yelling, screaming stream of humanity roaring past him.

"What is it? What's happened?" he shouted.

Before he could get an answer, an explosion shook the
ground on which he stood. Adam grabbed the arm of a wild-
eyed, white-faced man who stumbled as he ran past. "Tell me,
man, what's happening?"

"Fire! A tank blew up, and the whole field's on fire!" He
tried to wrench loose, but Adam held him fast.

"How? How did it start?"

"They say some ignoramus took a lighted lantern and tried

to see how much oil there was in a tank! Is that a stupid stunt, or what?"

"Was he hurt badly?"

"Who?" The man stared at him, then said, "If you mean the guy who started the fire, I hope so! Now let me go. I've got to see what's left of my crew. Say, aren't you the Doc?" Evidently he'd calmed sufficiently to recognize Adam, who nodded. "Well, there'll be plenty for you to do this night."

Adam released him and watched as he ran off. The full implications of his last statement hit him as he stared at the sky, lit by a big ball of fire. As the explosions followed one after the other, sounding like charges of dynamite, the flames shot hundreds of feet into the air, illuminating the dense, rolling, oily smoke. Escaping gas formed blazing balls which also exploded high in the air, making an unholy display of fireworks.

A mother's agony brought Adam from his mesmerized state; she held a crying child in her arms. He touched her shoulder gently and said, "Bring him into my office, madam. I'm a doctor."

"What?" She looked up at him, dazed; then what he'd said penetrated her dulled senses. "Oh, please, you've got to save him! My other baby, he's . . . he's dead . . ." Low sobs wracked her body, and she allowed Adam to guide her into the office where she let him take the child, whose arm had a nasty break.

By the flickering light of three oil lamps, he set the little arm, hoping that his cleansing of the wound where the skin was broken would keep it from becoming infected.

That was only the beginning. Throughout the remainder of the long night—he'd glanced at his watch and seen that it was a little after one o'clock in the morning—Adam's office was filled with hysterical burned men and women. Some were more concerned with the fact that their entire fortunes were literally going up in flames, in the stinking, greasy smoke, than they were about their burns and broken bones.

Adam worked feverishly, mending the burned, bruised, and broken bodies, until dawn when he fell exhausted onto his cot. An hour later the morning light, even filtered as it was through the haze of the smoldering blazes in the oil fields, was still harsh enough to pain his gritty eyelids. Someone was pounding at the door.

It was Jeannie, and with her, Carrie, whose face showed her concern for Adam.

"Adam," she said, "are you all right?"

"Sure, and he's only feeling the effects of working most of the night, am I right, Dr. Adam?" said Jeannie as she eyed Adam. He'd stood aside to let the two women come into the small, horrible smelling office; the stench of the night's work hung over it.

Adam ran a hand over his thick black hair. "What are you two doing here?"

"We've come to help," answered Jeannie, already gathering up litter.

Carrie took a step closer to Adam, her eyes full of undisguised pain at his weariness. "Oh, Adam, you look so . . . so terrible!"

Before he could respond to the unabashed pity in Carrie's tone, Jeannie sang out from the inner office, "A cup of mum's coffee and a stack of her flapjacks and he'd be right as rain, I'll wager."

While he'd been about to succumb to the sympathy Carrie offered, Adam found himself scowling. "If you'd worked half the night on charred, half-crazy people, you wouldn't be so—"

Jeannie interrupted him, saying, "You think I didn't, hmm? Well, we'll not go into that. By the way, my guess is that there'll be a new wave of patients on your doorstep shortly, so you'd best get this place in order." She wrinkled her small nose. "It's a mess."

With the three of them working, they soon had the place neat again and all the doors and windows open so the air could make its way through. It was an ill wind, however; Jeannie's prediction was true. Most of the men and women who walked haltingly into the office were not seriously injured, at least not physically. But their minds were stunned with disbelief at their terrible misfortune.

The fires were, for the most part, out, except for an occasional explosion of gas. Even Carrie forgot her preoccupation with Adam as she sat close beside a woman who'd lost her husband and all her possessions; she had nothing left but the little boy she held tightly. The child's expression was dazed, blank, though he seemed not to be harmed physically.

As Adam helped a man out the door, he overheard Carrie's soft words, "You have strength you've never used, and you can call on it now."

"No, no, I don't." The woman's tone was dull and lifeless. "I don't have anything left."

"You have your son, and he needs you."

The woman's eyes went to the child. "He needs me." The words were only a breathy little echo.

"What's his name?"

The woman hesitated a long while, then replied, "His name is Arlen, after his father. But his father's dead—" Her words rose until they were almost a shriek.

"Calm yourself," said Carrie firmly. "If not for your sake, for your son's. You're an adult, and children depend on adults not to act like children."

The low, firm command had the desired effect. "Yes, you're right, miss. I mustn't act like a child. He needs me."

"Where is your home? Can we help you contact your relatives, your husband's relatives?"

Adam's expression was thoughtful as he said, "I believe there's a group that's been set up to do just that, Carrie. It's a couple of blocks east of here."

To his pleased surprise Carrie said, "I'll take her over."

"Thank you, Carrie. We . . . I appreciate your being here, and your help."

Her smile at Adam's words of praise and encouragement was brilliant. She glanced back at Jeannie, who was busy in the inner office, then said, "In case you go back to the hotel before I return, don't worry. I can manage."

"No, we'll wait for you." He watched her tenderly help the woman to her feet, and then pick the little boy up in her arms. "We'll get through this if we stick together."

Her eyes met his, the vulnerability that was always lurking there plain now. "Yes, Adam, we must stick together, mustn't we?" And then she led the woman out.

Adam watched her go, and as he had so many times in their relationship, he admitted that he admired her very much. She was a strong, admirable woman in many ways. But when Jeannie Gallagher called out, "Dr. Adam, I think you should look at this," he turned, and in a little while all thoughts of Carrie left his mind.

It was late afternoon before the three of them were able to return to the hotel, only to find the chaos there hadn't abated at all. Though fires in the fields were either out or under control, the night's happenings had made a difference in the attitudes of those involved in the oil business. The trading was even more frantic, with men trying to sell before everything they'd invested was lost and buyers trying to get the best possible deals. The noise in the lobby of the hotel was almost deafening. Over it all were excited conversations about the production of the gushers in Saratoga and Batson.

"It's not Spindletop, but they say it's bringing in over five hundred barrels a day," one man said to his companion.

"Spindletop?" he snorted. "It'd be nearer to the truth if they called it *Swindletop!*"

"Lost your stake, did you?"

"That, and more. I borrowed an ungodly amount . . ."

Adam and Carrie, following Jeannie, missed the remainder of the man's lament as they made their way to the kitchen.

However, once around the huge oak table, the conversation centered on the same topics: the fire, the fact that the boom here in Beaumont would soon be on the downward side, and agreement between Mrs. Gallagher, Jeannie, and Jude that all three were more than ready to return to the Thicket.

Mrs. Gallagher poured coffee all around again, and placed a huge platter of doughnuts on the table. "To tell the truth, it's not just the fire. I been ready to go home for a spell now. Been thinking I'll maybe set up my own boardinghouse, even."

Jeannie's eyes were thoughtful. "If things are slowing down here and starting in Saratoga, it makes sense. I'm for sure ready to go home. How about you, Uncle Jude?" She glanced fondly at him; he had poured his coffee into a saucer and was blowing on it delicately.

"Honey-gal, I was ready before I left. I just come along to keep an eye on you womenfolk. Figgered Sean'd haunt me if I didn't. How about you, Robbie boy? You going to the Thicket with the rest of us?" He ruffled the child's hair.

"Can I have a yaller cur dog?" Rob asked, his eyes shining.

"Shore you can. I'll git you a pup myself—"

It was Carrie who broke in. "With Adam doing so well here in Beaumont, I doubt very seriously if we'll be leaving."

"But I thought you wanted to leave," said Adam.

"I . . . what's important is that you do well, Adam, and have plenty of work." She glanced at Jeannie, who spoke now, her voice calm and matter-of-fact.

"Well, Dr. Adam, it's for sure we don't know when Melrose is coming back, so she's right; there'll be plenty for you to do here." She rose from the table. "I, for one, am going to pack right now, for I've been feeling the call of the Thicket for a good while. Carrie," she added with a smile, "you'll most likely be glad to have the room to yourself and Rob. It's a bit small for the belongings of the three of us."

Carrie tried to keep her face from showing just how glad she did feel; she didn't quite manage to. "I'm very grateful to you, Miss Gallagher, and we appreciate your hospitality."

"I know you do." Jeannie's brown eyes were thoughtful. "Well, the sooner we're out of here, the better I'll feel. How does tomorrow morning suit you, Mum?"

"Fine as frog's fur," said Mrs. Gallagher cheerfully, grinning at Rob when he giggled. "Give me a hand with the packing, you two?"

Jude muttered something to the effect of having to see to his horses, but Jeannie immediately set about separating her mother's things from those that belonged to the hotel.

At Adam's nod to Jude's questioning glance, Jude took Rob with him, and Adam followed Carrie into the hallway. "Adam," she said earnestly, "it's going to work out, you'll see. You'll get a better office, one here in Beaumont, and . . ." She trailed off as she saw the frown on his face. "What's wrong?"

"I don't understand why you changed your mind so quickly. Not very many hours ago you were begging me to leave."

"But things are different now, don't you see?"

Neither she nor Adam voiced the reason for the difference aloud; Jeannie Gallagher was leaving, so now they could stay. He nodded, wondering at the feelings that disturbed him. One thing was certain, as long as Melrose was gone, he'd have plenty of work.

The next few weeks went on pretty much the same as they had before, with only a couple of differences. The new cook at the Crosby Hotel was not quite up to average, and Adam missed the Gallaghers to an alarming degree. He persuaded himself it was because Reba Gallagher was such a good cook, that Jeannie had been so much help to him; that he needed her knowledge of midwifery. He might have gone on as he was for a long time, treating an amazing variety of patients every day, had it not been for two happenings. The first was Dr. Melrose's return.

Shocked at his sudden appearance, even more surprising was the fact that he was cold sober. Dr. Melrose was also neatly dressed in a new suit of clothes, his eyes were clear, his mustache trimmed, and there was no trace of tobacco juice.

"Been busy, Dr. Jarrett?" he asked, those clear eyes taking

in the full, clean waiting room, the neat inner room, the fully stocked shelves.

"Very." Adam knew the resentment he felt at the man's proprietary glance wasn't altogether unreasonable. After all, the office had been a shambles, much the same as the man, when he'd left.

"Well, I'm back, so I'll take over now."

"Just like that?"

"I'm not saying I'm not grateful you took over, but the fact remains, it's my office and my practice."

"That's so, Dr. Melrose, but—"

"Made plenty of money, did you, while I was gone?" asked Melrose shrewdly.

Adam had been about to say the practice was more his than Melrose's now, but instead he said, "I did, and I thank you for the opportunity, Dr. Melrose."

"Don't mention it." Seeing he wasn't going to have to persuade Adam to leave, he said magnanimously, "Heard good things about you, son. You won't have any trouble setting up somewhere else, I expect."

"I'm sure you're right." As Adam gathered together the instruments and supplies he'd brought with him or bought since, he wondered what Carrie would say about this turn of events.

As it turned out, she was pleased. That evening, having finally found someone who came up to her standards to stay with Rob, Carrie insisted they have a celebration supper. Though the meal itself was no better than usual—watery potatoes and stringy beef—she'd bribed one of the maids into putting a clean cloth on their table, which was tucked into an almost intimate corner.

In her excitement at Adam's news, she reached across the table and caught his hand in hers, oblivious to the noisy crowd around them. "Oh, Adam, you have a following. It doesn't matter that Melrose is back. They'll keep coming to you. Now you can get a real office, a nice one here in Beaumont instead of that hole in Gladys City, and we can get a house."

Adam didn't reply immediately, nor did he withdraw his hand from her grasp. He knew as well as Carrie that she meant a house for the three of them, not just for her and Rob as they'd had before. It was in her face, in her eyes—the hope that their time had come. He had to admit she looked exceptionally lovely. Her shiny black hair, parted in the middle, was caught in a chignon low on her neck. And he noticed now what he hadn't before, that she had on a new dress, made of some dark blue, rich-looking material that made her eyes look even bluer. The neckline was decorously high, but the soft fabric subtly emphasized the curves of her body. Not sure exactly what he wanted to say, he murmured, "Your dress is new, isn't it? I like it."

She flushed with pleasure. "Thank you. It's been a long time since I had a new one. I'm glad you like it."

Smitten by the fact that she rarely asked for anything, he said, "You're a good, loyal woman, Carrie, and you deserve better. I just don't think of these things."

Her voice was low and full of emotion. "I don't expect you to, Adam. You're a busy man." She stopped and her eyes met and held his. "And a busy man should have a home, where he can come after a long, hard day, where he can have a proper meal with his son. Don't you agree?"

"Carrie, I—" She leaned forward, her face bright with expectancy. "Look!" he exclaimed; "it's Jeannie Gallagher!" He missed the flare of disappointment, of near panic on Carrie's face as they both watched Jeannie thread her way between the crowded tables toward them.

Adam pulled his hand from Carrie's and stood, then brought a chair from the adjoining table. "Sit down, Miss Gallagher, and tell us how things are in Saratoga."

Jeannie's smile was warm as she sat down, nodding her thanks to Adam. "How pretty you look, Carrie. And as for Saratoga, that's exactly what I came to talk to you about. I've heard that Dr. Melrose is back."

"That's true," said Adam. "Showed up today."

"Sober?" asked Jeannie. "I'd heard that, too, but didn't know whether or not to believe it."

"Not only sober, but dressed like a gentleman and ready to take back his office."

"Adam has decided to open up an office of his own," put in Carrie, her chin lifted slightly as she met Jeannie's eyes.

"Is that a fact?" said Jeannie slowly. "And may I ask where?"

"We'd thought here, in Beaumont—"

"I haven't decided yet, Miss Gallagher," Adam broke in.

Jeannie's smile was brilliant. "Good! Then I want you to consider coming to Saratoga."

"Tell me why."

"Because of the need," replied Jeannie simply. "There's no doctor there now, and as more and more outsiders, the oil folk, come in, the need grows. And . . ." She hesitated, then added, "My own people, the people of the Thicket, *need* a doctor like you."

"No doctor at all, hmm?"

"Not living there. And many's the time they do without, or make do with the likes of me."

"I'm sure you do very well." Carrie smoothed her dress and kept her eyes on Adam, "And I'm also sure you'll find someone, another doctor, to come to Saratoga."

The little silence was filled by the sounds all around them: silver clinking, business being conducted, women laughing. Then Adam stated slowly, "No, Carrie, they won't need to find someone else, because I'm going to go."

"But, Adam—" Carrie broke off as she saw Jeannie's troubled gaze.

"Sure, and I'm sorry if my asking you to come to Saratoga causes any problems." She shrugged, her smile apologetic. "I guess I was so glad to get back home and away from Beaumont, I figured you would like it, too. Well, I'd best leave the two of you to discuss the matter."

"No need for discussion, I've made up my mind," declared Adam. "It will be good to get Rob out of this madhouse, and he's missed you . . . and your mother and Jude."

"Yes. Well, I can believe that. Uncle Jude mopes around, always talking about how Rob would like this or that. By the way, Mum's opened her own boardinghouse in Saratoga like she wanted, so there'll be room aplenty for you all. Unless, of course, you'll be wanting a house instead. Carrie told me a while back that you're going to be married soon. We're all happy for you."

Carrie, her face impassive, said nothing. Finally, Adam replied, slowly and thoughtfully, "Tell your mother to reserve a room for Carrie and Rob. I intend to set up an office as soon as possible, and stay there. It worked out well at Melrose's."

Jeannie rose. "We'll be looking forward to your coming, you and Rob especially, Carrie." She smiled warmly again at Carrie, whose answering smile was tight and forced looking. Then she moved away into the crowded room.

It was several moments before Adam spoke, his voice low. "When did you tell Miss Gallagher we were to be married?"

Carrie bit her lip, but she met his eyes squarely. "It was the day you brought her home at dawn."

"The day you came to the office to ask me to leave Beaumont, right?" She nodded, and he said, "Carrie, I haven't been fair to you, have I?"

"What do you mean?"

"Just that I've been unbelievably selfish. You said you weren't concerned with what people say, but you are, aren't you?"

Blue eyes brimming, Carrie said, "It's not that she's ever said anything, or been anything but kind . . . but Miss Gallagher makes me feel not . . . not quite respectable."

"Oh, Carrie, I'm so sorry."

"It's all right, Adam. It really is. I love you." A smile trembled on her lips. "And you said you loved me, that day in your office." Her voice quivered as she dabbed her eyes with her napkin.

He nodded slowly. "Yes, I did, didn't I?" Adam thought again, as he had so many times before, that he would never love any woman again the way he had loved Bethany. But his life seemed inextricably twined with Carrie's; they'd shared so much in the past three years. She loved his son, and she loved him. "If I could just be certain it would be enough for you . . ."

"What, Adam, if what would be enough?"

His breath caught at the look of hope on her face. "I care deeply for you, Carrie. But you know how I loved Bethany, that I'll never feel that way again."

"You don't have to say any more, Adam, and you don't know that for sure! And yes, it will be enough."

Adam knew there could be no more stalling. Something in Carrie's eyes told him so. They'd been moving toward this for a long time; there was a feeling of inevitability in the moment that he couldn't deny. "All right, Carrie, we'll be married, if that's what you want."

"It is, Adam, it is!" Her smile was tremulous, but her voice was steady as she said, "You won't be sorry, I promise you. Oh, it's going to be so wonderful!"

He nodded, listening as she made plans, thinking how very beautiful she was in her happiness.

CHAPTER 8

And God said, Behold, I have given you every herb bearing seed,
which is upon the face of all the earth, and every tree, in the
which is the fruit of a tree yielding seed; to you it shall be for
meat.   *Genesis 1:29*

Jude spat into the mud as the wagon he was driving lurched
crazily. "Doc, I told you the road from Beaumont to Gladys City
was a royal highway compared to this here road to Saratoga."
He winked at Rob, who tried valiantly to wink back. The little
boy, clinging to the rough seat beside Jude, grinned at his
friend.

The road to Saratoga from Kountze was only twelve miles
long, but it was also not much more than sandy ruts, with tree
roots thrown into the worst mud holes. Carrie, who'd been quiet
up until now as Jude regaled Rob with mostly acceptable tales,
said, "Is Saratoga a very big town?"

"Town?" Jude snorted. "Little lady, before this oil craziness
started there probably wasn't many more'n a dozen folks living
there."

"And now?" Adam asked as he put his arm around Carrie
when the wagon—loaded to capacity with medicines, supplies,
even an operating table he'd located—swayed dangerously. She
leaned into him, a look of gratitude on her face that was far
more intense than the small gesture warranted.

Jude spat again. "Them loonies're pouring in so blooming
fast if I was a panther I'd light out for Mexico! I oughtta think
about it, at that. Those fool oil men don't care nothin' for the
critters in the Thicket, two-legged or otherwise. Poison gas
everywhere, salt water and that black oil scum messing up the
pastures, fouling the bayous."

85

"Sounds terrible," murmured Carrie. "Adam, are you sure we're doing the right thing, moving there from Beaumont?"

"Little lady, when Jeannie told you the Doc was needed, she wasn't just a'whistling Dixie. The only Doc I ever heerd tell of settling in the Thicket was Dr. Mud." He glanced down at the small boy at his side, who'd been taking in every detail of the surrounding countryside. There were tall, thin pine trees that grew close together, graceful palmetto fronds, a lush profusion of drooping gray moss, Virginia creeper-hung hardwoods, bay-gall groves with vines as big as a man's hand looped low over the green brown bayou water. And as Jude had commented earlier, the underbrush was so thick a ribbon snake couldn't wiggle through.

Rob giggled. "Dr. Mud? That's funny!"

"Folks took him serious, son. That's how Saratoga got its name."

"Is it a story?"

"Yup."

"Tell it, tell it!" Rob bounced exuberantly on the seat.

"Well, set still, you little tadpole. Set still, or I won't!" But the words were said affectionately as Jude scowled at the child. "It was like this, you see. A hundred years ago the Injuns found out that the mud round about Sour Lake would cure up sores, even eyes that was all pussed up. They'd put that ol' mud on 'em—"

"Mud, in their eyes?" asked Rob incredulously.

"Yup, and it cured 'em. Anyhow, this feller who called hisself Dr. Mud was half Injun and half Negro, and he got pretty famous for curing folks with that old mud. Had hisself a regular dress suit and a top hat, and all the ladies swore by his mud packs for their rose-petal complexions," he said, exaggerating his words.

"Ugh," was Rob's disgusted comment. "Mud on their faces, too?"

Jude grinned. "Ladies'll do pert near anything to look more beautiful. "Course," he added gallantly, with a glance at the pair behind him, "if they're pretty as Miss Carrie, they don't need mud or nothing. Anyhow, long about '67 some fellas built a bathhouse over them sour springs and called it Saratoga Springs."

"There's a Saratoga Springs in New York, I believe," said Adam.

Jude nodded. "The very ones they named this'n after. It weren't a big success, though folks still swear by that smelly ol' water for ulcers and arthritis, and the like. Anyhow, most of them buildings have done fallen in, and business kind of petered out."

"Until they discovered oil." Adam's thoughtful statement fell into the little silence that followed. The only sounds they heard, except the sucking sounds the wagon wheels made as they pushed through the mud, were the calls of birds and the sighing wind in the pines.

"Right you are," agreed Jude. "Old Fletcher Cotton kept noticing that when his hawgs came out of a certain part of the Thicket, they was allus slick and glossy. He follered 'em one day, and found a slough full of bubbling, stinking mud. He drove a two-inch pipe down, and it wasn't too awful long afore oil came right up in that pipe. Sold that piece of property to the Hooks brothers from over at Kountze, and they drilled the first producing well here in the Thicket." He sighed noisily. "Hope it'll poop out afore too long, I surely do, afore they ruin the Thicket."

"In the meantime, there's money to be made." Adam reached to steady Rob as the wagon lurched again. Softly he added, "And I'm going to get what I can."

Jude glanced back at him shrewdly. "Sound like the rest of them wildcatters in Saratoga."

"Wildcatters? Where we're going?" asked Rob timidly. He liked hearing stories about panthers and wildcats, but the thought of living in the same place with them was scary.

"Son, I'm talking about two-legged critters now, the men who're on the prowl looking for oil."

"Oh." Rob leaned against Jude trustingly. Whatever kind of critter they came up against, he knew his friend Jude would protect him. And in spite of the roughness of the ride, he fell asleep.

An hour later Jude hauled up on the reins and announced, "There it is, folks, the Hotel Saratoga. Leastways that's what Reba's calling it."

Adam didn't know what he'd expected, but the name seemed pretentious. A two-story frame structure, the hotel had a deep gallery on both stories. At the back, a narrow boardwalk connected it to a smaller house. Jude explained that Reba Gallagher did the cooking there. Tall pine trees crowded the building, making a dense shade that was welcome after the heat of the fierce sun they'd endured throughout the trip. A couple of log houses and a general store were the extent of Saratoga—except for several new buildings which had a raw, unfinished look beside these older, more comfortable ones.

After asking Jude to see that Carrie and Rob were taken to the hotel and delivered into the care of Mrs. Gallagher, Adam began his search for a suitable place for his office. It didn't take long. There obviously wasn't much available unless he waited for one of the new buildings to be finished. One side of the general store was being used as a storeroom, and the owner, Cy Young, responded instantly to Adam's generous rent offer. As Adam was hauling in the supplies they'd brought from Beaumont, he heard a familiar laugh. When Jeannie Gallagher appeared a couple of minutes later, still laughing with the owner of the general store, he nodded to her. Her red hair was straggling a little, but her face was wreathed in a welcoming smile as he heard himself say, "Miss Gallagher, I'm not at all sure you've done us a favor. This place is primitive, to say the least."

Her smile faded a bit, but not for long. "Why, Dr. Adam, where in the wide round world did you get the idea I was trying to do you a favor? We need a doctor and you're a good one, it's as simple as that." Somehow during her little speech her expression had changed from warm joy at seeing him, to guarded politeness, much like his own. "You've rented Cy's storeroom for your office, I understand." When Adam nodded she asked, "Would you be needing some help to set up, then?"

Adam could not have told what prompted him to say, "No thanks. I can manage."

She gazed thoughtfully at the piled up supplies, the dusty shelves. "Whatever you say. I'll go on over to the hotel and see that Carrie and Rob get settled in." And with that she turned and walked quickly away.

As he watched her make her way across the street, Adam felt a sharp pang of regret, and wondered why he'd been so abrupt. He was remembering how much help she'd been when Melrose had handed over his office. And when he looked at what he had to do here, he cursed softly under his breath. Whatever had possessed him? He shrugged and set to work.

When he came across the wooden sign that a grateful patient in Beaumont had carved—it read Adam Jarrett, M.D.—he nailed it up outside with the hammer Cy Young had graciously loaned him. The sun was slanting from the west, and shone warm on his back as he tried to decide if the sign was straight on the rough plank wall. Suddenly the irony of the situation hit him: Adam Jarrett, M.D., top of his medical class, pride of his professors, promising research scientist, was hanging his shingle in the wilderness.

For it was wilderness. To call it anything else would be a lie. Although man was scratching furiously at the earth only a few miles away in the attempt to force the land to yield her black treasure, Adam could feel the wilderness waiting, saying, *Go ahead, do what you will to me. But I am here, and I will be here when you are gone, when your oil fever subsides and your head is clear enough to tell you to leave, to get away, and I will slowly cover the desecration you leave behind. I will not forgive it, but I will cover my shame.*

Adam had heard many tales of the Thicket since he'd been in Beaumont, and had there been anyone he was close enough to confide in, at that moment he would have confessed that he felt drawn, compelled, even, by what he'd heard. Tales of bears, wild and vicious, panthers, snakes of all kinds, including every poisonous variety known to be in North America; tales of men coming deliberately into the Thicket to hide from the law and their dark pasts. With bogs of quicksand, impenetrable groves of baygall and vines of every kind, the Big Thicket was off the known path, the most hostile environment to be found.

Strangely, perversely, knowing all this, Adam drew a deep breath of the warm, musky air, and knew he'd been right to come. As he was about to go inside to tackle setting up again, a towheaded girl, who looked to be twelve or so, came running by.

"Hey, Cy," she called out, "you seen Jeannie?" She was dressed in a faded pair of overalls over a ragged shirt, her feet bare. "I gotta find her!"

Cy came out of the general store, wiping his hands on the apron tied around his skinny middle. "Hey, Polly, is it your mama's time?" The girl, out of breath, nodded. "Well, you're in luck. This here's the new doctor in town, Dr. Adam Jarrett."

"How far away do you live, Polly? Can we walk?" Adam had already turned to go inside and fetch his bag when the girl spoke up.

"Yessir, but . . ." Her pale blue eyes glanced at Cy. "Mama told me to get Jeannie."

Adam felt that pang again; he told himself it was ridiculous to be jealous of a woman. "I'll get my bag, Polly, and if you feel your mother would want Jeannie, too, you go and get her. She's over at the hotel."

The girl stared at Adam, her face troubled. Finally she said softly, "We don't have much cash money."

"Don't worry about it. Go get Jeannie, and I'll wait for you here." As he watched the girl run across the street, he thought several things at once. In a way, he was trespassing on Jeannie Gallagher's territory; she was, after all, an experienced midwife whom everyone trusted. But *she* had asked him to come here, and he might as well establish himself with the people of the Thicket as soon as possible.

Just then the youngster came out of the hotel, Jeannie close behind her. Adam's involuntary thought as she walked briskly toward him was how very different she was than Bethany. Beth had been tall and willowy, her delicate blond beauty soft and appealing. This little woman, with her fiery hair and peppery speech, was more like Landra. Fleetingly he wondered how Landra was, if her pregnancy was progressing well.

"Dr. Adam," Jeannie's greeting rang out on the still afternoon air. "Are you ready to deliver your first Thicket babe? Polly tells me we'd best hurry, and I don't doubt she's right. Mrs. Dalton is like it says in the Bible about the Hebrew women when they were in Egypt."

As he fell into step with the two, Adam said, "I'm afraid you'll have to explain yourself, Miss Gallagher. My knowledge of the Bible is sketchy at best."

Jeannie glanced at him, her mouth curved in a smile. "Dr. Adam, you may have thought your education was finished when they turned you loose from that fine New York medical school. But believe me, it's just begun. Those Hebrew women knew they'd better birth their babies fast before the midwives arrived, because ol' Pharaoh had told the midwives to kill them." Her face grew serious as she added, "Polly's mama has her young'uns fast, but they don't always make it. She's had several—"

"Six," was Polly's terse, grim comment.

"And only Polly and little Sarah made it. It'll take the both of us to make sure this one makes it; that's why I was glad you came along."

He nodded, but he felt a stab of something very near anxiety as he saw how quickly they were in deep woods, for he knew they'd only come a few hundred yards from Saratoga proper. The green closed around them, and the path they were walking on single file—with Polly in front, Jeannie between them—was just that, a wispy path that looked as though it might not be there tomorrow if someone didn't walk on it today. Because he had never been in such dense woods before, Adam was unsure of the distance they covered before they came to a small clearing in which a low log cabin sat.

A tiny girl's face was at the window, then disappeared as they came into view. "Mama," they heard her yell, "Jeannie's come, and there's a man with her'n and Polly!"

Inside the cabin everything was neat, except for the bed upon which Mrs. Dalton lay. It was a tumbled mess, and she tried to sit up as they entered, but she fell back.

"Jeannie . . . better hurry," she panted. Jeannie moved quickly toward her while motioning for Polly to take the fair-haired, round-eyed little girl outside. They left, but not before the child said, "Is my mama gonna be all right?"

Jeannie went to her and hugged the scrawny mite close. "Of course, Sarah. Now you and Polly go and pick some flowers for your mama and the new baby. You hear me?" The child nodded, her eyes on her mother, but she obediently followed her sister out. "Poor Sarah. She's seen what happened to the other babies," she said as the woman cried out—a low, unwilling growl of pain. She went back to the bed, her hands deftly straightening the tangled bedclothes, smoothing Mrs. Dalton's forehead. "I've brought a doctor, June, Dr. Adam Jarrett. He's very good, and we're going to have a good baby, aren't we?"

"Oh, Jeannie," June Dalton said, her breathing shallow, her words breathy, "do you think so? Oh! It's coming . . . the baby . . ."

As Jeannie had said, things happened very quickly after that. She carefully deferred to Adam as he delivered the child— a large, perfect baby boy. He lifted him high and gave him a couple of little smacks between his shoulder blades, but there was no cry. The arms and legs of the infant looked strangely flaccid. And his color was not good at all.

"Dr. Adam," said Jeannie, her voice low, "see if there's any water heating on the stove. And find a couple of basins big enough to put a baby in."

Adam stared at her. "Miss Gallagher, I—"

"Now! One warm, one cold, and hurry." Jeannie's quiet words were a command and both of them knew it. Her brown eyes stared into his for a second, and his frown deepened, but as he went to do her bidding she did an amazing thing. She grasped the limp, blue baby by his feet only and spun around. Then she held him close and examined him. No response. "Hurry, Dr. Adam, hurry!"

Clumsily he poured cold water into a dishpan, found a big soup pot hanging on the wall, and filled that with a mixture of hot and cold. Before he was finished Jeannie lowered the baby into the cold water, then quickly into the warm. Into the cold again, and then the warm, a look of fierce concentration on her face as she first rubbed the small body, then slapped his feet lightly. Finally she whispered, "Look, he's turning pink . . ."

Adam was close beside her. The baby was, indeed, turning pink, and his face was moving, his tiny brow wrinkled as if in concentration. Then a faint "Ahhhhh" came from his mouth. "He's alive," said Jeannie, "June, he's alive!"

Brisk and gentle at the same time, she rubbed the baby dry and wrapped him tightly in a strip of flannel laid out in hope earlier. When she'd placed the baby in June Dalton's waiting arms, she said, "I'll make you some raspberry leaf tea, Juney girl, and we'll get the rest of this business done up so the children can see their new brother. Dr. Adam, would you like to tell them?"

Knowing from the smile she directed at the mother and child that he was being dismissed—however politely—he nodded and left. Outside he announced to the two little girls, waiting in equal amounts of patience and anxiety, that they had a baby brother. Both of their faces lit up, and though they were too shy to speak to him, they whispered together. Adam, feeling more and more an outsider in this society of females, thought with sympathy that the bit of male humanity who'd just made his difficult entrance into the world had better watch his step.

Later, as they were returning to Saratoga, he made a comment to that effect.

Jeannie, because of the narrowness of the trail, stopped, as did he. She looked up into his eyes, a speculative expression in her own. "Dr. Adam, it sounds to me as though you think men and women are on opposite sides in the game of life."

Through the green, deep odors around them, he caught a hint of the fragrance of Jeannie Gallagher herself; a faint suggestion of something fresh and clean. He wanted to move away from it, but something he couldn't explain prevented him. He'd noticed it before, but somehow it was more compelling here. "Miss Gallagher," he replied slowly, "you can't deny we often are."

"For instance?" Her face was turned up; her eyes held his. They were extraordinary eyes. Adam had thought they were just brown, but now he could see tiny flecks of gold in them, and they were more than a little challenging just now.

"For instance back there with Mrs. Dalton, and every time we've worked together in a childbirth, it's really you who's been in command, whatever you try to tell them, or me."

"You believe that's true, do you?" She lowered her lashes, which were long and flashed tiny golden shafts in the sun's few penetrating rays.

"I know it is. The simple truth is, you are far more capable, more knowledgeable in these situations than I am."

"And are you offended by the idea that a woman could be better than a man at something?" There was that challenge again, no mistake about it. But there was also something else, an undeniable desire to know what he would say.

There was the far-off sound of the *thud, thud, thud* of a drilling rig, an occasional shout that carried in the still, humid air. But mostly there were only bird sounds: a mockingbird, beginning his concert early, the fluting of a red-winged blackbird, the sassy quarreling of a pair of jays and the low, sweet-sad mourning of a dove.

"No, I'm not offended by you, Miss Gallagher—not you, nor your obvious skill. On the contrary, I admire it, and am grateful. We seem to . . . work well together."

"My sentiments exactly." Her low, musical laughter joined the bird sounds. "And how fine that you can admit it." She turned and began to walk again, and he fell in step.

"You sound surprised. Has your experience with men driven you to such a low opinion of us? Do you *expect* us to be pompous and unreasonable?"

The sound she made was suspiciously like a chuckle, but she stifled it. "Doctor, that's an understatement! However, I also find men necessary, interesting, and—" She glanced at him, then said, "I have to stop by my house to get some more raspberry leaves. I gave the last in my bag to June. If you want, you can stop with me. If not, I'll see you later." She stood at the fork of the trail and waited, her expression neutral, as though it didn't matter what he did.

Adam found he wanted to go with her, and that he didn't want to examine the reasons very closely. "Perhaps I should go with you. The raspberry leaf tea and some of the other things I've seen you use are new to me."

"And you're really interested in knowing herb remedies." It was more a thoughtful statement than a question.

"Yes, I am. Does that surprise you?"

She was silent for a few moments, then broke a glossy, dark green leaf from a nearby shrub, crushed it, and held it out for him to smell. "Sweet bay. I give it sometimes for stomachache." He took the fragrant leaf from her small hand, his eyes holding hers as she added slowly, "Yes, it surprises me. A lot of things about you surprise me, Dr. Adam."

He wanted to ask her if being surprised was a pleasant thing or unpleasant. Instead, he put the leaf into his pocket and said, "Well, let's get on with the tour of the famous Miss Gallagher's medicine show."

"Now you're making fun of me."

There was a long rattan vine dangling in the path, and Adam held it aside for her. "I assure you, I'm not."

Before she passed beneath his outstretched arm, Jeannie looked up into his face, as if to see for herself. It was an unguarded moment for them both. The secret green woods around them was a world apart from the cabin where they'd been, from the settlement at Saratoga, and most especially from the mad chaos of Gladys City and Beaumont. It was as though in this wild place they were different people, and must begin their relationship from the beginning. A slim ray of sun caught in Jeannie's hair just then, firing it for a brief second. Her lips were parted, as though she was about to say something. It seemed an eternity before she murmured simply, "Thank you. It's . . . my cabin is not far, just over there." She indicated the direction with a nod of her head, and once again her bright hair flashed.

Adam followed her as she began to walk again, refusing to allow himself to think about, to even name the feeling that had flooded him a second before.

Jeannie's cabin was larger than he'd expected, and he commented. She looked around and said, "My mum would tell you it was entirely too small for a family of four young'uns, I expect.

But she did the best she could. It was hard when my dad died, though."

"There were four of you? Where are they now?"

"Two of my brothers died of typhoid fever when they were little," she said, a frown creasing her brow. "The other one, Mike, went to California a couple of years ago to make his fortune. We hear from him now and then, and he sends money."

Adam was watching her thoughtfully. "So you, as the only daughter, decided you needed to stay with your mother."

Jeannie shrugged. "She needs me. Besides, the Thicket is home to me. I only went to Beaumont because she wanted to. I can tell you this for sure, I'm glad to be back." Her glance around the room mirrored fondness.

Adam's eyes took in the amazing array of filled shelves, which covered every inch of wall space except where a massive fieldstone fireplace mounted from floor to ceiling. The hearth was swept clean now, with a huge bouquet of wildflowers gracing the opening. The shelves held a variety of bottles, large and small, vials, jars of many sizes. They were all filled with leaves, bark, and powders, whose colors made a fascinating collage— greens both dull and bright, browns ranging from muddy to rich, reds, yellows in subtle variations.

"This was your parents' home, then?"

"Yes, it was," she replied, "before my dad died and my brothers died. Mum managed to get the hotel building in Saratoga, though, and I think she'll do well enough." She had gone to the side of the big front room which served as kitchen and dining room and was rummaging in her leather bag. Obviously failing to find what she wanted, she dumped its contents onto the square oak table.

"What are you looking for?"

"The little bag I keep my raspberry leaves in," she said, rummaging in the pile. "Ah, here it is. I need to refill it." She went to a large glass jar which contained dark green leaves.

"That's what you gave Mrs. Dalton, isn't it?" She nodded. "May I ask for what purpose?"

She finished filling her little bag, then glanced at him. "I use it for other things too, but in June's case it was to aid the coming of the afterbirth."

"I see." His expression was thoughtful, still faintly skeptical. "And you really believe it does?"

A smile curved her mouth as she pulled the drawstring of

the bag, then went to the table and began to tuck it, and the others she'd dumped out, back into her simples bag. When she'd finished, she met his eyes. "I wouldn't give it if I didn't."

She hesitated, as though remembering their conversation that first evening at the Crosby Hotel. Then she said steadily, "I do believe God's world has laws, laws He gave for our good. And I believe He provided plants for our good, too. Some even think that for every ailment there's a plant remedy, that the use of the plant depends on its shape."

"Its shape? I don't quite understand," said Adam, interested in spite of himself.

"If a plant is kidney shaped, then it would be good for kidney trouble," she said. "There's an old saying along the same lines, too, that many remedies grow not far from their causes."

"And you believe all this?" he asked again.

"There's one thing I am certain of." Her brown eyes looked directly into his now.

"What is that?"

"The time I spend with a new mother as she drinks her raspberry-leaf tea is well spent. I don't ever force the afterbirth to come, and that woman can ask questions and tell me how she's feeling if she's got a mind to."

"So you feel your simples are merely a tool to use with your patients, not that they are medically efficacious?"

Jeannie's laughter rang out. "Dr. Adam, that's a ten-dollar word if I ever heard one! No, I can't say for sure my herbs and remedies are always—what did you say, medically efficacious?—but I've seen them help. I know they do. Just tell me this, can you doctors say without a doubt that every medicine you use does what you want it to?"

He looked a little sheepish as he admitted, "You do have a point."

"Come on now, haven't you ever read some outrageous 'medical' cures?" she challenged, her expression merry, even mischievous.

His face was as near smiling now as she'd ever seen. "I did read one in the *Beaumont Enterprise* the other day by a foreign doctor—"

"And?"

"He said the cure for—um, distempered spleen, whatever that is—was a hot drink in which two black spiders and a cockroach have been boiled."

Jeannie made a face. "Ugh. I don't think I'll try that one!"

"Now to be fair, you should tell me a folk remedy to match." Surprised at the lightness of his mood, Adam watched as her brow wrinkled in concentration, then, as her face was lit by that bright smile.

"The third-day chills. Do you know how to cure them?"

He shook his head. "I'm not even sure what they are."

Jeannie leaned back against the table, her hands resting on its worn surface, her chin lifted, showing the clean, pure lines of her throat. "Just before it's time for the chill to come on, the sick person is supposed to wrap himself tightly in a blanket, run around the house three times just as hard and fast as he can, then into the front door and dive under the bed. The chill will jump *into* the bed, and he'll miss it!"

This time he laughed with her. "If I get desperate, I may try that. What other miracle cures do you have?"

"Mullein, to break up a cough and ease a sore throat; willow bark for a headache. Wild ginger for indigestion, mint and camomile for all sorts of things, sassafras bark and roots made into a tea against fevers . . . the list goes on, to be sure."

His eyes were intent on her face. Once more he asked that question. "And you believe in all these?"

"Remember little Susie, that awful sore on her arm?" When he nodded she said, "It's almost entirely healed, and it was the comfrey that did it. Yes, my simples work."

Adam had certainly not known what to do for the child. He was about to admit it aloud when she spoke again.

"Dr. Adam, I accept the abilities God has given me—and the fact that He intends for me to use them to help others. These," she indicated the bag, the shelves of herbs, "are tools, like you said, and some work better than others. The most important thing is, I care about people, and they know it and respond to me."

"I can see that. Somehow, when I hear you say you believe in your abilities to help them, I think you're right."

She softly replied, "I . . . thank you, Adam. It means a lot for you, a doctor, to say that."

He found it hard to break away from her steady gaze. "We both want to do the same thing, Miss Gallagher—to help others. I'd hate to be so thickheaded I couldn't recognize that in someone else."

There was a silence between them then; it was punctuated

only by the seductive cooing of a whip-or-will, calling for its mate. "Dr. Adam, you're an unusual man. But I sense something in you that bothers me, that has bothered me since that first day at the train station."

"Have you got a cure for it in all these bottles?" The question was half-joking, half-serious.

Jeannie's face was completely serious as she said, "I get the feeling something terrible happened to you, that it's festering in your soul like an infected wound." She ignored the look of warning that flashed across his face, the lowered black brows. "What ails you is anger or grief—or both."

"Let me get this straight. You're saying I'm ill and my emotions have caused it?"

"Does that surprise you? Surely even medical men know a fit of anger can make a person sick on his own bile, that fright can make you tremble, even stop your heart."

"That may well be, but I'm as healthy as you are."

She sighed; his tone was cold and challenging. "No, Dr. Adam. Don't you see, you're not. And only God himself can cure what ails you."

"Let's leave God out of this discussion," said Adam bitterly.

"Sure, and how can you leave God out?"

"He's left me out, I'm convinced of that."

"Ah, it's as I thought. You're in deep trouble. Well, no matter what it is, you'll not be right until you've given it, and yourself, completely over to Him."

"Are you ready to go, Miss Gallagher?" was all he said. Even with the late afternoon sun slanting in through the windows on the west, the room seemed chilly now.

"Yes, I'm ready." Jeannie picked up her bag and went to stand by the door. "I . . . I'm not sure I should be saying this, but . . ."

He waited, but he did not voice the question.

"If you ever need someone to talk to, Dr. Adam, someone who cares, I'll listen."

Still without speaking, he walked past her, and she had to walk quickly to catch up with him on the trail outside.

CHAPTER 9

*But unto you that fear my name shall the Sun of righteousness
arise with healing in his wings.*   *Malachi 4:2*

In the weeks that followed, Adam realized that he had come
to Saratoga at just the right time. What had been a trickle of
people coming into the area became a great flow of humanity,
of every kind and description.

The sawmills operated day and night, cutting derrick tim-
bers as well as lumber to build the booming town of Saratoga.
The inevitable ox and mule teams, with their loads of pipe,
heavy machinery and various kinds of oil-field supplies,
crowded the place. Adam often heard a saying attributed to
teeming contractors: Kill a mule and buy anuthern', kill a man
and hire anuthern'. He privately decided it wasn't far from true.
Men and animals were driven furiously in the haste to cash in
on the boom.

Whiskey and beer arrived with as much regularity as oil-
field supplies, and saloons and gambling houses sprang up almost overnight, prolific as the mushrooms that grew in the
Thicket. The original little sawmill had been joined by another
to keep up with the demand for lumber to build the gambling
houses, saloons, and tommy-joints. For with the wave of men
came women, and those women were as eager to make money
as any roughneck.

Prostitution was not legal, but that certainly didn't keep
the pimps from setting their businesses right alongside the others. One of their schemes to get around the law caused Carrie
an intensely embarrassing moment. One evening after supper
she and Jude, with Rob between them, were walking from the
hotel to Adam's office.

Rob pointed to a treadle sewing machine on the rough board sidewalk. "Look, Mama," he cried. "Sewing?" Evidently he remembered the sewing machine she'd had to leave behind at the house near Indian Camp.

Before Carrie could reply, a red-haired young woman sauntered out from the half-board, half-tent structure behind. She probably wasn't any more than nineteen, but with her heavily made-up face—kohl-ringed eyes, rose rouge on her cheeks, lip paint applied in an exaggerated bow—she looked much older. The woman wore a low-cut dress of green satin, and her milky skin was dusted with pale freckles. For one shocking moment Carrie thought it was Jeannie Gallagher; then the girl spoke.

"Whatcha staring at, honey?" The redhead winked at Rob. "Need some sewin' done? I reckon somebody here could do it, but I'd rather work for ol' Whiskers, here. He's probably got more money anyhow." Her bold gaze rested on Jude.

"I . . ." Carrie stared at her for a long moment; then she pulled Rob close and began walking, the laughter of both Jude and the girl ringing in her ears as she ran to Adam's office. He met her at the door just as Jude caught up, still chuckling.

The look on Carrie's face prompted Adam to inquire, "What happened?"

It was Jude who answered. "Miss Carrie was about to get herself some sewing done, over at the um . . . sewing place!" He slapped his knee, still snickering.

"Jude! It's not funny, and why in the world do those . . . those creatures have a sewing machine out there?"

"I can tell you," supplied Adam, glancing at Rob. "There are some peppermint drops in the cupboard for you, son. You can have two." When the little boy ran off eagerly, he continued, "Prostitution isn't legal here, Carrie. And if those girls can't show—how does the law put it? 'any visible means of support'— they can get arrested and fined. So they set up the sewing machines, and a couple of times a day they go out and run up a seam. Look for the sign next time you go by."

"What sign?" Carrie asked, still embarrassed and just a little angry.

"Sewing Done Here. Come in an—" He broke off as Jeannie Gallagher entered. Their eyes met briefly, but neither did more than nod.

Jeannie said, "Hello, Carrie, Uncle Jude, it's good to see you. I've just been to Grannie Annie's. She asked about you, Uncle Jude."

"She did, huh?" Jude switched his wad of tobacco from one jaw to the other. "I'd best drop over."

"Yes," said Jeannie, "I wish you would. She fell the other day and is having some trouble getting around."

"Anything broken?" asked Adam. "Maybe I should go by and check on her."

Jeannie shook her head. "You can go, but not as a doctor. It's just a sprain, and she takes pride in doctoring herself. The only thing is, she knows she has to stay off her feet for a spell, and that means I do her collecting as well as mine."

"Collecting? Oh, you mean your herbs," said Adam.

"That's right. How's your business been? I've been so busy myself I haven't had time to check in on you."

"Oh," said Carrie, her voice a shade too bright, "Adam has been busy, too. So busy we haven't had a free minute to discuss our wedding plans."

"Really? That's too bad." Jeannie had turned slightly away from Adam and missed the look on his face. "Well, have you at least set a date?"

"We thought maybe Thanksgiving," said Carrie.

"Thanksgiving!" The surprise in Adam's tone made both women turn and look at him. "Are you sure you can get ready by then, Carrie?"

"Of course, Adam," assured Carrie. Her bright eyes teamed with victory. She and Adam hadn't discussed a date, and they certainly hadn't mentioned Thanksgiving, which wasn't far away.

"I'd be happy to do what I can to help," said Jeannie. "Folks hereabouts love weddings, or any excuse for a party."

Carrie's expression was mixed; Jeannie Gallagher was the source of most of her distress, and yet, she'd never met a woman who seemed more honest, or sincere. Somehow, though, she sensed the affinity that existed between Adam and Jeannie, that had existed from the very beginning. Yet she was also convinced that Jeannie intended only good to her. It was a puzzle she couldn't solve, for her strong woman's instinct assured her Jeannie was attracted to Adam, no matter how she might deny it. "Thank you," she murmured. "I . . . it would mean a lot to me to have help planning the wedding."

"Then of course I'll help," said Jeannie. "We'll have to get started, though, if you intend to marry at Thanksgiving." She glanced at Adam as she and Carrie walked to the other side of the waiting room, an area they'd curtained off.

Adam watched the two women, their heads together, and though he believed he was carefully hiding his thoughts, Jude said quietly, "Boy, if you ain't certain sure you want to marry that purty little gal, think on it some more while there's still time."

With his eyes still on Jeannie and Carrie, Adam shook his head. "I've committed myself, Jude."

"The knot ain't tied yet, friend."

"No, but—" He was suddenly interrupted by a short bald-headed man bursting through the door. Adam immediately recognized him as the one everyone called Buzzard.

"Doc! They're bringing in an ol' feller over from the Wooden Nickle! He . . . he—" Buzzard stopped; his eyes were wide with the horror of what he'd just seen. "He was gamblin', and he lost, George did. Lost everything he had, and he called the dealer a cheat! And that dealer just . . . he just took out a long knife and quicker'n you can say *scat*, he sliced George's belly clean open! And he—"

"You say they're bringing him here?" Adam asked, glancing at the wide-eyed Rob. The man nodded. "Carrie, will you take Rob back to the hotel? I'm sure Jude won't mind escorting you."

Jude looked as though he'd rather watch the little drama unfolding here, but he nodded. "Shore I will, Doc. But I'll be back."

Carrie didn't want to leave any more than Jude did, but common sense won out. Even though she knew Jeannie Gallagher would stay to assist Adam, she caught Rob's hand to leave. "Say goodbye to your papa, Rob, and we'll go and see if Mrs. Gallagher has any more doughnuts." Then, before the child could protest, she scooped him up and left, knowing that the injured man would be there at any moment.

It was only a couple of minutes later that he stumbled in, a man on either side of him. "Doc," he cried feebly, "my guts are cut out. Do something for me quick!"

Adam gave quick instructions, and without speaking, Jeannie carried them out. By the time they got him laid on the operating table, there was blood everywhere, and Adam saw that the man's bowels were, indeed, lying outside his body.

"Everybody clear out," he said, and at the low command the two who'd brought the injured man, as well as the pack of on-lookers, hurriedly left and returned to the Wooden Nickle.

After turning up the lamps and washing his hands, Adam began the grim task of taking care of the wound. Whether from shock or loss of blood, or both, the man mercifully passed out. Quietly assisted by Jeannie, Adam tucked the intestines back in and began stitching the gaping wound.

When he'd finished he allowed himself one deep, low sigh. "It's a miracle, but the knife didn't cut through any of his intestines, at least not any that I saw."

Jeannie nodded as she went about the task of cleaning up. "It would have been a lot worse if it had, I suppose."

"He might not make it anyway, depending on how much blood he's lost. But if one of the intestines was even nicked, peritonitis will surely set in. It may yet." He rubbed his eyes. "Miss Gallagher, you're good help."

"Thank you, Dr. Adam."

For a long moment they faced each other across the inert George. They said nothing aloud, but the unspoken words were as plain as though they'd been said.

Both Jeannie and Adam were startled when Buzzard burst through the door yet again. "Doc, I sure hope you're finished with George, 'cause Long Jim has got his head split clear open!" Wildly waving his stubby hands, he breathlessly added, "After they brung George here"—he nodded toward the man on the operating table—"Long Jim said he believed George was right, that dealer *was* a cheat! And he was gonna draw on him, but Mac, the owner of the Nickle, he took out his own pistol and let Jim have it right across his noggin. Never seen so much blood in all my born days. When it commenced to gushing, it looked like a new well blowing, or a hawg killing!" he said with relish.

Adam had been washing his hands again as the man related his story. "Is Jim unconscious now?"

"Yep, but boy watch out when he comes to; he's gonna be mad, for sure. He's liable to wipe up the floor with the first face he sees—" He stopped, a funny look on his own face. "Now, I don't reckon he'd mess with a doctor; leastways I don't think he would." But his eyes glittered with excitement at the prospect.

"Don't be too sure," cautioned Jeannie, who was packing Adam's bag just as though she'd done it forever. "You say he's unconscious?"

"Wal, mostly."

"Be careful, Dr. Adam," she said, so softly Buzzard didn't hear. "I'll watch George until they come for him."

He nodded, then followed Buzzard, who seemed to thrive on bringing bad news.

The Wooden Nickle was one of the several gambling establishments that had appeared almost overnight. But unlike many of the others, it had a roof, and the owner had brought gaming tables instead of the usual tarpaulins spread on the floor, and a gramaphone as well. It was grinding out loud music as Adam paused at the swinging doors, where the owner, a man named Mac, dressed in a well-cut blue suit and white shirt with a neat, black string tie met him. He was not smiling.

"Thanks for coming, Doc. These fellas have made a mess of my place, that's for sure."

Adam slowly nodded, seeing the gun on the man's hip and the cold, hard look in his eyes. "Where is Long Jim?"

"Follow the blood," came the laconic reply.

Buzzard had been right; it did look like a hog killing. The bench, the table before him, the dirt floor, Long Jim himself were all soaked with it. Jim, who was unconscious so long that some of the other men had thought he was dying, was finally coming to. He was half sitting up, and the barrel of the gun he held looked to Adam as though it were two feet long. However, Adam's voice held steady and cold as he said, "Put the gun down, Jim."

"Says who?" snarled Jim. "I ain't gonna put my gun down for nobody! Who are you, anyway?" His eyes were bloodshot, firing out a dangerous mixture of pain, rage, and fear.

"I'm Dr. Jarrett, and I'm here to sew up your head." Then turning to a bartender hovering nearby, he told him to bring a pan of hot water while Adam proceeded to lay out his instruments. "Put the gun down," he repeated.

The answer this time was a string of oaths and a violent wave of the gun that started the blood flowing again from the hideous gash on his head. As Adam dabbed at it, trying to get a clear field to assess the extent of the wound, the gun barrel came down hard on his shoulder.

"Gone kill him, kill the dog that hit me!"

Suddenly Adam was very angry. All the frustration and anger he'd felt for—it seemed forever—focused on the ugly, cursing man before him. "Put that gun down immediately or I'll walk out of here and let you bleed to death!" The only answer was another spate of ugly curses, and Adam began calmly packing away his instruments.

A hush had fallen over the room as all the men watched, and Long Jim saw that Adam would do exactly as he said. With blood streaming down his ugly, unshaven face, he began to cry and whine, begging Adam to fix the cut, to stop the bleeding, to save his life.

Adam coldly replied, "Put the gun down."

They stared at each other for a long moment—shifty blue eyes into hard black ones. Then Long Jim laid the gun between his feet on the floor, within easy reach. Before he knew what was happening, Adam gave it a hard kick, and it skittered over in front of Mac, the owner.

"Put that thing away," he ordered, and set to work on Long Jim, who was now as docile as a baby. Angrily, Adam took Long Jim's chin and twisted his head so he could clamp it with his arm, and he set to work.

As he pulled the first stitch together Jim let out a blood-curdling yell that caused snickers of laughter to ripple through the gamblers, the thugs and pimps and drillers watching. One hard, sweeping glance from Adam, and they quieted down. After that Long Jim settled into a low, steady stream of foul cursing, threatening to kill Adam as soon as he finished, but he sat very still as he cursed.

Calmly, deliberately, Adam finished the job, packed away his instruments, and walked out, leaving Long Jim, as well as all the other men staring after him. A stream of excited comments broke out—before he got out of earshot he heard a few.

"Never seen anything like it. The Doc don't carry a gun, but he don't need one!"

"Nerves of steel."

"One tough hombre, that Doc . . ."

And a last parting, particularly colorful oath from Long Jim, ending with "You stay outta my way, Doc, or I'll *kill* you!"

The night air was almost cool; Adam breathed deeply as he strode across the street to his office. There was a hint of honeysuckle still blooming somewhere, and something else. It was the smell of the Thicket, wild and free, and it taunted Adam, for he felt anything but free. And yet, he knew there was no other place in the world he'd rather be.

Jeannie Gallagher was still in his office when he pushed open the door, and he saw that she'd made good use of the time he'd spent at the Wooden Nickle. The last of the supplies, which he'd never gotten around to putting away, were arranged neatly on the shelves, and the mess he'd left after treating the man with the knife wound was gone, as was the man himself.

"You didn't have to do all that."

She stood in front of the lamp, the glow outlining her slim, small figure. "It needed to be done." Silence reigned for a few moments; then she continued with a slight smile. "They came by and gave me a report on the fearless physician. It seems you've made a start toward becoming a legend. Did you really kick his gun clear across the saloon and threaten to let him bleed to death?"

"He kept threatening me." Adam rubbed his hand over his eyes. "I'm tired."

"There's a pot of tea made." She hesitated, then said, "Well, I'd best be going."

Adam watched as she gathered up her shawl and bag, then paused at the door. "Miss Gallagher, I do appreciate your help."

"I know you do." Just before she went out she said softly, "Good night, Dr. Adam."

Adam's head rested against the door frame as he watched Jeannie Gallagher disappear into the woods leading to her cabin. With a deep sigh he turned and quietly closed the door. An empty silence filled the room as Adam was overcome with a deep sense of loneliness. His heart longed to cry out to someone for help. But whom?

CHAPTER 10

*For the earth which drinketh in the rain that cometh oft upon it,
and bringeth forth herbs meet for them by whom it is dressed,
receiveth blessing from God. But that which beareth thorns and
briers is rejected and is nigh unto cursing; whose end is to be
burned.*   *Hebrews 6:7–8*

Standing at the tall corner windows of her upstairs room in
the hotel, Carrie watched Saratoga wake up the next morning.
She'd stood at this spot last night as Adam made his weary way
from the saloon to his office, on the other side of the general
store. She'd also seen Jeannie Gallagher leave his office a while
later, and told herself it hadn't been very long, that they
couldn't have been alone together for more than ten minutes.

Carrie bit her lip against the sudden pang of intense jeal-
ousy that shot through her. *If only I could hate the woman!* she
thought. *But no, at every turn she's helping with Rob, doing
things that make life easier for me.* Just yesterday, Jeannie had
brought in that bouquet of wildflowers that were so lovely
they'd taken Carrie's breath away.

And her comment as she'd handed them to Carrie . . . "I
always thought these would be so pretty in a bride's bouquet."

The memory of her bright face as she held the flowers was
like a physical pain to Carrie. *How could Adam not fall in love
with her?* She hugged herself tightly. *It's me he's going to marry,
me . . . and I'll make him happy, I will. We'll go far away from
here, from the memories of Greenlea, of Indian Camp . . . and
here.* She must have made an audible sound, for Rob sat up on
his little cot, rubbing his eyes.

"Mama?" Carrie went to him and tried to coax him back to

107

sleep, but he resisted. "Jude's waiting! We're going to see Grannie Annie today."

"It's too early," Carrie protested. But the little boy eluded her grasp and ran to where his clothes were laid out, and she relented. "All right. But you have to eat all your breakfast."

His solemn black eyes, so like Adam's, sparkled now as he sang softly, "Jesus loves me this I know, for the Vible tells me so."

"Bible, Rob, say Bible." She pulled off his nightshirt and, as always, was unable to keep from hugging his sturdy little body. "Who taught you that song?"

"Jeannie. I love Jeannie. She tells stories, too."

"What kind of stories does she tell? Are they like Jude's?"

He shook his head. "Nope. Stories about Jesus." And he began to sing again, loudly this time, "Jesus loves me, this I know!"

Carrie held out his little blue checked shirt as he thrust his arms into it, a maneuver he did with vigor. Jeannie Gallagher had not only been telling Rob about Jesus; just yesterday she'd casually mentioned something to Carrie about how He helped her when she was afraid. *If only she was pushy or offensive about it*, Carrie thought; *then I could tell her to keep her beliefs to herself. But it's always so . . . so natural, and . . .* She frowned, knowing her irritation was mostly with herself, because she'd wanted to ask questions. She had wanted to know more and hadn't had the nerve to ask.

"Stand still, Rob," she said, "or we'll never get you dressed."

"Never?" His eyes showed alarm. "But Jude said we're going to meet Mother Nature today!"

"He told you that, did he?" Rob nodded, squirming as she buttoned his shirt, wanting to be away. To herself she added, troubled, *Jude didn't say anything to me . . .*

And once they were downstairs Carrie had the uneasy feeling that the Gallaghers and Jude were taking her place with Rob. Mrs. Gallagher looked distracted as she set out plates for the first batch of boarders.

"Get the silver, will you, Carrie? I'm running late again. We may have to hire a couple more if this keeps up. Robbie, lad, your breakfast is out in the kitchen." The child ran out before Carrie could say a word.

She nodded to Mrs. Gallagher; she didn't mind helping at

all. Her own family had shunned her after she'd run off with the mayor's son. The brief escapade had lasted only three days, until the boy's money had run out. But after that, though there'd been no other men, the rumors that she was a bad girl had persisted. Those rumors were the main reason Adam had brought Rob to her. He'd felt that no one would think it strange that a young woman with her reputation should turn up with a baby.

Her lips curled in a faint, bitter smile as she thought of the incident with the sewing machine outside those women's quarters. Until Rob had come to live with her, and with him Adam's generous payments, she'd taken in sewing herself . . . so she wouldn't give in to the occasional offers to set her up that she received from men. She laid the silver out beside the thick white china plates on the blue checked cloth and thought of the gentlemen who'd made those offers. As she had so often, she wished there were some way she could bring the subject up to Adam, so he would know she had refused them. With a little spurt of frustration she put the last knife down much harder than she'd intended.

"What's wrong, Carrie?" asked Reba Gallagher, her eyes bright with curiosity. "Did you get up on the wrong side of the bed?"

"I . . . no, Mrs. Gallagher, I was just thinking about something." Carrie stood back as the first of the men began straggling in. She would never get used to their sidelong glances, the slight but recognizable speculation in those looks. They certainly never looked that way at Jeannie. Head held high, she assured herself that once she and Adam were married, they wouldn't look at her that way, either. As Adam's wife, they would respect her. "Anything else you want me to do, Mrs. Gallagher?"

"No thanks, girl. Seems like you're taking on more and more every day as it is. You go on out and see to the young'un." She was dishing up the hearty breakfast from the covered dishes on the huge sideboard, and waved Carrie out. "Get yourself something, too. You're getting thin as a rail!"

Carrie left the room, but not before she heard a couple of the comments.

"If that's thin, I like it!"

"Umm, forget the flapjacks, I'll have her!"

"You fellers cut that, or you won't get any grub!" came Mrs. Gallagher's sharp retort.

Cheeks burning, Carrie almost ran to the cookhouse, where she found Rob eating his breakfast, as usual to the accompaniment of another of Jude's tales. Grateful that Jude only winked and went on with his story, she poured a cup of coffee and sat down, willing herself to calm down. "And I was just a tadpole like you when my daddy brung us here from Mississippi. He built just a little bitty one-room log cabin, so me'n my sisters had to sleep on quilts outside the house 'cause it weren't big enough."

"Outside all night?" Rob's eyes grew big.

"Yup. Well, Daddy and the others had killed a couple of hawgs that first day, and they just throwed all the trash and bones out near the cabin. Way into the night we heard something gnawing them bones, and fighting and spitting. My oldest sister Josie looked, and what do you think she saw?"

"What?" The whispered word expressed delighted fright.

"Three panthers. Well, I gotta tell you, we got so skeered we ran into the house, screeching like banshees. Know what Daddy said?" In wordless horror Rob shook his head. "You young'uns go on out and get to sleep; you gotta get used to it." Jude grinned and spat into a tomato can. "We went out, all right, but we shore didn't sleep much."

Carrie shivered a little; these stories always made her uneasy. "Jude, don't you think you ought to tell stories that are less frightening?" The Thicket seemed to her a forbidding place, almost an enemy. Jude spoke of it as though it were a friend; Adam obviously had found refuge here, and Jeannie . . . Jeannie had no fear whatsoever. On the contrary, she went wherever she liked, gathering herbs and treating people. The Thicket was home to them all—all except Carrie.

Jude looked at her keenly. "Hmm. Mebbe you're right. Rob, tomorrow I'll tell you how to find a bee tree. But today, we're gonna visit Mother Nature and Grannie Annie, like I said." When Rob let out a yell of delight and started to get down from his chair, Jude said, "Whoa, now, I don't take no boys who don't finish their flapjacks."

"One more story?" asked Rob hopefully.

Jude glanced at Carrie, hitched up his pants, and moved the cud of tobacco over to the right side of his mouth. "One more, and you got to eat up all your breakfast." The boy began eating, his eyes on Jude. "This here's not exactly a story, it's sorta more like, umm, a nature talk."

Carrie couldn't keep from smiling a little. "That sounds nice, Jude."

"Well, shore," he said self-righteously. "Anyhow, wood ducks, they nest in the holler of a tree and raise their families there. And when it's time for the little 'uns to learn how to swim, the mama and papa ducks carry 'em down to the water by the scruff of the neck."

"Like a mama cat?" asked Rob wonderingly.

"Don't stop eating," commanded Jude. "Yup, just like a cat carries kittens. They put the little critters on their backs 'til they get the hang of it; then they swim out from under and leave 'em to it."

"Jude!" said Carrie, laughing.

He held up both hands. "It's the gospel truth. I seen it myself lots of times. Well, looky here, the boy's cleaned his plate. Ready to go, partner?"

Rob jumped down, shouting, ran to kiss Carrie, and then went out with Jude. Alone in the cookhouse now, she began to straighten up the chaos Mrs. Gallagher had wrought, amazed as always that the woman was able to cook and serve not only three meals a day, but six. The salesmen—Mrs. Gallagher called them drummers—ate at eleven, the roughnecks and everybody else after that. Not only did she manage the meals, the rooms in the hotel had to be cleaned twice a day—once for those who slept in the daytime, then for the ones who slept at night. She'd hired extra help, but the work seemed beyond them all.

Carrie helped in the kitchen when she could, for she admired the woman . . . as long as she didn't ask personal questions. But she thought often of the time when she and Adam would be married and have a place of their own. So deep in the familiar daydream was she that she didn't hear Adam's footsteps when he came in.

"Carrie?"

At the sound of his voice she spun around, dropping the blue willow plate she held. It broke into three pieces, and she stared at them, appalled at the tears that welled up in her eyes. Adam came and picked up the neat blue and white triangles. "Here, now, what's this? Tears for a plate?"

Carrie knew that Adam Jarrett was not the kind of man who teased. So the gently teasing attitude he now showed touched her. She'd never been able to hide her feelings, for she loved him deeply; he was the only man she'd ever wanted to marry. "I have been sort of on edge lately, I guess. And we don't . . . I haven't seen much of you lately."

He poured himself a cup of coffee and leaned against the long wooden drainboard as he studied Carrie. She wore a deep blue dress that made her eyes even bluer, and as usual he couldn't deny she was very beautiful. "That's so, and I'm sorry. But it's difficult setting up a new practice, especially in a place like this. As it is, I only have a few moments now."

Carrie knew she had to choose her words carefully. She squeezed the dishcloth out and began to wipe down the long, crudely made table on which Mrs. Gallagher prepared most of the food she served. "Have you been here long enough to know whether or not it's what you want, or is it just a place to make enough money so we can move on?" She was wise enough now not to ask him to leave. Carrie had learned that Adam Jarrett was the kind of man who made his own decisions.

He took a cautious sip of the black, hot coffee. A shaft of golden sunlight slanted in through the open door and he seemed to be concentrating on it. "I can't say why, exactly, but the Thicket has caught my imagination, my . . ." He smiled slightly. "My heart is what I was going to say. Can you believe I even thought that?"

Before she could stop herself Carrie blurted out, "But it's full of all kinds of undesirable people!"

He nodded. "That's so. But the oil boom won't last forever. And when it's over, most of them will be gone, to the next boom or back to their own homes. And then, the people of the Thicket will still need a doctor. I think I want to be that man," he finished simply.

Carrie wrang out the dishcloth and hung it neatly on a rack near the pump. The slump of her shoulders spoke the words she didn't have the courage to say. *But, Adam, I hate it here . . .*

Adam finished his coffee, and set the cup in the copper-lined sink. "I've got to go, Carrie."

"I know." Suddenly an idea dawned upon her and she said, "Let me come with you."

He gave a startled look. "On my call?"

"Yes, why not?" she insisted. "It's time the Thicket residents started getting acquainted with the woman who's going to be your wife."

"But, Carrie, I have to go over to Batson Prairie. The trip itself won't be easy, and I'm not sure what I'll find when I get there."

"Please, let me go," Carrie said firmly. A sudden vision of Jeannie entered her mind, challenging her to carry out her request.

"I just don't think it would be wise." Adam frowned.

"I'll go and ask Jude if he has a horse and saddle I can use. He's taking Rob on a walk today." She stood at the door, and the look of pleading hope on her face must have touched a chord in Adam.

"I'm afraid we'll regret this," he replied slowly.

"It'll be great, you'll see!" And she was off in a flash, leaving him scowling.

A while later Carrie thoughtfully admitted that Adam had been right; she shouldn't have come. But it was too late to turn back now. They'd left the so-called "road" that the oil companies had cut through the Thicket and were on a trail. The trees were so close that Carrie had to follow Adam, and her heart sank almost as deep as the horses did in the soggy, swampy earth. When they came to a slow, sluggish bayou, Adam called for her to keep to the right, or the horse might bog down as they crossed.

Though it took every ounce of willpower she possessed, Carrie kept silent. She just held on tighter, grateful beyond words when the horse she was riding followed Adam's mount out of the bayou on the other side.

She'd just breathed a sigh of relief when she heard a strange, terrifying noise. Her horse spooked and started to gallop. The pounding of Adam's horse behind her, of Adam shouting, "Pull him up, pull him up!" all became a part of a horrifying rush of sound that seemed to color the air. Carrie was afraid she'd faint and fall off the horse. Fortunately she had the sense to lean low over her saddle to keep from being dragged off by low hanging limbs. But the vines and briers seemed to snatch and grab at her, and she was all too aware of the painful scratches they inflicted.

When Adam finally caught up to her, he couldn't pry her hands loose from the reins. "I'm sorry, Carrie. Are you all right?"

"What is that noise, Adam?" Her words were scarcely audible.

Horses blowing, Carrie's breathing almost as heavy, they waited. Suddenly, a flood of hogs burst out of the Thicket and thundered over the trail, making an ungodly noise of grunts and squeals. It was like a roaring wave of animals, oblivious to anything in its path. Carrie drew in her breath sharply and would have screamed, but Adam laid a warning hand on her arm.

He drew a pistol from his jacket, and both watched in silent horror as the dark shape of a bear materialized, and with one swift, deadly movement wiped out the life of a small pig. A squeal of fear, then pain, and the creature was dead on the ground.

In the softest of whispers Adam said, "I'll not shoot unless it's absolutely necessary. If we can remain totally still, he may not notice us. He may just carry off his prey . . ." She had to try very hard to block out the disgusting sound the bear made as he devoured the pig.

Trembling violently now, she closed her eyes and was silent. When she felt Adam's hand grip her arm tightly, she was intensely grateful for his nearness. It seemed an eternity before he spoke again.

Finally, Adam whispered, "He's gone, but we'd better leave while we can, because he may not be far away."

Only too willing to leave, Carrie touched her heels to the wild-eyed, jittery horse and followed Adam down the trail. After a tense ten minutes, Adam evidently felt it was safe to speak normally again. "Jude told me the hogs belong to the people here in the Thicket. They call them 'piney wood rooters.' "

"They just let them run wild?" questioned Carrie, still feeling weak from the aftereffects of fear.

"That's right. After they let the hogs forage for themselves until winter, they decide on a good place, build a large pen out of logs, and keep corn in there for a month or so to let the animals get used to it. Then, they close up the pen and later begin to slaughter."

"Sounds dangerous," Carrie responded, trying to dodge the low hanging rattan vines.

"I gather it's very dangerous, especially for the dogs, because they sometimes get ripped up pretty bad by the hog's tusks. But if a dog survives a serious confrontation with a boar, he never gets that close again, at least that's what they tell me."

Carrie was about to reply that she didn't doubt that was true when she felt something crawling on her face. In panic she slapped it off, her stomach twisting in revulsion as she saw it was a huge, ugly black spider. As she cried out, Adam reined up and looked back anxiously.

"What is it? Are you all right?"

"I'm fine, it was just a spider," she managed to say. Carrie had just decided two things: she would die before she cried out again, no matter what happened; and she'd never again ask to accompany Adam on a call. Had she known what was in store for her, she never would have insisted on coming this time.

They finally came to an open space, perhaps the size of a garden, with a cabin built at the far side of it. "To tell the truth, I'm glad I was able to find the Hamilton's place again."

"You mean we could have gotten . . ." Carrie trailed off, unwilling to even say the word 'lost' aloud. At that moment there was born in her such a fear of getting lost in this wilderness that she shoved it far, far back into the dark recesses of her mind. She was grateful when they reached the plank house. It was built up on stilts, which was certainly not surprising in such swampy country.

Their approach was announced by the baying of a pack of hounds, long ears drooping, their ribs countable through their hides. A woman appeared at the door and watched silently as Adam tied his horse, then helped Carrie down.

Though Carrie wasn't certain she'd be able to walk, she managed to get up the steps unassisted, and stood quietly, trying not to shake as Adam introduced her to the gaunt, unsmiling woman, whose name was Gussie Hamilton.

"How do," nodded Mrs. Hamilton. She didn't smile even yet, but stood aside to allow them to come into the large room that spanned the front of the house. The walls were rough, unpainted planks, with a huge stone fireplace at one end.

On the crude, heavy timber which served as a mantel, Carrie was surprised to see an old, beautifully carved clock and some silver candlesticks. The rest of the furniture was rustic and homemade; there was a large square table in the center of the room and a half dozen rickety chairs. Carrie ventured to say, "That's a lovely old clock, Mrs. Hamilton."

"Belonged to my folks, back in Kentucky. My man Henry's in yonder." She gestured to the door on the left. "You his nurse?"

"Why, I—" Carrie hesitated, for at least two reasons. She hadn't thought to ask what ailed Mr. Hamilton, and she'd always been a wretched nurse.

"She is today," put in Adam smoothly.

"He ain't good, Doctor. I done everything you told me to, give him all the medicine you left. But he ain't good." She spoke in a low, almost monotone voice, but her inner feelings were betrayed as her rough-workened hands smoothed the fabric of the homemade blue dress that hung loosely on her gaunt frame. And yet, there was something about her, the way she held herself, the lift of her chin, that was at odds with the way she was dressed.

Gravely Adam said, "The wound became infected, then."

"I reckon. And he's got a turrible cough."

"Probably pneumonia," muttered Adam as he rummaged in his bag. "I was afraid of that."

Carrie reluctantly followed him, and when she entered the dim sickroom, she wanted to run out again. The man on the bed most likely was no more than fifty, but he looked far older. A straggly gray beard rested on his thin, barely moving chest. His eyes were open, but they did not focus even when Adam spoke to him.

"Mr. Hamilton, can you hear me?" Adam pressed the stethoscope to the man's chest, and frowned. "The rales are much worse than I expected."

Carrie, pressed against the wall on the opposite side of the room, whispered, "Is he dying?"

"I'm afraid he may be." He shoved the stethoscope back into his bag and began to remove the bandage from the man's chest. The rotten smell, which had only been subtle before, now permeated the entire room, having a nauseating effect on Carrie. Adam dropped the soiled cloths into a wooden box placed at the head of the white iron bedstead. Then, even as the man's rattling, dying breaths filled the room, he cleaned the pussy wound and placed a fresh bandage on it before he called, "Mrs. Hamilton, I think it would be best if you came in."

There was a knowing look in the woman's eyes as she came in slowly and took her stand at the head of the bed opposite Adam. Her thin mouth was clamped shut, her eyes were lowered, but she took the man's hand in both of hers and held tightly. "I'm here, Henry," was all she said. Her husband's face, wracked by pain even though he was unconscious, smoothed a bit.

There was no sound in the room except that awful breathing for several moments. Then there was no sound at all. The woman didn't cry, and the look on her face was unreadable. But her eyes were so full of pain and grief Carrie's own breath almost stopped.

"Reckon you did all you could, Doctor," Mrs. Hamilton said, and placed her husband's hand on the faded coverlet. "Henry was a man who allus lived by the gun. 'Spose it's fittin' that he died by the gun." She allowed herself one long, deep breath. "Reckon I'll need someone to help lay him out. Your woman be willing?" She was looking at Adam, who glanced quickly at Carrie and nodded encouragingly.

"Of course Carrie will help." He was replacing things in his bag and missed the expression of pure panic that crossed Carrie's face.

Mrs. Hamilton nodded, her face, even her eyes, totally impassive now. "I'll git the things we'll need. It don't do to let a body set . . . got to get 'em ready and in the ground afore too long in this country," she said as she left the room.

Adam finished packing his bag and lifted his face toward Carrie. The look in his eyes was gentle, and giving her a reassuring nod he picked up his bag and quietly stepped from the room, leaving Carrie alone with the dead man.

Cold beads of sweat began to pool and trickle down her back, sending chills throughout her body. She closed her eyes, trying hard to shut out the vivid scene in front of her. Deep inside, Carrie wished desperately that she could pray. She'd heard Jeannie speak of it with so much peace and assurance. She even wished Jeannie herself were there. Quietly, Mrs. Hamilton appeared at the door carrying a basin of water and some cloths. She handed one to Carrie.

"Henry don't even own a suit, but we'll put his clean overalls and his blue shirt on him. He allus liked that blue shirt." And as though he were a child—who was alive and well—she tugged the nightshirt off her husband's body and began to wash him carefully, beginning with his face. She closed his eyes gently and stroked the grizzled hair back from his high forehead.

Carrie managed to dip her cloth once into the tepid water and to wash one arm and hand, but no more. Even though he was not yet cold, she could feel the heat of life ebbing, and it made her violently nauseated. She managed by a supreme effort of will to keep from retching, and when Mrs. Hamilton asked with motions, not words, that she help pull the overalls on, she did it. She was never able to remember how. Numbly she watched as the woman tied a ribbon under her husband's chin to hold the gaping, toothless mouth closed, put his favorite blue shirt on him, then, placed a saucer of salt on his flat stomach.

Mrs. Hamilton left, and it seemed a very long time indeed to Carrie before she returned with a small handful of cape jasmines in one hand and a Mason jar of water in the other. The sweet fragrance of the gardenia-like flowers overlaid the other smell in the room—the smell of death.

When she and Mrs. Hamilton emerged from the bedroom, Adam assured the woman that he would send someone right away. Nodding soberly, she thanked them both. Carrie was somehow able to murmur her sympathy and follow Adam out of the house.

It was only when they were mounted on their horses and a few hundred yards from the Hamilton cabin that Carrie spoke, her voice low and urgent. "Adam, I have to stop!" She made it off the horse, but just barely before the vile, churning contents of her stomach forced itself past the constricted throat. It was a very long time before she felt strong enough to climb back on, even with Adam's help. She nodded, eyes closed, when he told her how sorry he was that she'd had to go through such an experience.

The trip back to Saratoga was a silent one. Carrie's thoughts centered around one thing: she was certain that Jeannie wouldn't have acted so stupidly.

As Adam took the reins of her horse from her at the rear of the hotel he said in a low and anxious voice, "Carrie, I hope you won't be too hard on yourself about what happened today."

She stared at him for a long moment, "I . . . I learned a great deal. About myself, and . . ." She trailed off, and sagged weakly against the upright post.

"Go on upstairs," Adam said. "You've been through a lot. I should never have let you talk me into taking you."

Carrie saw the compassion in his eyes, and wished it was more than compassion. But when he leaned toward her and brushed her cheek with his lips, she swayed toward him, her arms wrapping around his neck. "Oh, Adam, surely there are other ways to prove my love!" She kissed him quickly, then pulled away and ran inside before he could answer.

CHAPTER 11

For I will pour water upon him that is thirsty, and floods upon the dry ground: I will pour my spirit upon thy seed, and my blessing upon thine offering: and they shall spring up as among the grass, as willows by the water courses.   Isaiah 44:3–4

That evening after dinner they were all seated in the big dining room at the boardinghouse. The room was empty except for family, which now seemed to naturally include Carrie, Rob, and Adam.

Jude, shaking his head, said, "Dr. Adam, what I'd like to know is, how in tarnation did you and that little gal *find* the Hamilton place so fur back in the Thicket, all by your lonesome?" He took a sip of his coffee, which had evidently cooled to his liking.

Mrs. Gallagher had been sneaking glances at Carrie. "And do you mean to tell me Carrie actually helped lay out old Henry?"

"You sound surprised, Mum." Jeannie was dishing up the apple betty her mother had made especially for the family, and she handed a plate to Carrie with a smile. "Carrie can do anything she sets her mind to."

Reba Gallagher saw the look of grudging gratitude Carrie flashed at her daughter. "Oh, I didn't mean to say she couldn't. Lord knows she works hard around here, too hard. It's just that the Hamiltons are a clannish lot. Why, that's what got the old man killed. Him and Luke Jordan have been feuding for a coon's age. One of 'em was bound to shoot the other'n dead sometime or another."

"You mean that's how he got the gunshot wound?" asked Carrie. "A feud?"

"Yup," put in Jude. "Goes way back. I bet neither one of 'em was real sure what begun the whole thing. But the Hamiltons, they was pert near royalty back in England, and protecting their honor seems mighty important to them."

"Mrs. Hamilton did look sort of . . ." Carrie hesitated, not having exactly the right word at her command.

"Aristocratic?" supplied Adam.

"I hadn't thought of it in just that way, but I think you're right," Jeannie nodded slowly.

"But the way they live isn't very aristocratic," said Carrie. "I did notice a beautiful old clock, and some silver things on the mantel. At the time I was too frightened to think much about it."

"I heard tell Henry left Virginia because he killed one too many men dueling. Also heard his family has been there since the Revolutionary War." Jude carefully cleaned up the last of his apple betty and eyed the dish which held the rest.

Jeannie nodded her head as she spooned another generous helping onto his plate. "Mrs. Hamilton will never forget what you did today, Carrie. Helping someone at a time like that is pretty important to Thicket folk."

Carrie's head bowed low. "I didn't do much. It was so frightening, and I haven't been around many sick people . . . or anyone who was dead."

"A lot of us are uncomfortable around death," said Jeannie gently. "But we have to hold on to the fact that if we love God, and have given our lives over to Him, He'll take care of us in the face of death."

Carrie hesitantly replied, "Then you believe there is something after we die? That it's not just nothing . . . black nothing?"

"Yes, I do. The Scripture tells us God has prepared a wonderful place for those who love and believe in Him," Jeannie said, her voice warm and firm.

"And is this wonderful place just for those of us who are 'good,'" Adam said in a cynical tone, "or does that include Henry Hamilton? Seems to me that a man who spent his life making moonshine and engaging in duels and feuds—who by the way, was killed by someone who was obviously a better shot than he was—might not find a welcome in God's wonderful place."

Jeannie gazed at him, her eyes not wavering. "Each of us, Henry Hamilton included, has to stand before God, and whether or not he'd given his life to the Father is something we won't know for certain on this side."

"I suppose you're saying that Hamilton is like that girl in the saloon, that God loved the old reprobate?"

"He certainly does." Jeannie's answer was as firm as her small chin, which was lifted high. "And, Dr. Adam, He loves you, too."

There was a sudden hush around the table. Reba Gallagher's bright eyes went from face-to-face, assessing reactions. Her own expression was not one of personal reaction to Jeannie's words, for she'd heard them all her life; it was just one of curiosity. And there was plenty on each face to feed that curiosity. Adam's was dark and strong, his unbelief plain. Carrie's held the same unbelief . . . mixed with a faint gleam of hope. Jude just grinned and shrugged. His faith was of a different kind. He loved nature, but had not yet come to know its Creator.

It was to Carrie that Jeannie spoke again. "Somebody told me one time that we've all got an empty spot inside us that only God alone can fill."

Adam got up so abruptly that he knocked over his chair. With firm determination he set it back up and silently, looking at no one, walked out of the room.

Jude broke the uneasy silence that fell after Adam's footsteps died away. "Jeannie girl, you gotta learn not to always go spouting off that religious stuff at people who don't keer to hear it." His words weren't harsh; he loved his niece very much.

Jeannie, still gazing at the door, said, "Maybe you're right, Uncle Jude. I guess I do have a habit of talking too much. I . . . I'm sorry."

Mrs. Gallagher rose and began gathering up the dishes. "At least things aren't dull when you're around." She winked at Carrie, whose expression was troubled. "Right, Carrie?"

"I . . . yes, Mrs. Gallagher, that's so." She got up and added, "Thank you for the special dessert. I'd better go and put Rob to bed. He was so tired he fell fast asleep on the floor next to the table."

"Me and the little feller had a good time today," said Jude

wistfully. "Never did want to marry—womenfolks is just too much bother. But I allus thought I might like a young'un, a boy to take around and show things. He's a fine boy, Miss Carrie."

Carrie's smile was real. Here was a sentiment she had no trouble whatever in agreeing with. "Yes, he is, Jude, and I appreciate your spending time with him." Then, with another troubled glance at Jeannie, she picked up Rob, whose little head naturally nestled into her shoulder, turned and carried him to their room.

Reba Gallagher halted in front of her daughter, hands on her hips. "Jeannie, Jude's right. You'd better learn not to keep spouting off stuff about the Lord that folks don't want to hear."

Jeannie's eyes were as troubled as Carrie's had been as she looked up at her mother. "You sound as though you think I do it on purpose, Mum, that I deliberately preached to them."

"Didn't you?"

"No, it just seemed natural for me to say what I did. It's the way I believe!"

"I believe it too, girl, but I also believe the best way isn't always to talk about it. A body ought to live it."

"But can't it both be right? It'd be wrong to always be thinking, uh oh, 'I can't say that about God, someone might get offended'. If I did that, I'd be a hypocrite." Her brown eyes shone with unshed tears now.

"Now don't get all het up," soothed Jude. "You're not a hypocrite, not by a long shot."

"And I never said you were, daughter. A hypocrite is someone outside the church, honey." Mrs. Gallagher's face was distressed at the turn the conversation had taken.

"No, Mum." Jeannie's voice was very low. "A hypocrite is a Christian who thinks one way and talks another, who says he believes something, but his actions show he doesn't."

Once again a silence fell on the three. Finally, Jude heaved himself out of his chair. "Well, I gotta be moseying on. Want me to walk you to your cabin, Jeannie girl?"

Jeannie nodded, and rose too. She hugged her mother. "Mum, forgive me if I seem disrespectful. I surely don't ever mean to be."

"I know that." Mrs. Gallagher held her daughter tight for a moment, then put her at arm's length. "You're everything a woman could want in a daughter."

A few tears began to roll down her cheeks as Jeannie said, "It's just that I think a lot about God, and when I read the Bible . . . I really believe He speaks to me. Can you understand that?"

Mrs. Gallagher's face showed that she didn't, altogether, but she could accept it. She hugged Jeannie again, then waved them both out.

It was a dark, moonless night as Jeannie and Jude stepped outside. The first thing her eyes were drawn to was the general store. Cy had long since closed up, but a lamp glowed in the window of the adjoining room that housed Adam's office. Though she said nothing, Jude's little grunt spoke volumes.

"You'd better watch yourself, girl," he warned, as he broke off a healthy plug of chewing tobacco. "I can shore see signs of trouble between you and that doctor."

Jeannie stepped off the veranda and began to walk briskly. "What in the world are you talking about, Uncle Jude?"

He hurried to catch up; it wasn't long before they were in total darkness, because the lights of Saratoga, even the bright ones of the saloons and fancy houses, were swallowed up by the Thicket. A few moments was all it took for their eyes to become accustomed to the black night. It wasn't cold, but it wouldn't be too much longer before a frost snapped the air and made the tallow trees, the sweet gums, flare with color.

"Hey now, honey'gal, don't get so riled up. I didn't mean you'd done something bad or wrong, or even that you was fixing to."

"Then what did you mean?" Jeannie walked quickly and silently as she always did, her stride long for such a small woman. Jude himself had taught her how to walk in the woods; he had the reputation that his feet could pick out trails you couldn't see. She tried to breathe deeply, to calm herself, because she knew exactly what Jude was talking about.

"I've known you all your life, and I can't remember a time when you wasn't honest. Honest with other folks or with your own self."

His quiet words smote her heart; she stopped and turned around. "Oh, Uncle Jude, what am I going to do?"

He spat off to one side and waited as she struggled for control.

Under cover of darkness the tears spilled down her cheeks. "I try, I really do. I'm as kind to Carrie as I know how to be. And it's not an act, it's not!"

"Nobody said it was."

"And Rob. He's such a fine little boy, the kind of child any woman would be proud of. He's no trouble, he's bright and lovable . . . and you know most of that is due to Carrie." The sound of a mockingbird's song was heartbreakingly sweet in the silence. The darkness all around them was almost like a living thing, but neither of them was afraid. The Thicket was home.

"Yup." Jude waited for her to continue, but she didn't. She started to walk again, very fast this time, and he didn't say anything further. He knew better than to push.

When they reached Jeannie's cabin her voice came low and troubled, "Come in for a bit?"

"Shore," Jude answered, still noncommittal, knowing she'd talk when she was ready and not before. He watched her build a small fire in the stove and put water in the black kettle. While it heated she stood before the shelves, a frown creasing her brow. She finally selected a jar of flower blossoms, another of small roots, and shook some of each into a round blue teapot.

The delicate aroma of apples filled the air, and when the tea was brewed Jeannie stirred a couple of spoons of Jude's own wild honey into their cups, then sat opposite him at the table.

"Uncle Jude, I'm in love with Adam Jarrett."

"I know that."

Her eyes widened. "You do? Is it that obvious?"

"Not to everybody, girl, but I know you. Mebbe even better'n your ma. She don't know yet, I reckon."

"Does . . . do you think Dr. Adam has seen . . . that he knows?"

Jude shook his head. "Nope. That man is too busy fighting whatever drove him here. But Carrie, she's a different story. She knows, all right. A woman who loves a man the way she does is on the lookout, has got feelers out for such."

Jeannie stared into her steaming cup. "I wish I could say you're wrong, but I can't." A question was burning in her heart, but she couldn't bring herself to phrase it aloud.

"You're wondering how the Doc feels about you, aren't you, gal?" Jude's quiet question was full of concern for her.

"Uncle Jude! No, I—" Jeannie stopped, her face stricken. "Yes, I was. Oh, they're going to be married; what I'm feeling is wrong!"

He reached over and took her clenched fists in his gnarled

hands. "I hate like everything to see you all tore up like this, I purely do."

"But you can't tell me it's all right, can you, for me to feel the way I do, that this will all work out?"

The soft light from the kerosene lamp flickered as Uncle Jude continued. He shook his head. "No, I can't! It's an awful situation, that's for sure. Worst part is, the Doc don't love that purty little Carrie, not like a man oughtta love the woman he's fixing to marry, leastways."

"How do you know that?" Jeannie whispered.

Jude grinned, showing tobacco-stained teeth. "Wal, don't you know, a bachelor allus knows everything about love and marriage. You know I'm right, though." Jeannie nodded numbly. "And I'll tell you another thing, too. The Doc could love you that way, the way a man oughtta love a woman."

"Uncle Jude!"

He shook his head. "I ain't saying he does. I'm saying he could. You two would make a good team."

"No." The word sounded quiet, forlorn, final. "He's spoken for, and I could never look myself in the eye again if I thought I did anything to . . . to—" She broke off, a lump welling up in her throat. "I'm tired, Uncle Jude. Thanks for walking me home."

"Any time, honey-gal," he said in a caring, loving tone as he drained his cup. "Hope I make it home afore I fall asleep on my feet. What was in that potion, anyhow?"

"Camomile and valerian root," Jeannie said, her back turned to him as she got up and went to the kitchen window. "See you tomorrow."

"Shore, honey." He went to the door, hesitated, then said, "It'll come out right, somehow." Then he went out, shutting the door softly behind him.

"No, Uncle Jude, it can't come out right; there's no way it can." The words echoed in the cozy little cabin, and for the first time she could remember, Jeannie Gallagher felt the aching pain of loneliness. She'd been born and raised in the Thicket, in this very cabin, and she loved both, and yet, had never felt lonely in her life.

But this feeling had nothing to do with place, at least not outside herself. It had to do with a person, a man whose dark eyes were filled with such haunting pain sometimes, such . . .

loneliness that his soul spoke to hers even when they were not together.

The tears flowed freely now. "Oh, God, help me! I don't know how to get hold of my feelings. Please, help me . . ."

It was a long time before she moved to get ready to go to bed. She stood unseeing, staring out at the darkness, waiting for God to answer her plea.

CHAPTER 12

*The hay appeareth, and the tender grass showeth itself, and
herbs of the mountains are gathered.*   Proverbs 27:25

In the short time since Adam had come to Saratoga, many
wells had been drilled and brought in successfully. Both Saratoga and Batson Prairie promised to be very rich fields. It didn't
take long for the heavy traffic to render the road between the
two communities almost impassable. The oil companies tried
to solve the situation by building a corduroy road, made of small
trees laid side by side. The problem was greatly compounded
by the steady rainfall in the flat, swampy terrain.

At first this worked fairly well, but it was too narrow for
wagons to pass each other, or even for a man on horseback to
pass a wagon without slipping into the treacherous mud. Adam
had the suspicion that the road would be sucked into the sticky
gumbo mud and disappear one day, along with whatever was
traveling on it at the time. Because the corduroy road was the
only way into the thriving little town, the people of Saratoga,
old and new, had been pleased to hear that the railroad was
coming. Unfortunately the surveyors later informed them the
station was to be located two miles from the Hotel Saratoga,
where many of them had already located their businesses.

A mad scramble had followed to get the best locations as
near the proposed station as possible. The new town site was
soon laid out along one main street which was to accommodate
businesses; on two side streets were all the hotels, gambling
houses, and red-light houses. Adam, for reasons he never really
tried to unravel, elected not to move his office to the new town
site. Although a new doctor had announced his intentions to
set up an office there, Adam knew he wouldn't lack for calls.

Since the incident in the Wooden Nickle when he'd sewed up Long Jim, his reputation had grown to almost epic proportions.

It was past midnight when Adam found himself hurrying to answer an urgent message from a man who owned one of the largest of the gambling establishments near the new sawmill, built three miles out of town. The "sawmill boys" and the "oil-field boys" had been involved in several skirmishes. The killings had become so frequent that a special deputy sheriff had been sent from Saratoga to try to keep law and order in the little settlement that had sprung up around the sawmill. Adam swung down from his horse and was looking for a place near the rear of the building to tie him when he saw a gun barrel pointed in his direction and heard a rough voice from the shadows.

"Who's there?" Adam immediately recognized the voice of Mr. Blake, the owner of the saloon.

"Put that gun away, Mr. Blake," Adam commanded. Since he'd been shot that day in Noirville, he was a lot more wary of guns.

"Doc Jarrett?"

"Yes, and we're wasting time. Where is the patient? Your note said it was urgent."

"Upstairs. She made a right proper mess of herself, I'll say that. Can't tell for sure if she really meant business, though. Those girls are always pulling something to get attention," he said as he holstered the gun. He motioned for Adam to follow him.

Blake had built his establishment like most other businesses of its kind: saloon in front, gambling rooms in the rear, with the upstairs divided into rooms barely big enough for a bed, a chair and a dresser. One small window let in a bit of light in the daytime, but now, there was only the dim glow afforded by the smoking oil lamps.

As Adam followed close behind Mr. Blake, he was struck again by the abysmal conditions the prostitutes tolerated, and wondered why, and how, they allowed themselves to fall so low. The dark-haired woman lying in the bed in the last room on the right was like so many of those he'd seen, except that this one had obviously tried to escape the life that so disturbed him.

She lay very still on top of the dingy covers, her hands placed carefully with the palms up to show the jagged cuts on her wrists. The blood had mostly coagulated, but there were a great many cuts, and the blood made it difficult to see how deep they were.

"I'll need a basin of clean water, and at least one full pitcher, maybe two," ordered Adam as he pulled the chair beside the bed and sat down.

Blake went to the dresser and brought over a plain white bowl and pitcher and set it on the floor beside Adam. "Fix her up good, Doc. The boys like her 'cause she's a fighter." He lingered a moment at the door. "Yolanda, you'd better promise me you won't try nothing like this again, or—"

The woman on the bed slowly lifted her head, her eyes blazing in her pale face. "You black-eyed vulture—"

Blake laughed and ducked out as Adam said, not roughly, but without much patience, "Lie still, or you'll start the bleeding again." He reached for her wrist and began washing it off. She jerked it from him.

"You think I care? I *want* to bleed, I *want* to die . . ." She didn't cry; there were no tears in her hard-looking black eyes. But something very near a sob choked her words.

"Then you should have done a better job," muttered Adam grimly, reaching for her wrist again. "Now be still."

She did as he said, but throughout the procedure she uttered short, hate-filled remarks. "I hate all those fellas, I hate them!" Then she would lapse into silence, only to erupt again. "I hate my old man, too. If I told you some of the things he did to me, you wouldn't believe it. And he used to whale on all us kids all the time. Men! None of you are worth the salt in your bread!"

After cleaning the multitude of jagged wounds, Adam saw that none had cut a vein seriously. "Miss, ah, Yolanda, if you'd really wanted to kill yourself, you'd have cut deeper. You're going to be fine." He began the painstaking process of stitching up the worst of the cuts.

"I wanted to!" she burst out. "I tried, I did, but . . . it hurt so bad . . ."

Adam steeled himself against the broken anguish and finished the job in silence. "These will all heal. They'll leave scars, however." He placed bandages on the wounds and taped them securely.

"I hate you! I hate all of you!" she spat, her voice low, hopeless.

As Adam repacked his bag he said, against his better judgment, "It's none of my business, but I'll venture to say you're in the wrong business." He walked to the door, mocked by her bitter laugh.

"You know, I do believe you're right, and I'm going to get out of this business." She stared at her bandaged arms.

"Are you talking about another suicide attempt?"

"What do you think?"

Adam thought he should just walk out, but his hand on the doorknob didn't move. "I think you might not be so lucky next time."

"Lucky? That's a laugh! If it hadn't hurt so bad, they would of called the undertaker instead of you. The next time I'll use something that won't hurt, something that will work, and I'll just go to sleep and not wake up . . ." Her eyes closed briefly as though she were already under the influence of a fatal drug.

"Yolanda, you need help—" began Adam, but her eyes flew open and she cut him off sharply.

"You don't know what I need! No man could, not even *God* knows what I need! Get out, get out of here and leave me alone!" She did begin to cry then, great wracking sobs that shook her scantily clad body, that young-old body that was still, despite the punishment she and countless men had done it, beautiful.

Adam slipped out, the awful sounds of her sobs ringing in his ears until he got downstairs where it was replaced by the din of business in full swing. Just as he was about to leave, Mr. Blake caught his arm.

"Come have a look at my place, Doc. We're doing right well." He grinned at Adam, who looked as though he might refuse. "You might oughtta let me escort you out, anyway. I wouldn't doubt that I got the meanest set of men and women in the whole world congregated here tonight, and that's no joke."

Reluctantly, Adam followed Blake into the gambling place at the rear of the building. It was thronged with Americans, Mexicans, Negroes, and foreigners of all sorts. Adam noticed that several of the Mexican women had thin, long knives stuck in their hair or into their belts. Most of the men wore pistols strapped to their legs, just as the owner beside Adam did.

"Now, Doc, ain't that the toughest looking bunch you ever saw? I've run gambling houses from Klondike to Venezuela, and I've seen a lot of tough hombres. But this is the wildest, meanest bunch of crooks I *ever* saw all together!" He grinned, and there was actually pride in his tone as he said, "I ain't saying everybody in Batson is a rat, but every rat is here who could get here!"

All of Adam's senses were assaulted by the odors of liquor, of unwashed bodies and sexual excitement, of bright clothes and exotic women, of the obscene curses and ribald laughter that filled the smoky, close air. Suddenly, he'd had enough. "Thanks for the tour, Mr. Blake. Call me if Yolanda has any trouble with her stitches."

Blake laughed. "That Yolanda, she don't have trouble, she gives it! I can't figure out why so many of the guys ask for her. She gives 'em fits, she does. Makes a lot of money, by the way. Glad she didn't do herself no permanent harm."

Blake's attitude that she was a commodity, that she existed to make money for him, made Adam so angry he found it difficult to speak. "I hope you won't have to call me again, Mr. Blake. I can tell you one thing, there are places I'd rather be called to."

Blake shrugged. "Don't be so all-fired high and mighty, Doc, I pay my dues. F'rinstance, I pay twenty-five dollars a week for every gambling machine you see here. And every one of my girls is fined twelve dollars and eighty cents per week. How do you like them apples?"

"Mr. Blake, I—"

"I suppose you know, if the judge needs a little extra scratch, he just ups the fine a little." His eyes narrowed, and he chomped a little harder on the unlit cigar in his mouth. "Don't you ever think I don't pay my dues."

"I'm sure you do. If you'll excuse me, I have to be going."

"Guess you do, Doc. But, I ain't paid you yet." He slipped a couple of bills into Adam's pocket. "Did you hear about the lady who was hauled into court for being . . . um, a vagrant, 'cause she couldn't prove she had a job?"

Because he was beginning to get the feeling he might explode, Adam moved past Blake, who let out a loud guffaw of laughter as Adam hurriedly made his way out the back door. He stood just outside, grateful for the clean night air; as he undid the reins of his horse he breathed deeply and told himself to calm down. The air was a welcome relief from the fetid, polluted atmosphere within the building, the singing, cursing revelry of the crowd floating out. Yet he felt a restless, pent-up surge of energy swell within him and slung his bag over the saddle horn. Knowing he needed to work some of it off, walking seemed more appealing than riding at that particular moment.

He'd put enough distance between him and the saloon so that there was almost no light except that from the waning moon when he heard a voice he immediately recognized.

"Well, all right! I won't get on you again, but you've got to let me look at the cursed thing or—"

"Miss Gallagher?" Adam asked in surprise.

"Dr. Adam, is that you?" She lifted a pale oval face in the moonlight, her hair falling around it as though she'd been struggling.

"What are you doing out at this time of night?" asked Adam, drawing closer.

"The same as you, most likely," followed the almost curt reply. "I've been helping to birth a baby, a baby too small for this cruel world, I might add."

The grim sound of her words was unmistakable. "Lost him, then?"

"No. We filled a couple of whiskey bottles with hot water—after I drained out the liquor, which won't set too well with the papa when he finally comes home, I'm sure. Then we put the poor little thing in a box with them and lots of blankets. I told the people to keep him warm, but . . ."

"But you're not sure they will."

She shook her head, the coppery strands flying out in her vehemence. "I'm not even sure they wanted the child in the first place, nor care if he lives. And then my mare picked up a stone, at least I think that's what's wrong. She won't even lead, much less let me get on her."

"And you're very tired."

"That I am, Doctor." Jeannie didn't even try to deny it. "It's been a long day, an even longer night; it was a difficult birth, and I'm about to kick this wretched beast from amazing grace to kingdom come!"

If Adam was tempted to laugh, he stifled it. "Don't do that. Hold mine and I'll take a look. Which foot?"

"What do you mean take a look? It's dark as the inside of a miner's boot, man!" She must have realized how sharp she sounded, for she quickly added, "Forgive me. They don't just make up stories about bad-tempered redheads, I guess. And it's the right front foot."

He said nothing as he handed her his reins, then bent the right front leg of her horse and felt for a stone. "I can't feel a thing. Could she have wrenched it?"

"Could be. That corduroy road is terrible on people riding; it must be even worse for the horses. I'd best get going if I'm going to get home by dawn. Thanks for stopping."

"I'll accompany you. This is no place for a woman alone." He'd taken the reins of his own horse. "Get on my horse, and I'll lead them both."

"No, I'll walk as well," she added testily as she took her reins from him. "As for my being out alone, you should know by now that I am a great deal of the time." She didn't say, *and without an escort,* but it was certainly implied.

Because she'd begun walking, Adam had to hurry to catch up with her. "Miss Gallagher, I'm not accustomed to having my suggestions ignored."

She flashed a smile that the moonlight, pale as it was, showed. "Suggestions? Orders would be closer, I'd say. And I'm too tired to play games. I don't want to ride while you walk. I want to walk with you." They were side by side now, and he'd narrowed his stride to match her smaller one. "Were you delivering a baby, too?"

Soberly he told her the nature of his call, and to his surprise even went on to share his reactions. "It's just that these people seem to be in such dire need of . . . something, though I'm not sure what. I've never been a religious man. Always felt my mother was religious enough for us both. And my wife was—"

She waited for him to go on, and when he didn't she said quietly, "She was religious enough too, I take it."

"Yes. Oh, I never minded. Bethany was so good, I figured if religion made her that way, how could it be bad?"

"But it's not for you."

Adam walked a long time before he replied. The silence around them, once they'd gotten out of earshot of the settlement, had a calming effect. There was even enough moonlight to enable them to see the path. "I know I've always been headstrong, Miss Gallagher."

Her laughter was low and quick. "After all this time, couldn't you see your way clear to calling me Jeannie?"

"Jeannie." He said the word softly, almost as though he were trying it out, to see if he liked the sound of it.

"Sounds all right, doesn't it?"

He glanced down at her. "Yes, it does."

She was quiet for a long moment, then said, "You're like a

lot of men. You feel that religious beliefs, belief in God, is for women . . . that men should be strong enough to fight their own battles."

Adam had to admit to himself that was pretty much the way he had always felt, though he hadn't really ever phrased it exactly. They were coming close to the bayou, and he slowed his steps. "Isn't that the way most men are? They . . . we feel it's not manly to need . . ." He didn't finish his statement, and he stopped walking entirely now.

"That's all well and good until a man comes across something that is more than he can bear. All of us, men and women both, need help sometimes, Dr. Adam."

Obviously choosing not to pursue that line of thought, Adam said, "I patch up their bodies, but it just seems they need a great deal more than I've got to offer in my medical bag."

"You're right about that. They need the love of God, the love of His Son Jesus."

His antagonism made him abrupt. "What they need is a cure for venereal disease."

"Doctor, are you trying to shock me? If you are, it'll take more than a statement like that."

Sheepishly Adam said, "Perhaps I was. But you'll have to admit it's certainly true. Why, we've got almost nothing to fight it with, nothing but potassium permanganate, and that certainly doesn't cure it."

"There are so many advertisements for medicines—"

"None of them any good, sheer quackery. Oh, we can fumble around, treat the first symptoms, even get rid of the acute condition. Some men even brag about catching it, of all things. They have no idea about what comes later."

"Which is?"

"Well, the tertiary phase can lull them into a false state of security."

"Beg pardon? What's the tertiary?"

"The third stage of syphillis. It appears after the secondary stage goes away, and the poor fool thinks he's beat it. But some develop gummas or tumors, of a gummy or rubbery consistency. Then comes involvement of the skeletal, cardiovascular, or nervous systems." He paused, then added slowly, "And then, of course, they die—horribly."

"It makes me ill to think on it," she murmured.

He nodded in agreement. "And these boom towns create a

breeding ground that will ruin the lives of men for years to
come."

"And the women?" she asked quietly.

Grimly he answered, "Ruined for life. Even if we get rid of
the acute condition, the chronic conditions plague them forever."

In the silence which followed it occurred to Adam that an
extraordinary thing had just happened. He'd been discussing
one of the most taboo subjects he knew anything about in an
entirely natural way. If this was not enough, it was not another
doctor to whom he spoke, not even a man; it was a young
woman, a most unusual young woman the likes of which he'd
never known before. Though it hadn't before, her name came
quite naturally to his lips now, "Jeannie, I—"

But before he even knew what he wanted to say, she exclaimed, "Look, something's on fire!"

It was, indeed. At first there was only a glow to the left of
them, toward Batson Prairie. As they walked, the horses skit-
tering nervously behind them, the glow grew brighter and they
could hear the sound of the fire crackling as it came nearer. A
broad strip of flame was racing along the ground, periodically
leaping up into the trees.

"Why, it's the bayou, the bayou is burning!" said Jeannie in
an awed, hushed voice.

"It does seem to be," Adam murmured. Even as they
watched, the vine-hung trees, the palmettos that bordered the
sluggish stream, flamed into startling beauty, etched against
the black sky. And, incredible as it seemed, the bayou was burning.

"How can water burn?" whispered Jeannie.

"I don't know for sure, but I suspect it has something to do
with oil."

"Do you think there's any danger that it will spread?"

"Not likely, with the heavy rains we've been having." And
then Adam was silent, as though he were giving himself to
experiencing the beautiful spectacle. It wasn't long before the
flames died down, and there was only the hush of night, the
soft darkness all around them. Some time during the scene
they'd just witnessed, it had felt entirely natural for Adam to
reach for Jeannie's hand.

It was a smallish hand, and slightly rough on the palm, as
though it was accustomed to hard work. When his fingertips

lightly brushed it she said, her voice low and husky, "It's from gathering roots and herbs. Not very feminine, I guess, to have callouses."

"You're a very feminine, ladylike young woman."

"Was your wife . . ."

"Yes. But she was different from you."

"In what way?"

He was quiet for a long time before he answered. "She always dressed just so; her hair was perfect and beautiful; her voice was always carefully modulated; she never said or did the wrong thing."

Jeannie was trying to tuck up her straggling hair with her free hand. "She sounds perfect."

"In some ways she was. Don't bother with your hair," he said; "it . . . it looks fine."

Her hand stopped in midair as she stared up into his face. His other hand came to rest lightly on her hair. "Adam . . ."

"Sometimes it looks like those flames we just saw, as though it were alive and could crackle and burn. But it's actually very soft."

"Adam . . ." This time the word was only a whisper. They both stood very still, not coming any closer, but the touch of his hand on her hair was so strongly binding that neither could nor wanted to move away.

It was Adam who finally broke the silence and gently murmured, "I'd better get you home before daybreak." He moved his hand away slowly and took her arm instead. It was a courteous, proper gesture, his hand on her elbow. But they both felt the current that flowed between them as they walked silently through the night.

CHAPTER 13

They that see thee shall narrowly look upon thee, and consider
thee, saying, Is this the man that made the earth to tremble, that
did shake kingdoms; that made the world as a wilderness, and
destroyed the cities thereof. . . ?   *Isaiah 14:16–17*

"Doc, did you hear about the feller with the red suspenders?"
Jude asked as they stood outside the general store the next
morning. A chorus of guffaws came from the tight little knot
of men gathered there.

Cy, Adam's landlord, nodded and took up the story. "They
say he was altogether a prideful man. Wore them red galluses
like he figgered they made him special or something. Getting
a lot of money quick-like goes to poor folks' heads, I guess." He
rolled his eyes. "And them checkered pants he wore—"

Another man, obviously relishing the story, spoke up. "Well
them galluses was what got him killed. I hear he challenged a
boomer in a saloon over at Batson Prairie, dared him to come
out on the street. Once they was out, ol' Red Suspenders hol-
lered, 'Draw!' and he couldn't!" Slapping his thigh, the man
continued. "Got his gun hung up in his fancy suspenders and
the other feller drilled him."

"Yeah, Dr. John Bevil carried him over to his office, but the
poor soul died," said Cy, trying not to look as though the story
tickled him. "Say, Doc, did you see that little fire on the bayou
last night? You was over that way, wasn't you?"

Adam, who'd only been half listening, looked back at Cy. "I
certainly did see it. Do you know what was the cause?"

"Shore do. An oil tank over at Batson Prairie sprung a leak
and it ran right down into the bayou. Covered the top of the
water with oil for several miles. Some fool tossed a lighted cig-

arette in, and that fire just raced right along. They say it was some kind of sight."

"Yes, it was," Adam said, and before he could add anything another man, who'd been silent up until now, spoke in a low, angry voice.

"Well, I consider it a heap more'n a crazy stunt! These fellers think they can come in here, make an unholy mess and then leave with all the money they made off the Thicket."

A couple of the others, obviously Thicket dwellers, muttered agreement. It was a theme Adam heard frequently—the Thicket dwellers' anger at the boomers for despoiling their home ground. Though many of the Thicket landowners had made a great deal of money off the sale of their property, or the sale of mineral rights, they bemoaned the havoc being wreaked.

"Doc, what do you think?"

Adam was saved from having to comment by two men who came thundering down the street on horseback. Stopping in front of Adam's office, they leaped off their lathered horses and came directly to him.

"Dr. Jarrett! The boss said we was to bring you right away!"

Adam was already moving toward the door of his office as he asked, "What's the trouble?"

The two men followed him into his office, talking excitedly as he gathered his equipment together. "You see, Doc, part of the drilling process is to let pipe down, then pull it up again. A big old hook is dropped from the top of the derrick, then, a man has to—quick-like, you see—fix it onto the gadget around the pipe that's to be pulled up again."

Adam didn't stop his packing as he said grimly, "And the man who operates that hook was injured."

With an emphatic nod the man added, "Don't know how it happened. Jake's usually purty speedy."

"Wasn't today," the other man commented.

"Nope. Instead of fastening the hook onto the ring on the pipe, the hook caught his arm and hoisted up Jake."

Adam scowled. "Extent of injuries?"

"Terrible, Doc. By the time they got the signal to the hoist man, poor Jake was flung around like a rag dolly up through the derrick."

Snapping his bag shut, Adam said, "Let's go." The two men nodded and quickly followed Adam out of his office.

The ride to the well, located outside Saratoga a couple of

miles, was a wild one for all three. Adam speculated on what he would find; he feared it would be bad indeed, if the man wasn't dead already.

As they approached the rig Adam could see a group talking, and when he swung off his horse, one separated himself from the others and came over. He shook Adam's hand. "My name's Pritchett; I'm the driller. Jake's in the tool shack, Doc, and he's tore up pretty bad. Awful shame. Come on, I'll show you where he is."

But before Adam could speak, there was a blowing, hissing noise, and the ground seemed to move.

"Don't let it worry you," Pritchett said with a shrug. "You see, there's so much gas near the surface of the ground it acts like it's gonna move."

"It certainly does," muttered Adam. It felt as though he were walking on a carpet laid over springs. "Is there any—"

"Danger?" Pritchett stopped at the door of a small shack, his smile grim, "We don't know for sure. I tell you I don't like the way the situation feels any more than you do, but I've got a job to do, and I'm not leaving. Jake's in there. Let me know if you need anything."

He strode off, leaving Adam staring after him. The tall pine trees all around were not moving, yet there was that eerie sensation of movement under his feet. Just then, mud and rocks started shooting forcefully out of the well, breaking limbs off the trees as they fell, landing on the tin roof of the shack like heavy hail. When Adam ducked inside, he confronted Jake, his patient, who was miraculously conscious and smoking a cigarette.

"Hey, Doc, you got a job here, patching me up." The words had a ring of bravado in them, feeble though they were.

"Then let's get started," replied Adam, for even without an examination he could see that the injuries were grave. The man's left eye was totally shut; there were multiple cuts and contusions all over his face and head and body; and his right arm, obviously the one which had been caught, was broken in at least three places.

It took almost two hours to "patch up" Jake, and during that time the rattling noise on the roof ceased. But when he finally put his equipment away and stretched, Adam was still reluctant to step outside. When he did, the earth seemed to sink and rise, and as he walked, the derrick again spewed a shower of mud and rocks hundreds of feet into the air.

Pritchett met him at his horse and tucked some money into Adam's jacket as he swung into the saddle. "Don't blame you for wanting to hightail it out of here, Doc. I don't know how long this will last." As he raised his hand in a goodbye salute, a man dashed up.

"Dr. Jarrett! We just got word they need you over at Batson Prairie! Bad bunch of poisonings—"

Adam nodded and wheeled his horse around. "Thanks for the message." As he rode, hard, in the direction of Batson Prairie, he thought over his experiences with patients around Saratoga who'd been victims of the insidious gas. Though he'd even written the dean of the medical school he attended, he hadn't been able to get much information on treatment for the poison gasses, and had had to devise his own, including finding medicines for possible lung and heart damage. With Jeannie's help he'd been able to develop a salve for their injured eyes, which along with the treatment of confining them to a darkened room for a few days, seemed to work as well as anything.

But when he ducked into the tent and saw the driller lying on a cot, Adam encountered a new problem altogether. The man looked dead. Though his eyes were open, his lips were parted and swollen, and dark as though they'd been burned with acid. It was with great difficulty that Adam could find a pulse or be sure that the man was even breathing.

After administering his usual treatment with no effects whatever, Adam had to conclude that the gasses in each location must produce different reactions. Although he fully expected the man to come out of his deep stupor in an hour or two, despite all Adam could do, he stayed unconscious for over twelve hours.

People wandered in and out during this time, and Adam had to go to a nearby house to treat another young man with even more puzzling symptoms from gas poisoning. The whites of his eyes bulged out, almost completely covering the iris. The medicine Adam gave him seemed to have little or no effect, but he promised Adam he'd keep applying it. Surprisingly enough, he seemed to be in no great pain.

It was well into the night when the driller regained even a semblance of consciousness. Exhausted, Adam accepted the offer of a cot there instead of returning to Saratoga in the dark again. He quickly fell into a deep, unrestful sleep, but his dreams were haunted by moving ground, and creeping, deadly poison gas that struck with no warning.

Early the next morning, he returned to Saratoga and went straight to the boardinghouse, where Carrie, her face full of relief, ran and threw herself into his arms.

"We were so worried! They told us you'd been called to Batson, and how bad the gas is there—" She stopped and withdrew slightly, seeing that Adam's eyes had gone to where Jeannie stood by the door. Defiantly she slipped her arm around his waist. "Aren't we glad to see him back safe, Mrs. Gallagher?"

"That we are, Carrie," agreed Reba. "Set down, Dr. Adam, I've no doubt you're in need of some breakfast."

"That's the best suggestion I've heard in a long time," said Adam. He hugged Carrie briefly and sat down. "Where's Rob?"

"Off with Jude, as usual," said Jeannie, the look in her eyes polite, suitably distant. "Tell us what you found. We've been hearing some pretty wild tales about the gas."

"Most of them are probably true," murmured Adam, rubbing the dark stubble on his face. By the time he'd finished a breakfast of sausage, eggs, and four of Mrs. Gallagher's mammoth hotcakes, he'd recounted the happenings of the previous day and night.

Jude, having come in with Rob as Adam was speaking, said, "Wal, Doc, I reckon you heard what happened to them folks over at Batson Prairie this morning early."

Adam crooked his finger at Rob, who came running to nestle at his father's side. "Which ones, Jude? I was near there all night at a well, but I left pretty early."

For Jude, his expression was extremely serious as he said, "It was a new well come in what done it. Near as I can figure, the gas in each one don't necessarily have to be the same kind."

Nodding, Adam pulled his son onto his lap. "I've noticed the same thing myself. Go on."

"The bad part was, the wind changed during the night and took that gas right into town. And it wasn't just people that died, all kinds of animals, chickens, cattle and horses was taken in their sleep."

"That's terrible!" Carrie cried. "And you go there often, Adam—"

"Now, Carrie, you musn't fret over things like that. I'm perfectly safe."

"Don't be too sure, Adam," put in Jeannie. "I've been hearing stories, too. Another doctor, George Parker, told how he was riding alone when a wave of the poisonous gas came across the path of his horse."

"What'd he do?" asked a wide-eyed Rob.

"He put the spurs to his horse and rode like a crazy man, holding his breath," said Jude with a sly grin. "He had to hold his breath for four days, I heard."

"Really?" Rob's head was half buried in his father's black jacket now.

"Don't tease the child," admonished Mrs. Gallagher. "More coffee, anyone?" She lifted the blue-gray graniteware pot, and several mugs were shoved in her direction.

Talk of the dangers the gas presented broke out again, and Carrie came to sit beside Adam. Shyly she leaned against him. "I don't care what they say, I'm afraid for you."

"Don't be. I can take care of myself," he said, more gruffly than he intended; he saw the shine of tears in her eyes.

"I didn't mean to say you couldn't; it's just that this is such a dangerous place in so many ways." She forced a little smile. "From all Jude had told us, I thought it would be quiet and beautiful here."

"I'm sure it is under normal circumstances," replied Adam.

Jeannie, seated at the other side of the table, was close enough to overhear. "And so it is. You've not seen it at its best. You should get Mum to pack you a basket and go on a picnic. Better take advantage of the weather, because it could turn nasty any day now. The sun is shining today, though, and it's even fairly warm." Her glance met Adam's briefly, then fell to her cup.

Adam wondered if she was thinking about the evening before, when they'd watched the bayou burn and he'd touched her bright hair. Knowing he shouldn't say it, but unable to hold it back, he said, "We'll need a guide to find the best spots, and I've been told often enough that if I get off the trail or road it's a foregone conclusion I'll get lost in the Thicket. You'll have to go with us." He felt the pressure of Carrie's fingers on his arm and knew as soon as the words were out he'd been right; he shouldn't have said them.

Jeannie's eyes were on Carrie as she rose. "Sure, and you do need a guide, but I can't go today."

"Why, daughter, what are you up to?" asked Mrs. Gallagher. "You could use a little rest, a nice picnic, yourself. What have you got to do that's so all-fired important?"

"I . . ." Jeannie turned her back and poured the remainder of her coffee down the sink. "I just can't go today, and besides, you'll need help at noon, with Carrie gone. I'm sure Jude will be glad to go along with them, especially if you pack a good lunch." Without another word, she left the room.

"I'll be glad to take you folks on a picnic," offered Jude, "but pack lots of food, 'cause I'm gonna have an oncoming appetite."

"Jude's always looking for an excuse to eat," said Mrs. Gallagher. "Jeannie usually likes to go, but I reckon part of the problem is just that she's been working too hard, what with her own work, and helping out here, too."

Carrie, her eyes on the door where Jeannie had just left, said, "Maybe we ought not go; maybe I ought to stay and help you."

"Horsefeathers! You go on. Jeannie's staying already. I will let you pack your own lunch, though. And this helps me make up my mind about something."

"What's that, Reba?" asked Jude, sipping his just-right coffee from a saucer as he always did.

Mrs. Gallagher, with her usual efficiency, cleared the table quickly and had the dishes in soapy water before Carrie could rise and help. "Remember Luce, that girl of Viona and John Barrett who's been off to who knows where this past year? Anyhow, I told you she come round a couple of times and was wanting to know if I'd give her a job. Couldn't make up my mind, but I told her to come back today and I'd let her know."

"Think she'd make a good hand?" asked Jude.

She shrugged. "I'll have to admit it was Jeannie who said I ought to give her a chance. Don't know as I would, otherwise."

"Why not, sis? Near as I can recall, she was a purty little thing."

Mrs. Gallagher scowled. "Oh, she's pretty enough, maybe too pretty. And the way she was dressed—"

Carrie, who'd seen Luce the first day she'd come to the hotel asking for a job, said slowly, "Like she might take in sewing for a living?"

With a little snort Reba Gallagher said, "If you mean what I think you mean, yes. The thing is, I sure wouldn't want her to wind up working at one of them places—" she glanced at Rob, who was listening raptly, as he always did. "At some of the undesirable places round here, so close to her folks. Her pa would hit the ceiling, for sure."

"What's 'zirable?" the child piped up.

"Never mind, Robbie," said Carrie. "Mrs. Gallagher, I'll make it up to you. I'll work twice as hard tomorrow."

"I know you will. Like I've said before, child, you're a good worker."

Adam rose. "I'll leave the picnic plans to you ladies, and you, Jude. If it's all right, I'm going to see if I can catch a little more sleep."

"Good luck, Doc," said Jude with a grin. "Bet you a dollar on a doughnut there's a line in front of your office already."

He was right, as Adam found when he went to unlock the door. There were already five people waiting. But four of them were not oil-field related; they were Thicket dwellers, which Adam also found pleased him. As he treated each in turn he tried to determine exactly why, and he decided that although he was, in a way, glad for the frenzied pace the boomers gave to his life, it was the people of the Thicket who really interested him most now.

Carrie had been waiting for almost an hour when he was finally free to go. When the last patient walked out, she put the "Back Later" sign in the window, grabbed Adam's hand, and said, "Come on before someone else comes! And I want you to promise you won't talk about poison gas, or boomers, or anything connected with it."

He looked into her lovely face, which was filled with anticipation, and had to admit to himself that the prospect of a picnic with her and Rob seemed attractive, even without Jeannie as a guide. "I promise, Carrie."

The spot to which Jude took them was, he said, one of his favorite secret places when he was a boy not much older than Rob. After they'd eaten lunch, Carrie coaxed Adam into laying his head on her lap while they both drowsed their way through Jude's enthusiastic recital of all the natural wild foods the Thicket had to offer.

"We never had to do any gardens if we didn't want to, 'cause there was always plenty around to eat. Why, there's all kinds of animals here that's good to hunt—wild hogs, wild cattle, deer, squirrel, turkeys. I'll shoot a couple for Thanksgiving. Boy howdy, it ain't far off." He ruffled Rob's hair. "And we got more kinds of berries than you can shake a stick at. Blackberries, dewberries, and strawberries, and mayhaws and plums besides. We did raise some cane—" He snickered and added, "Both kinds, I can tell you! We used the one for making syrup and sugar, and we had lots of honey."

He glanced thoughtfully over at Adam and Carrie, who seemed, for the first time since he'd met them, relaxed and at ease with each other. "Right now might be a good time for me to tell you about how to find a bee tree, Rob. You like honey, don't you?"

"Yea!" shouted Rob, then clapped his hands over his mouth at Jude's warning scowl.

"Settle down, for pity's sake, you little wiggleworm. Now set here by me." The boy nestled close, and Jude stared down at his round, cherubic face for a long moment, thinking again he wished the child was his own. "Well, sir, you got to put out a bait—that's sugar 'n water, not too thick and syrupy, with a tad bit of honey in to make it smell good, and some twigs on top so the bees'll have something to light on—then you got to wait 'til bees happen on it. They'll load up, then head right on for their tree."

"They will?"

"Yup. You got to have a eagle eye, and watch how they go. They don't always go straight, like some fellers claim. Them bees'll go round stuff. They ain't dumb, and they don't take kindly to your robbing their tree, neither."

"Do they sting?" asked Rob. At Jude's solemn nod he changed the subject, obviously deciding that bee coursing was not for him. "Tell me about your secret place again."

Jude, like Carrie, was sitting on the ground with his back to an oak tree. He looked around the little open space enclosed with trees, which made it like a small green room. "This here is the very place, boy. How do you like it?"

"I do, Uncle Jude, I do! What else grows here?"

"Why, all kinds of nuts, boy."

"What kinds?"

"Hickory nuts, walnuts, beech, pecans. I like hickory nuts the best, but they're the dickens to crack."

Rob made a muscle with his arm as Jude himself had showed him one time. "I'm strong, I can crack 'em," he bragged. Jude snickered, but he covered it well.

Adam, who had been watching his son and Jude, spoke quietly to Carrie, "Jude is very good with Rob, isn't he?"

"I suppose, in some ways," admitted Carrie. "But he tells such wild tales, I'm concerned. Rob has such a vivid imagination." She hesitated, then added, "I've been wanting to talk to you about that, Adam."

He sat up and locked his hands around one knee, the other stretched out before him. "What?"

She saw that the relaxed look of a few moments before was gone, and regretted her words. But she took a deep breath and said, "I'm not at all sure it's going to be good for Rob if we stay here much longer. That business with the gas frightens me. Maybe we should be thinking about moving."

He frowned, and it was a while before he answered. "I'll admit there are a lot of things about living here that aren't the best for Rob. But there are some advantages, too."

"What in the world could they be?" The words were a good deal sharper than she intended, but she couldn't seem to help herself. "We live in a tiny room with rough men all around, some of them drunk no matter what Mrs. Gallagher's rules are, and I have to work like a hired hand. It's hard trying to keep Rob with me, and wondering where Jude has taken him to when he's not—" She stopped, suddenly aware that she'd said far more than she'd intended, that she was complaining bitterly, something she'd sworn not to do.

Adam's face was set. Not angry, just closed. "I'm sorry, Carrie, I didn't realize how hard it's been on you since we came here."

"You've been busy." Her words were small; she'd have given anything to take her earlier ones back, to think of something to make the mood light and happy as it had been a few moments before.

"I have," he agreed, "but that's no excuse. I need to provide for you better."

"It's all right where I am, really, Adam. And it won't be long before we're married. Like Jude said, it's almost Thanksgiving—" She stopped, for she'd promised herself she wouldn't mention it again until Adam did.

He rose and extended a hand to her. "It's time we got back. I'm sure there are patients waiting."

"Adam, I'm so sorry."

"For what? You haven't said or done anything wrong." He turned and said, "Jude, we should be getting back."

Carrie had already packed up the leftovers of their lunch

earlier, so nothing remained to be done but to dust off Rob's little bottom and admonish him to watch where he stepped. And as they walked back, all silent except for the chattering child, she wondered if she would ever learn to say the right thing, to know when and when not to speak.

CHAPTER 14

All his days also he eateth in darkness, and he hath much sorrow
and wrath with his sickness.   *Ecclesiastes 5:17*

For the next few days Adam brooded on what Carrie had
said, that Saratoga was no better place for a child than Beaumont had been. Fights erupted at all times of the day and night,
making an endless parade of lacerations, smashed noses, damaged eyes and broken bones, not to mention the gunshot
wounds. And the oil field presented many unusual dangers,
such as gas poisoning.

A large part of the problem concerning the oil-rig accidents
was due to the fact that, as in all rapidly expanding industries,
the primary consideration was to get the job done as quickly as
possible. It was standard procedure to allow newly drilled wells
to flow unchecked in order to clean them out, with no effective
blowout preventives. Men wore no gas masks or steel helmets
as they worked capped flowing wells, using steel tools that could
easily cause sparks. Firefighting equipment was almost non-
existent in the fields. It had to come from Beaumont and was,
in Jude's words, "slower'n Christmas." As with the disastrous
fire at Spindletop, men used lighted lanterns unwisely, smoked
carelessly as they worked, and seemed to disregard their own
safety almost totally.

Adam listened as he patched up the men, as he mingled
with them on the streets, as he ate beside them at the boardinghouse. The conclusions he drew were fairly accurate. Part
of the careless attitude toward the dangers involved came from
the attitude of the previous generation. They'd been an adven-
turesome lot who'd stretched the boundaries of the nation west,
and casualties were considered part of the price of that progress.

149

Those frontiersmen, with a lust for adventure in their souls, had not only accepted danger as part of their lives, but many of them had done it eagerly, scorning their safe brothers who stayed at home.

Adam also knew that although the bosses and drillers were not unconcerned for the safety of their men, they were not legally liable for that safety. They took risks they considered necessary to get the job done. So he accepted the daily multitudes of medical challenges that the situation provided, and worked sixteen, even eighteen-hour days, glad for the exhaustion that allowed him to sleep at night.

It was certainly not for his own sake that he'd begun to search his heart, to see if perhaps Carrie was right, that they should consider moving on to a more stable environment. It was because of Rob. Adam never let himself admit that Jeannie Gallagher was one of the reasons he'd stayed this long. But when he'd gone to get Rob one morning, determined to spend some time with the boy, he'd had to quickly suppress the feeling of dismay when she'd merely smiled and said she'd love to stay and talk, but the Daltons had sent word that Polly's little sister Sarah was ailing, and left.

Somehow being denied the opportunity to be the one to keep their relationship cool made him perversely resentful that Jeannie had done exactly as she should have. Carrie, who'd volunteered to help Mrs. Gallagher train Luce, the new girl, saw the little exchange between Adam and Jeannie, but said nothing about it. For when she asked about his excursion with Rob, he told her rather shortly that he didn't know how long he intended to keep Rob with him. Her face troubled, she watched him walk off, carrying the child on his shoulders.

Once outside the boardinghouse, Adam felt the tension within him ease a little as he strode toward the stable. Though it was only about nine o'clock in the morning, the sidewalks and street already had a fair amount of traffic. Rob was a friendly child, and he spoke to several of the boomers by name. Adam supposed he knew them from Mrs. Gallagher's, and the men seemed to be tickled at being singled out, for they responded jovially.

Suddenly Rob cried out, "Look, Papa, there's Jimbo! He's all tied up! Why is he tied to that tree?"

They'd come to the edge of town, near the stable, and Adam saw that Jimbo was indeed chained to a pine tree, as were two others. He walked over to where he saw the sheriff's deputy, Les Newton, standing.

"Newton, what's this all about? Be still, Rob," he commanded, for the boy was clamoring to get down.

"Let him down, Doc," said Les, aiming a brown stream of tobacco juice over his shoulder. "He just wants to see his buddy Jimbo. I've et over at Miz Gallagher's a few times, and they're buddies for shore."

But Adam stilled the child by placing his hands on his legs firmly. "Stay put, son. Why do you have these men chained? What have they done?"

"Oh, the usual. Fighting and drunken brawling." He grinned, showing brown-stained teeth. "The sheriff over at Batson Prairie tried it, so I figgered I would, too. By gum, it works. I 'spose you know the jail's over at Kountze, it being the county seat?" Adam nodded. "Well, the wagon got too full of prisoners and these was left over."

"I see," said Adam, frowning. "You transported the men you arrested to Kountze by wagon, and didn't have room for these three?"

Another brown stream of tobacco juice shot out of the deputy's mouth. "That's right, Doc. Purty good idee, huh?"

Adam shook his head. "Seems barbaric to me."

Rob, who'd been obedient except for a few wiggles, said, "Papa, why is Jimbo tied?"

"Because he broke the law, Rob," said Adam, still slightly shocked by the sight of men chained to trees. All except Jimbo were peacefully sleeping off their drunk in the weak sunlight. Jimbo waved at Rob, who dared to wave back, then clasped his arms tightly around his father's neck as Adam walked away.

Fall was in full swing; in fact, Indian Summer was a better description of the weather they were having. Though November would soon be half over, the temperature had not dropped below freezing yet. However, several nights of near frost had been enough to blaze the sweet gum trees, the sumac vines with crimson.

Excited by the rare prospect of some time alone with his father, Rob jiggled up and down a couple of times. "Where are we going, Papa? Where?"

"Be still! You'll dislocate my neck." But Adam was laughing as he said, "We're going to see a friend of Jeannie's—and mine, and yours."

"Who? Who?" Rob gave a couple more little jumps, and Adam swung him down as he came to the stable.

"Grannie Annie," answered his father, smiling at the look of delight on the boy's face. He wasn't really sure why he'd decided to take Rob to see the old lady. He suspected it had something to do with the fact that his own mother had died many years ago, and Marie, Bethany's mother, had also died before Rob had gotten a chance to know her.

A few minutes later Adam set off toward Grannie Annie's, Rob perched in front of him on his saddle. They rode slowly because the corduroy road was easier walked on than ridden on with a horse. "It could jar your liver out," as Jude put it. Adam found that the closeness of Rob's sturdy little body to his was deeply satisfying.

"Rob, I'm glad you came along."

The little boy, starved for his father's time and attention most of the time, glanced up, adoration plain on his face. Then he burst into song, making Adam smile again.

"Jesus loves me this I know, for the Bible tells me so!"

Encouraged by the response, Rob sang his complete repertoire, ending with "Leather Britches," a song that obviously Jude, not Jeannie, had taught him.

Both father and son were laughing as Adam dismounted from his horse in front of Grannie Annie's cabin, then swung the child down.

She was in the doorway, propped on her homemade crutch. "I heard you a'coming! What's so all fired humorous?"

Adam strode up the clean swept dirt path, Rob in his arms. "Grannie Annie, I've brought Rob to see you." He set the boy down.

Rob ducked his head in a sudden fit of shyness, but the old woman smiled, "Howdy do, son. Would you keer for a sweet?" Rob's head came up and he grinned. "That gits 'em every time. Men, little or big, are patsies for sweet things, whether they're in a jar or in a skirt," she chuckled. "Well, you know where I keep 'em, so go get one. And you come in this house, Doctor, afore you take root!"

Adam did as he was told, marveling as he always did at the amazing, seemingly unlimited profusion of Mason jars and bottles and boxes filled with herbs of all kinds, much as he'd seen at Jeannie's house.

But there wasn't the same sense of order here. The leaves

and roots and bits of bark were in all stages of preparation; bunches hanging from strings in gently waving bundles from the low rafters; leaves stripped from stems and laid out on clean flour sacks; tall sprays stuck in crocks and cans on the floor. Overall there was that slightly musky, clean medicinal odor that Adam liked very much.

Rob's black eyes were wide as he stared around, reflecting the feeling his father had every time he came here. But where Adam asked questions, the little boy just licked his peppermint stick and watched the wizened old lady solemnly. He liked her. She didn't pinch his cheek, or pick him up or squeeze him like most grown-ups did.

"Jude 'n me was talking about you the other day, boy," said Grannie Annie as she hobbled to the back door. "Wait'll you see what I got out here on the porch. My dog Queenie had that litter of pups I told you she was gonna. Remember?" Rob nodded eagerly and followed her, and when she showed him the bunch of squirming puppies, his face was all delighted smiles. "Now don't you be mean to these here pups, 'cause their mama won't like it if you are, you hear?"

Rob glanced at the huge, sad-eyed hound that lay nearby sunning herself. The old dog raised her head and eyed the child, who had the good sense to realize the puppies were to be handled with care.

Grannie Annie came back into the kitchen just as the kettle began to sing on the stove. Ten minutes later she placed a fragrantly steaming mug in Adam's hands. "Drink this ginseng tea, Doctor; it'll cure what ails you. I've heard tell the Chinese folks say it does all sorts of wondrous stuff for a feller. Now tell me why you come, and don't worry none 'bout the boy. He's fine out yonder with them pups."

He took a cautious sip and found he liked the bitter taste, which surprisingly turned slightly sweet after a moment. "I came to see you, Grannie Annie. From what I hear, you're somewhat of a legend in these parts."

She chuckled. "Can't deny it; for a little bitty ol' woman I cast a long shadder!" Though her vision was failing, the look in her dark, deep-set eyes was still shrewd and knowing. "Doctor, it's plain as the nose on your face that something's on your mind." She didn't question, didn't insist he talk, but her calm watchfulness did its work.

The old Seth Thomas mantel clock ticked the moments away

in the silence that followed. Adam thought of the night before, of the kaleidoscope of happenings since they'd left the quiet of the placid Louisiana village near the fledgling leper hospital. The hotel in Beaumont, the boardinghouse in Saratoga. . . . The thoughts came flooding through his mind.

Grannie Annie, who'd "saucered and blowed" her tea like Jude did his coffee, had a thoughtful scowl on her face. "So I take it you're wondering if the Thicket is a proper place to raise a young'un." Adam shrugged and she said, "Folks do it all the time, I reckon. But you being from a big city and all, you probably figger it'd be best to take him back there."

He shook his head. "No, I don't by any means. I'm well aware that there are as many dangers and pitfalls in raising a child in a big city as in a place like this, maybe far more."

"Shore there is. And I'd a heap sight druther live where I kin hear birds instead of the humble bumble of a great throng of folks. Now I'll admit as how this oil business has changed things considerable."

He nodded. "There are elements, certain types of people, certain situations that I feel are . . . not suitable."

"Why, Doctor," Grannie replied, all innocence, "I wouldn't a thought you was a snob."

"Where a man's son is concerned, I should think he ought to be," Adam said stiffly, until he saw the teasing glint in her eyes.

"Well, shore!" Grannie's laugh was none too subdued. "I'll grant you, Doctor, a little 'un needs a certain amount of pertection, 'til they can pertect theirselves. But they see more'n you think they do, even in a nice house with a nice nanny in a nice town, and don't you never forget it."

"I suppose. It's just that I'm not sure I shouldn't find that nice house in a nice town and get him away from all this."

"The little woman I heard tell you had with you, what's her name?"

"Carrie," murmured Adam.

"Carrie. She wants you to leave, don't she?" Adam nodded. "But you don't want to."

He knew her words were a statement, not a question, and started to deny it. But he found he couldn't. "The problem is, I'm not sure why I don't want to." There was a note of desperation in his voice.

"I could make a stab at it, son, but you wouldn't like it

nohow." She sipped the last of her tea from her saucer, then set it down and fixed him with her steady gaze. "The Lord brung you here, Doctor, I'm certain sure of it. I'm just not sure yet what for."

Adam got up from the table and went to stand at the front window. Even here, placed closely together on the wide sill, there was a pleasant profusion of green, growing plants. He stared out at the dense growth in the woods outside for a long time before he responded, "She says that, too."

"Our Jeannie." The words, spoken softly, hovered in the air. After a long moment Grannie Annie added, "I'd bet a pretty penny she's the main reason you can't leave."

He wheeled around. "How can you talk in one breath about God bringing me here for some lofty and noble purpose and then suggest in the next that I'd be interested in Jeannie Gallagher when I'm to marry another woman?"

"Don't get so het up, Doctor Adam," Grannie said mildly. "I didn't say you'd committed some awful sin or nothing; though a man's sins are between him and God."

"I don't have a god." Adam's words were hard and low.

"Land sakes, how do you even get through the days, son?" She shook her head from side to side, the gray, wispy hair gently moving. "Why, ever morning I get up afore the sun does, and I go out on the porch to watch and see if it's gonna come up, or the Lord's coming back! Well, if He hasn't yet, I just come back on in and make the coffee. I don't never make it 'til I check though." She had a smile on her wrinkled face, her eyes twinkling as she spoke; but now her expression was sweet-sad, and he knew it was for him.

"Dr. Adam, I raised seven young'uns, lost five in miscarriages, and have helped to birth so many I can't count 'em. Why, if I hadn't had the Lord with me, if He wasn't with me now, life wouldn't be worth living."

"Is it?" Adam asked, so softly he thought perhaps her hearing was too poor to hear him.

But she had. She pushed herself out of the cane-bottomed rocker, hobbled over to him on her makeshift crutches, and placed her hand on his shoulder. "Son, it ain't without Jesus. Why, when I was a girl my soul hungered after something so bad I thought I'd die of it before I found out it was Jesus." Adam's long, painful sigh was a wordless admission that he had an inkling, at least, of what she spoke.

The quiet, homey, cluttered room was broken only by Rob's giggles, his chuckling words to the puppies on the porch. Finally Adam spoke, his head bowed low. "I don't want to offend you, Grannie, or your God. But I just don't believe He's the answer to every question, every problem."

Her answer was firm. "Just 'cause you don't believe it don't mean it ain't so. He *is* the answer, son."

Adam shook his head. "There are things I've seen, things I've done, that are beyond what He can forgive, or even stand to think about. If there is a God, He has surely turned His back on us all."

"Lots of folks have felt that way, I reckon." Her hand on his shoulder gripped harder.

Adam's mind was suddenly besieged with the memory of Bethany's frenzied, hysterical weeping as he took Rob away; of her endless, hopeless weeping for those long weeks; of her empty face before she calmly took herself out into the rain to die.

He saw the blind, mindless prejudice of the men at the council meeting who decided the fate of the hospital at Elkhorn, the hospital that would have been so good for his patients; the hate-filled mob that killed Anson dePaul. A terrible parade of events flashed before his mind's eye: the hundreds of people he'd already treated, the ones he'd seen die . . . the horrible things they did to themselves and to each other; the hopelessness he'd seen in that woman's face when she said, next time she'd be able to kill herself.

He buried his face in his hands. "If there is a God . . . and I don't believe anymore there is, why are things in such a mess? Tell me that, *why?*"

Her hand, gnarled and twisted, still gripped his shoulder. "Oh my, Doctor, you got misery enough in your soul to fill a whole army of men. You got to recognize it ain't God causing all the mess; that makes all the difference, you know. Why, ever man makes his own paths, decides for himself what—"

She was interrupted by a quick knock at the door, and then Jeannie stuck her head in. "Grannie Annie?" Adam straightened and ran a hand through his black hair. "Oh, Dr. Adam, I thought that was your horse outside. I'm glad you're here." She'd come in as she was speaking, and Rob, who'd recognized her voice, came running in too, a puppy cradled carefully in his arms.

"Jeannie, Jeannie, look! Grannie let me play with the pups, and I like this one!" He leaned against her skirt, his chubby fingers tickling the woebegone-looking yellow hound pup under the chin.

"He's a fine pup, Rob," agreed Jeannie, her hand going to tousle the child's hair much as Jude had a habit of doing. "Grannie, I came to tell you that Barretts' boy Danny has taken sick. I'm afraid from what Luce told me it's a bad fever of some sort. It's her little brother. I'm on my way over there now." Her glance rested on Adam briefly; then she knelt to speak to Rob.

Adam said, "If you'd like, I'll ride over with you."

Jeannie's voice was quiet and matter-of-fact as she said, "That might be a good idea. I've a notion it could be serious, from what Luce says."

"And what is *it*?" asked Adam, his tone professional.

"Nosebleed a couple of times during the night, ringing in the ears, a temperature last evening."

Adam frowned. "Any headache?"

"She didn't say," answered Jeannie. "Why do you ask?"

"Never mind," said Adam, already at the door. "I'll have to take Rob back to the boardinghouse."

"Never you mind about the young'un," said Grannie Annie. "I may be old and broke up, but I ain't too old to take care of one little bitty boy! Leave him here, I'll enjoy his company. 'Sides, he's taken a shine to that yaller dog pup. Seems like I recollect Jude said he wanted one."

"He'll be fine, Adam," assured Jeannie.

"All right," said Adam, the decision made quickly. "How far is it to the Barrett place?"

"About four miles as the crow flies, but it's a rough four miles on horseback."

He followed her out, after a hug from preoccupied Rob. He was still entranced by the pup and seemed more happy to be left behind.

The ride from Grannie Annie's was a silent one, for although Jeannie was deeply concerned for the child who lay sick, she was also determined to keep a pact she'd made with herself after the other night's experience with Adam. She'd had no sleep at all after he left that early morning. Dawn had found her curled in the old bent willow chair in front of the east window, her eyes not seeing the gradual lightening of the day.

Jeannie's feelings as Adam's hand had held hers, as he'd

touched the callouses on her palm . . . and her hair, were like
the leaping flames they'd watched as the fire raced over the
bayou. She knew she must put out that flame, but it was not
as easy to do as to decide.

Adam rode ahead of her, and his ramrod straight back, his
square, broad shoulders, the very way he held his head were
etched on her heart. Her mind told her something else; that no
matter how strongly she was attracted to him, there were two
unsurmountable obstacles to her love. The first was obvious
even to Jude: honor. Adam belonged to Carrie; their wedding
was very close now.

The other reason was not as plain, but it was planted deep
in Jeannie's soul. She knew that even if Adam Jarrett had been
free, that second reason would be enough to keep them apart.
For she had the self-knowledge to realize that she could not
marry a man who did not share her faith, and Adam did not,
by any means. Added to that devastating truth was the fact
that he was consumed by the shades of the past, of old wounds,
old griefs and guilts that drove him, made him bitter. No, Adam
Jarrett was not a free man in any sense of the word, and she
knew only a man free in Christ would do for her.

She tried to take comfort in the familiar tangle of bright
autumn colors, the cool green of the plants that grew all around
and never turned brown. A blue heron crane, standing haughti-
ly on one foot in a small slough off to the right, flew off in his
ungainly fashion as they approached, and there was the ever-
present chatter of squirrels and small birds.

He's not the man for me . . . the words cut like a knife of
truth in her heart. And still, when they reached the split-log
cabin where the Barretts lived and Adam helped her from her
horse, the touch of his hand on hers made shivers run through
her.

"No telling what we'll find. It could be anything—influenza,
malaria, or pneumonia." The cool, detached tone of his voice
was like cold water in her face.

"That's true. Of course, it could be typhoid," she responded
as coolly as he.

As they walked up the leaf-strewn path, he asked, "What
makes you say so?"

"Oh, I suppose I was thinking of your question about
whether or not he had a headache. We've had our share of the
summer scourge, as some folks call typhoid."

"But it's almost Thanksgiving!" protested Adam.

"And it's been unseasonably warm," Jeannie countered. "I'm afraid it's a possibility. Don't tell me you didn't have the same thought."

Adam's glance at her just before she knocked at the door of the Barretts' cabin was sharp, almost antagonistic. But it disappeared as Viona Barrett, her face registering surprise at seeing Adam, opened the door and said, "Oh, I didn't know you was bringing the doctor; my man left only enough cash money for groceries—"

"If you're worried about my fee, don't be, Mrs. Barrett. What we need to do is see what's wrong with your son."

"How is our Danny? Luce told me you were both really worried." Jeannie led the way to a curtained-off area to one side of the room, where a little boy not much older than Rob lay in an alcove just large enough for a straw mattress. She laid the back of her hand to his cheek and touched her lips to his forehead. "Warm," she murmured, smiling down at him. "Not quite up to going bear hunting with a switch, I take it?" He managed a small smile, and shook his head from side to side once, then stopped as though it hurt.

"I'm awful worried, Jeannie. He's thirsty all the time, and I'm grateful to the Lord that awful nose bleeding stopped, but he says now he's got a headache something fierce." Mrs. Barrett, her hands twisting nervously, added, "After that girl Luce of ours got so crossways in her life, my husband sets a right smart store on this boy. I suppose it's 'cause I ain't likely to have another. Though God knows I tried!"

Jeannie nodded sympathetically. She'd been almost as downhearted about Mrs. Barrett's repeated miscarriages as the woman herself. "I'm sure Danny will be fine."

Adam, who'd pulled up the child's nightshirt and was gently palpating his abdomen, was watching Danny's flushed, pink face. The little boy winced in pain, his dark eyes widening in reproach, though he didn't make a sound. Adam did, though— a sort of grunt of regret at causing the pain. "I'm afraid it could by typhoid, Mrs. Barrett. I'm sorry, because if it is, we're in for a fight. Is Danny a healthy child usually, able to throw off colds and such?"

Mrs. Barrett's eyes were wide with fear, and she ignored Adam's question. "Typhoid? Are you sure?"

"No, as a matter-of-fact, not totally. We will be in another day or so." He pulled the faded little nightshirt down and smoothed the fair hair back from the boy's forehead. The gesture seemed to reassure Danny somewhat, but his fingers still picked nervously at the bedclothes, almost as though there were invisible insects there that he was trying to remove. "Typhoid can fool you; it has so many variables. It can look like malaria, nephiritis, colitis, meningitis, endocarditis, or—"

"Oh, them sounds awful!" burst out Mrs. Barrett. "But typhoid does, too," she added in a whisper.

"We'll do everything we can, Viona," assured Jeannie, "whatever it is. Won't we, Dr. Adam?"

"Of course. And for now, I want to impress upon you the importance of boiling every drop of water you or your husband, as well as Danny, drink."

"What on earth for? Our spring is as clear and pure as God's own rain."

"It's very important that you do it. And I'll leave you some alcohol to wash your hands with after each time you touch Danny. If and when we do find it is typhoid fever, you must also bury all stools and urine in a trench. Tell your husband; I'm sure he'll help."

"Don't be too sure about that," murmured Jeannie, but he went on as though he hadn't heard.

"Where is your husband now?"

"He's got a job roughnecking, over at High Island."

"Does he come home at night?"

"No. He's staying there most nights. That's why . . . why Luce was here. She knowed he'd be gone for a few days, and come to see me and Danny. I reckon he'll come home when he finds out Danny's took sick, though. He thinks the sun rises and sets in that child." She glanced at the pale-faced boy, whose eyes were open, but who seemed to be staring at nothing.

"Mrs. Barrett," said Adam, "it's still possible that what your son has is not typhoid. But if it is, you've got a stretch of very hard work ahead of you."

"I'll do it, Doctor," the woman said, her voice low and frightened, but steady. "Whatever it takes, I'll do it."

"And I'll help, Viona," said Jeannie warmly.

After Adam had finished going over a careful list of do's and don'ts with the anxious woman, he and Jeannie left.

Just before he swung onto his horse, Adam said vehemently,

"If only I had my laboratory equipment—" He broke off without even looking at Jeannie.

She started to ask what he meant; he'd never mentioned a laboratory before. But his face was closed and set, and he looked so forbidding she remained silent. Throughout the ride back to Grannie's, her mind was racing. If Danny had typhoid fever, it was highly unlikely he'd be the only one stricken. Jeannie had seen enough cases of typhoid and knew only too well that it was a nasty, difficult disease; and more often than not, even after a vicious, hard-fought battle, death was the victor. Two of her own little brothers had been lost to typhoid and although she'd not been very old, she remembered the long battle for their lives, the feeling of bitter loss when they died.

The sky was cloudy, the day gray with the promise of rain. As they neared Grannie Annie's, Jeannie shivered slightly, thinking of Rob, of the other children. She hoped with all her heart it was something besides typhoid fever.

CHAPTER 15

Instead of the thorn shall come up the fir tree, and instead of the
brier shall come up the myrtle tree, and it shall be to the Lord
for a name, for an everlasting sign that shall not be cut off.
                                                    Isaiah 55:13

It was late the next afternoon before Adam was free to go
back to the Barretts' home. The dread he felt at what he might
find was intensified even further as he rode by the gatepost and
saw the draggled spray of myrtle, hung bottom side up, tacked
there. Only once before had he seen that; Jeannie had explained
it was a sign of sickness, or other trouble, and at times a plea
for the passerby to stop. He strongly suspected it was Viona
Barrett, not her husband, who'd put the myrtle there. When
John Barrett answered his knock, he could see almost immediately this was not the kind of man who asked for help easily.

"Yes, who're you?" were Barrett's first curt words. Then he
saw Adam's black bag and his expression changed slightly. "Oh,
you must be the doctor Viona told me about."

He still didn't invite Adam in, however, though he stood
aside slightly. "Yes," said Adam. "I'm the doctor, and I've come
to check on Danny." Without saying anything further, except
to speak briefly to Viona Barrett, Adam went directly to Danny
and examined him. A few minutes later he made the announcement he'd hoped he wouldn't have to. Danny definitely had
typhoid.

"Just how can you be so sure?" Barrett's question was very
close to hostile. He was not a tall man, probably no more than
five eight or so, but he was broad-shouldered and his arms and
chest were well developed from hard work. His clean-shaven

162

face was scowling, and though he tried hard he couldn't keep the fear from his eyes as he came and stood by his son's cot.

Adam knew the hostility stemmed from the fear. "From the symptoms, Mr. Barrett. The nosebleeds, the raging headache, the terrible thirst, his tender abdomen, which now has red spots, by the way. Also, your son has a fever that has been steadily rising, and I'm afraid it's almost 104 right now. Touch his face."

The man's jaw clenched, but he reached down and placed a work-roughened hand on the boy's forehead. He jerked it back. "He's burning up! You gotta do something, Doc!"

"Pa . . ." Danny's small voice sounded frightened. "Pa, my toes hurt, the covers hurt my toes, and my head hurts."

A dreadful look crossed John Barrett's face, a look Adam had seen before. He'd known many men who were not only helpless in a sickroom but also terrified of sickness itself. Adam got a chair, then leaned it against the edge of the cot with the bedclothes draped over it to make free space for Danny's feet. "Some typhoid patients seem to develop a severe sensitivity in their feet and toes. He'll sleep better if they aren't confined."

"What else can we do for him, Dr. Adam?" Danny's mother asked. She'd been mostly silent since Adam had come, and showed an extreme deference to her husband that he seemed to think was normal.

"Give him as much to drink as he'll take. Broths, gruel, water, tea—" He stopped, then said slowly, "I'm sure Miss Gallagher has some suggestions, and would provide you with some soothing varieties of herbal teas."

"She already brought some," said Mrs. Barrett as she moved over to the kitchen table. "See? There's mint, and some camomile, and she said she'd bring over some white willow bark if you said it was all right."

"I suppose. When did she come?" Adam asked casually. He shook his thermometer, wiped it with alcohol and put it back in its case.

"Early this morning was the last time. She told me she'd give a hand with the nursing since John, here, has to get on back to the rig." She glanced at her husband, who still had an intense look on his face.

"A man's gotta work," he said defiantly.

"Of course. And we'll do our best to see that Danny is taken care of while you're gone, Mr. Barrett." Adam's voice was fairly neutral, but he meant the words, and his sincerity pierced the man's protective armor.

John Barrett's face sagged and for one terrible moment he looked near tears. "That boy means a heap to me, Doc. It ain't her fault, I reckon, but my woman Viona didn't have such good luck birthing young'uns. None of 'em seem to live long, 'cept that oldest girl, and she's no count."

Adam snapped his bag shut. "You mean Luce." The man nodded. "I've met her at Mrs. Gallagher's boardinghouse. Perhaps she'd come and help your wife with Danny's nursing—"

"No! Viona can do whatever has to be done," retorted Mr. Barrett sharply. "She don't need Luce, and neither does Danny."

"Mr. Barrett, there's going to be a lot to do. The child's clothes and bedding will have to be changed often and washed carefully. Boiled, as a matter of fact. And he'll have to be bathed a lot to bring the fever down, his mouth kept swabbed out . . ." He opened his bag again and rummaged around. "I forgot this. Here's some glycerine for his lips, because they'll get dry from the fever."

Mrs. Barrett took the little brown bottle. "Dr. Adam, Danny'll be all right, won't he?"

Adam met her frightened eyes squarely. "We'll do everything we can to make sure of it."

"You'd dern sure better," muttered John Barrett, punctuating his words with curses.

"Mr. Barrett, let me assure you—"

Surprisingly, his wife interrupted Adam. "Oh, Dr. Adam, he don't mean no harm; he's just worried about Danny, aren't you hon. You didn't mean nothing by it, did you, John?" She went over to him and tentatively touched his arm.

Mr. Barrett didn't make a move toward her, but neither did he move away. "No, Doc, I didn't mean no harm," he said gruffly.

Snapping his bag shut again, Adam eyed them both, his gaze sober. "We have to work together on this, all of us. I think you should reconsider asking your daughter Luce to come home, Mr. Barrett."

"No! I told that girl she wasn't never going to set foot in this house again, not after the life she's been living." His face was dark with anger now.

"But, John, she's our daughter—"

"She ain't mine, not no more!" was his short reply to his wife's timid protest. He went back to his son's bedside, for the child had made a whimpering little sound. "It'll come right, boy; don't you frash yourself. You'll be right as rain in no time."

"Pa?" The boy's eyes opened for a moment, and he raised up, then fell back dizzily. "Pa . . ."

Adam saw the look of anguish on the man's face; he also saw how quickly Barrett suppressed it, as though showing his feelings was somehow not manly. Just as Adam went out the door he heard the man say, "T'won't be no time afore you're out squirrel hunting with me again, son. We'll get us a mess, and your mama here'll cook 'em into the best stew ever. You like squirrel stew better'n anything, don't you, boy? It won't be long . . ."

Many thoughts were running around in Adam's head as he rode back to Saratoga. The men who lived in the Thicket seemed to have a code that, though different from what he grew up with in the north, was no less honorable in its own way. It was obvious that Barrett didn't treat his wife with the warmth, even the simple courtesy, that Adam thought essential in a relationship. He treated her more like a possession, and his feelings toward his son were also the same, in a way. But the man also felt a strong obligation to provide for his family, going so far as to work at a dangerous, hard job away from his home. Though he was curt to her, Adam suspected John Barrett loved his wife deeply. He most assuredly loved the towheaded little Danny. Adam felt a twinge of anxiety; what if the child didn't survive the fever? He touched his heels to the horse, vowing he'd do everything in his power to see that Danny pulled through.

At Mrs. Gallagher's boardinghouse he deliberately sought out Luce. When he told her about Danny, the quick spasm of fear on her face, which reminded Adam strongly of her brother Danny, showed how much she cared for her little brother. She recovered quickly, however, and the fear was replaced by a careless bravado.

"Oh, he'll be all right. Won't he, Dr. Adam?"

"I won't lie to you, Luce. He's young, and typhoid is hard on youngsters. Whether or not they recover depends a lot on their physical condition before they contract the disease."

She ran her fingers through her long, silvery blond hair,

which hung halfway down her back. Mrs. Gallagher insisted she twist it up and pin it back tightly when she was serving or working in the kitchen, but whenever she could, she let it fall free as though she knew how beautiful it was. She wasn't working now, and the dress she now wore was snug, and much lower in the neck than Reba Gallagher would allow. There had been several confrontations between the two about Luce's hair and clothes—usually refereed by Jeannie—and Adam wondered if Reba would allow the girl to continue to work for her, even with Jeannie as her defender. A rebellion seemed to be lurking just beneath Luce's pretty surface.

"Well," she said now, "Danny just has to get all right, that's all."

"I hope he does, for his sake as well as your father's." Adam saw her eyes harden, her mouth set when he mentioned John Barrett. "I suggested that you go back home and help your mother nurse Danny, but—"

"I'm not ever going back, not after the way Pa talked to me!"

Adam's expression grew grimmer. "Luce, typhoid victims require dedicated nursing if they are to have even a fair chance of surviving. Your mother is going to need help."

For the first time a look of uncertainty crossed Luce's face. "But he doesn't want me there."

"I know." With a little sigh Adam continued. "It's just that even after the worst part passes, after the fever abates, Danny will have to be kept on a soft, almost liquid diet. Patients who were on their way to recovery have died because they ate solid foods too soon."

"That doesn't seem right."

"I assure you, it is." He felt sorry for the girl; he could see the indecision on her face, and knew she was struggling with the knowledge that her mother and brother needed her.

Finally she murmured, "Well, I guess I'd go, if *he* said so, if . . . he asked me."

Mrs. Gallagher came in then, with an admonition that Luce fix her hair "proper," get on a decent dress, and get back to the kitchen, because the drummers would be coming in at any moment. With one last anxious glance at Adam, Luce flounced out, ignoring Reba Gallagher's scowl of disapproval.

Adam went across the street to his office with the heavy knowledge that very rarely was there one isolated case of typhoid; there were almost always more.

However, when the next cases made themselves obvious, it was not at all in the way he, or anyone, expected. Very early one morning almost a week later Jeannie came to Adam's office and knocked softly at first, then banged loudly until he came to the door, bleary-eyed and groggy-looking from too little sleep.

"Jeannie! Why are you here so early? What's happened?" He raked his fingers through his thick black hair.

Resisting the sudden, treacherous urge to smooth it, as she had Rob's so many times, Jeannie made quite certain her voice was low and neutral as she said, "I'm sorry to bother you so early, truly I am. But a couple of the men at the house are ill."

Suddenly wide awake, Adam asked, "What are their symptoms?"

"I know what you're thinking, that it could be typhoid." Adam nodded slowly. "I'm afraid it could very well be. Three of the men—regulars, by the way—have developed fevers, and are complaining of headaches. One of them threw up all over his bed. Mum was alerted when the other man in the room complained." She still was standing outside, her small figure barely illuminated in the gray, early morning light.

"Come in. I'll get my things together."

Jeannie shook her head. "I'll just wait out here."

"Why?" The low word seemed to hang in the air between them. "Don't you trust me to behave like a gentleman?"

She winced at the harsh sound of his words. "Don't," she whispered.

"Don't what?" He stared down at her, aware that they both knew exactly what he was talking about. "Don't be careful, don't try never to say anything, or act in such a way that might make people think we're—"

Stricken, Jeannie stared back at him. She could think of nothing to say that would make the situation any better.

"I'm sorry, forgive me," he finally said.

"There's nothing to forgive," she said, her voice low.

"Then come in while I get ready, please?" He didn't look to see if anyone was watching; it was as though he didn't want to know.

She hesitated a moment longer, then stepped inside. "Dr. Adam, if it's typhoid we'll have to get Rob out, and right away."

He nodded as he tucked his white shirt into his black trousers, tied a thin, black string tie beneath the collar, and ran a comb through his unruly hair. Shrugging into a jacket, he said, "You're absolutely right. But where?"

"He likes it at Grannie Annie's." Jeannie was dismayed that, even as they were calmly discussing what they should do with his little boy, she was thinking about how she'd like to watch Adam shave now, how she wanted to touch the creamy lather after he smoothed it onto the dark shadow of his square jaw . . ."

He must have been thinking of the same thing, though not in the same way; he ran a hand over his jaw. "If they're as sick as you say, they probably won't mind if I shave later."

"I don't think they'll mind," said Jeannie softly. "And . . . Carrie is awake, too. She's worried about Rob, naturally. She loves him very much."

"I know. Well, let's go see what we've got."

What they found was a crowd of anxious men, muttering warily among themselves as they stood outside the room where the ill roomers were.

"Charlie says it's typhoid, Doc," one of them said when Adam came up the stairs.

"I ain't staying in no place where there's typhoid!"

"Me, neither!" was the chorus of several others.

"Now, don't panic," ordered Adam. "We don't even know for sure that it is typhoid." He glanced down the hall and caught a glimpse of Carrie, her face white and frightened at the door of her room before she disappeared, slamming it loudly.

When he examined the three men, he reluctantly had to conclude they were all in the first stages of typhoid fever. For although the clinical manifestations of the disease varied from patient to patient, all had that telltale tenderness on palpation of the lower left quadrant of their abdomens. One of them, a driller from Oklahoma, also had moderately severe muscle pains, or myalgia, and the man who'd sounded the alarm by vomiting earlier was still quite nauseated.

As he prepared to go out and face the men outside the room, the sound of an unproductive, dry cough came from the man in the bed nearest the window. Without even being aware that he was doing so, he sighed. They were in for it, all right. And there was no telling how many other boarders had the fever as well.

At his announcement to that effect, the faces of the men

showed a variety of emotions, but the predominating one was fear. Firmly Adam said, "Now, please don't panic. Above all else it is important that you keep cool heads about this."

"Yeah, it's easy for you to say, Doc!"

"How can we tell if we even got it?"

"How'd they get it, is what I want to know?"

"Wait, wait!" said Adam above the sudden spate of questions. "I'll answer all your questions, I promise."

There were only a dozen or so men left; Adam suspected the others had quietly left at the first hint of typhoid. And the last question—where they'd gotten it—was one he really couldn't answer himself, and wanted very much to know. He raised his hands in a calming gesture. "Let's go downstairs where we can talk about it."

But by the time Adam gathered them together, to his dismay there were just three men left who listened with scowls that only partially disguised their dread. All the other men had slipped out. He hoped there were none among them with the incubating disease . . . carrying it with them wherever they went.

Mrs. Gallagher, lips drawn tight, and a solemn-faced Jeannie stood silently in the doorway to the dining room as Adam carefully went over the early warning signs, and asked that each man undergo an examination. He also outlined the sanitation rules and the reasons for them, much the same as he had with Mrs. Barrett. Finally he said, "Are there any questions now?"

"Yeah, how'd them fellers get it?"

There it was, the one question he couldn't answer, the one he desperately needed to answer. "We don't know for sure, but I'm going to make every effort to find out," Adam assured him. "Mrs. Gallagher, you're going to need help. Nursing typhoid patients requires a lot of time and energy."

"Jeannie will be here," reminded Mrs. Gallagher.

"What about Luce?" asked Adam.

"I looked in her room a while ago, but she wasn't there," said Jeannie, her eyes troubled. "She might have gone home after you told her about Danny."

Adam shook his head. "Not likely," he disclosed. "Her father was set against it, and she vowed she wouldn't if he didn't ask her. Probably she was like the other men who slipped out, and was afraid of contracting the disease."

"Can't blame her, Doc," muttered one of the three remaining boarders. "I sure thought about it."

"What made you decide to stay?" asked Adam.

"I was scared that maybe I had it," he admitted. "But I felt like I oughtta do like you said, too." He glanced at the other two men, who nodded; obviously their reasons for not defecting were much the same.

Adam took a deep breath. "Thank you for your honesty. I'll examine each of you closely, and watch for signs of the fever. You may be needed to help with those stricken."

"I'm willing," said Joe, the youngest of the three, who scarcely looked to be out of his teens. "One of 'em is my buddy. We came to the fields together, and I ain't leaving him."

"We'll get through this fine if we do the same, stick together," encouraged Adam. "Mrs. Gallagher, I'm going to go up and speak to Carrie about taking Rob to Grannie Annie's."

"Good idea, Dr. Adam. He'll be safe with her, that's for sure."

It was a frightened Carrie that answered Adam's knock, opening the door only a crack until she saw who it was. "Adam! Is it true? Do those men really have typhoid fever? What are we going to do? I'm afraid for Rob!"

"Let me in, Carrie, that's what I want to talk to you about."

"Oh, I'm sorry . . ." She opened the door wide and he came in.

"Papa!" shouted Rob. He raced across the room toward his father and clasped him around the knees. "Can we go and see the pups again Papa, can we?"

Adam, his hand resting lightly on the boy's silky black hair, thought of Danny, so sick and pale. "How would you like to visit Grannie Annie and the pups, and stay for a while?"

"Can I? Can I?" The child danced around at Adam's nod of consent not paying attention to his father explaining the situation to Carrie in a low, tight voice.

"But, Adam, I don't like the idea of his being away from me . . . from us," Carrie whispered. "I don't know . . ."

"It's the best thing for him," Adam said firmly. "If you'd feel better about it, perhaps you should go to Grannie's, too." He could see the struggle she was feeling, the pull to go with Rob, to be away from the boardinghouse. He felt a surge of admiration when she spoke again.

"You're going to need help here, aren't you?"

"Yes, we certainly will."

"If only I wasn't such an awful nurse—"

"Carrie, you don't have to stay," Adam said gently. "It's going to get tough around here in the next couple of weeks."

"I know that. But . . . I want to help." She looked into his eyes and was rewarded by the smile of gratitude on his lips. "I'll get Rob ready. Come on, son, let's pack your clothes." She turned around when he tugged at her skirt.

"I already packed, see?" He proudly held up a pillowcase stuffed with knobby objects.

In spite of the gravity of the situation, Carrie and Adam smiled at each other. After a moment's hesitation, she caught his arm and pressed close to him. "It'll be all right, Adam, as long as we face things together, won't it?" She leaned her face against the smooth black fabric of his coat sleeve.

For a moment he didn't speak; then he assured her, "Yes, Carrie, it will."

"Let's go, Papa, let's go see the pups!"

Adam lifted the excited child into his arms and lovingly held him tight for a brief moment. "We'll go just as soon as Carrie gets the rest of your things together."

She nodded and set to work.

A quiet, eerie atmosphere invaded the dining room that afternoon as Adam called them together. Although Mrs. Gallagher had made a peach cobbler, the dish in front of each went mostly untouched—except for Jude's—as Adam told them what lay ahead.

Mrs. Gallagher's question brought them to the main point of the meeting. "Dr. Adam, I suppose even if we could get word to the families of the three men upstairs in time, it wouldn't be good to move them. Is that right?"

"Yes, that's correct." Adam's expression was grave. "I'm aware it's asking a lot to expect you people to take care of strangers, but I'm not sure we have any alternatives." He glanced at Carrie, who sat at the end of the table, her eyes on him. "I'm proud to say, Carrie has told me she's willing to help." And he was proud of her; only he knew how very difficult the time ahead was likely to be for her, with her extreme dislike of sickness. She was a great deal like Danny's father, he realized; only Carrie was going to stay in spite of her feelings.

"I'll be available part of the time, as much as I can manage," said Jeannie. "I've promised to help Mrs. Barrett with Danny, and if we have any more cases, I'll probably be called."

"So most of the nursing will fall to me, Carrie and Jude, I reckon," said Mrs. Gallagher practically. "Well, tell us what you want us to do. I lost a couple of young'uns to the fever, but I can't say as my memory is good concerning what to do and what not to do. I've heard tell garlic is good to prevent its spreading. Might as well give it a try. One thing I'm sure of, I don't want any of us to catch it."

"I don't know about the garlic, but our staying healthy is one of our primary concerns," said Adam. "All right. As I told Mrs. Barrett, you must boil all drinking water. And I'll make sure there's a good supply of alcohol and bichloride solution to cleanse your hands after every single time you care for one of the patients, or touch anything that has come in contact with them.

"You must remember that urine and stools of a typhoid patient are like pure cultures of typhoid bacilli. Jude, it's a dirty job, I know, but can I count on you to bury all wastes in a spot we decide on?"

Jude, his face still and serious for once, said slowly, "I reckon you can, Doc."

"Good. Now as for nursing care, we must keep fluids going into them, and make sure each patient and their bed linens are as clean as possible. By the way, everything must be washed as usual, preferably in lye soap, then boiled. And when the fever gets high the men must be bathed in tepid water to bring it down."

"We have only three; that shouldn't be too hard," said Carrie; the hope in her voice was clear.

As gently as he could, Adam said, "It will take everything all of us can do to bring these three out alive. For many reasons, the clinical manifestations vary a great deal from one patient to another."

"Speak English, Doc," said Jude.

Adam shrugged. "Sorry. I just mean that one may not get very sick, and the man next to him may die. The incubation period varies, too, apparently, according to how much typhoid bacterium he was exposed to." He saw the frown on Jeannie's face and said, "Do you have a question, Jeannie?"

She nodded slowly. "I keep wondering how we can find out where it came from."

"That's the one question I'm very concerned about," Adam acknowledged. "I'm going to do everything in my power to find that source before it spreads. A typhoid epidemic is a terrible thing, something we want to head off at all costs. And I feel that it's up to me to do that. We can only hope that none of the men who left so hurriedly has carried the disease with them."

"Merciful heavens!" gasped Mrs. Gallagher. "I never even thought about that. Guess I was too concerned about losing all my boarders," she admitted ruefully. "Well, we'll be busy without 'em, looks like."

CHAPTER 16

He healeth the broken in heart, and bindeth up their wounds.
                                                    Psalm 147:3

And busy they were. The next couple of weeks were filled with hard, backbreaking work for all of them. It was Carrie who surprised everyone, especially Adam. She never shirked any duty, particularly the abominable task of nursing the men during the most acute stages of the fever. She had to keep them clean when their bowels produced quantities of the typical greenish "pea-soup" stools of typhoid patients. Without complaint she did whatever was necessary, as Mrs. Gallagher often reported to Adam, who was in and out a great deal of the time.

Having determined to find the source, he tracked down every clue, no matter how slight it seemed. He knew that water supplies—creeks, wells, springs—were often where the typhoid germs were found, where they spread their poison to an uneducated populace who never gave a thought to their privies if they didn't fall down. And the influx of people brought by the oil boom had added to the problem immeasurably. He knew he was facing awesome odds, but still he tracked down every clue, no matter how small—to no avail.

Because he was the doctor who'd been called in the first case, little Danny Barrett and the others at Mrs. Gallagher's boardinghouse, Adam found the problem was left to him alone by the other doctors who'd come on the scene as the population swelled. He suspected this was in part because they were making a great deal more money by treating boomers. He also found that he was being called less and less by the oil men. Strangely enough, this suited him. It left him more time to attend Thicket patients, as well as the typhoid victims.

174

One day a couple of weeks later, he and Jeannie met by chance at Barretts'. Little Danny, his face still pale, was, as the people in the area were apt to say, "sittin' up and takin' nourishment."

Adam examined Danny and found that he was very weak, but his temperature was almost normal. "Mrs. Barrett," he said, "you must remember what I told you. Danny should not have solid or bulky foods of any kind for ten days after his fever is gone."

"But, Dr. Adam, he's always saying how he's starving now," his mother said, intensely grateful that her son was on the mend. "What can I give him?"

"Thick soups mashed up, like pea or potato. Milk toast is fine, or mashed potatoes, even soft boiled eggs. But not hard boiled. You do understand how important it is, don't you?"

She nodded, but there was a little frown on her brow. "I reckon."

Adam could see that she didn't really understand. He hesitated. How could he explain to this woman that after the terrible battle the body waged against the typhoid infection, the walls of the intestinal tract are treacherously thin, with ulcerous-like patches; that even without eating hard or bulky foods, those walls could possibly perforate? And if they involved blood vessels, the patient, thought by that time to be on the road to recovery, could begin to hemorrhage and die in a very short time.

Aloud all he said was, "Mrs. Barrett, it is of the utmost importance that you follow my instructions if you want Danny to recover."

The gravity of his tone must have impressed her. "I promise, Dr. Adam, I promise I'll do just what you said." She glanced at Jeannie, who'd been standing nearby, quietly watching Adam as he talked to the woman. "And I'll tell you something. If it hadn't been for Jeannie here, me or Danny, neither one woulda made it."

"You did all the work, Viona," said Jeannie.

Adam doubted that statement, but keeping his tone entirely professional, he merely said, "Miss Gallagher, I need to speak to you about something."

"Certainly, Dr. Adam." She placed the ever-present bag of simples over her shoulder. "I'll be back, Viona." The woman nodded.

"Bye, Jeannie," said Danny, his eyes clear and bright again. "Thanks for the flowers. I can't hardly wait 'til I can get out and find some my own self. I'll bring you a whole bunch."

"I'll be waiting, Danny," she replied, smiling at him.

Adam hadn't noticed the lovely little bouquet of wildflowers at Danny's bedside before. He saw now that it included a half dozen flowers he'd seen as he rode the trails, and a couple he had never seen. Jeannie Gallagher must know some secret places, some beautiful, hidden places where—He broke off his thought and strode out, leaving her to follow.

At Jeannie's suggestion they led the horses for a while, to enable them to talk more easily, but from then on she was silent, having decided to say nothing until he did.

Finally he spoke, frustration plain in his tone. "I've had no luck whatever in finding the source of the typhoid contamination. Of course, everyone insists his water is sparkling pure, and if it weren't for those four cases of typhoid, I'd be inclined to believe it."

"Could it be that having only four cases has something to do with the source?"

He stared at her. "You're right, you know. I'd just about come to the same conclusion. Somewhere in the back of my mind a fact has stuck, that I'd almost forgotten until now. If there are only a few cases, and they're fairly isolated, as ours are, it could indicate a carrier rather than a contaminated water source."

"A carrier," said Jeannie thoughtfully. "Someone who would have been at Barretts' and at the boardinghouse—" Her face came alight with the sudden realization. "Luce."

"Right."

"But she's gone. She and her father quarreled and when the men at the boardinghouse fell sick, she couldn't get out fast enough."

"Probably afraid she'd contract the fever again," he said, scowling. "Of course that's impossible, but she wouldn't necessarily know that, even if she is the carrier."

"But, Adam, she wasn't sick when she was working for Mum, or, as near as I can tell, when she was at home, either."

"She could have had typhoid as recently as six weeks ago, or even as long as a year ago, and still harbor the organism within either her gallbladder or her intestinal tract."

Jeannie said slowly, in dawning comprehension, "And she helped Mum fix and serve the food . . ."

"If it's Luce, it's a wonder more of us didn't come down with it." Adam stepped closer to her. "Here, let me help you up on your horse."

She started to say it wasn't necessary, but her need to be near him stifled the words. The light, slightly astringent odor of his cologne seemed finer than her favorite flowers; she fought the urge to slip her arms around his neck. "Thank you," was all she said, very softly, as he helped her mount her horse.

"I'll need to go into Beaumont for a couple of days, or as long as it takes, to find Luce and talk to her." He didn't look at her as he spoke; his eyes were gazing off into the wild, tangled brush.

"Yes, that's a good idea." The thought of him being away for only a couple of days dismayed her. She vowed to pray harder, to dispel the powerful emotions he stirred within her.

Neither of them saw Carrie at the window when they rode into Saratoga together, side by side and close, now, discussing Luce and the possible implications if she was indeed a carrier. Adam was almost convinced she was, and reluctantly Jeannie agreed.

The first problem Adam faced was finding Luce among the mass of humanity in Beaumont. Because she had worked for Mrs. Gallagher, he decided to check all the boardinghouses and hotels first, hoping she had chosen to get a job in one. Mrs. Gallagher's concern that Luce not fall prey to the lure of the saloons, or worse, nagged at the back of his mind.

It took most of a day, going from place to place, until Adam caught sight of her in a fairly nice hotel, standing quietly at the table of a prosperous-looking pair as they studied their menus. Her long blond hair was demurely pinned up and would have pleased Reba Gallagher. She wore a dark, plain dress with a white collar and cuffs and the half-circle white apron tied around her trim waist was spotlessly clean. But he knew that she was most certainly a danger to the people around her, and that she had no idea of it. Without hesitation he strode over to her and laid a hand on her arm.

Startled, she looked up into his face. "Dr. Adam! What are you doing here?"

"I need to talk to you right away, Luce."

The command in his tone made her eyes widen; she glanced

at the two men at the table, who were watching with interest. "But I—"

"Now, Luce," Adam said quietly, firmly.

"Go on, miss, looks like he can't wait!" one of the men chuckled. The other chimed in, "Yeah, and he looks like he'd pay more for your services than we would . . . for being a waitress, anyway!"

Adam's quick, hard glance silenced them. "Where is your employer's office?"

"In the back, but why?" She was walking with him because his grip on her arm was firm, but her eyes were filled with frightened questions. "Is it my little brother?"

"He's better."

"Then what is it?"

He refused to tell her until they'd spoken with her employer, who highhandedly refused when Adam asked if Luce could take off the rest of the afternoon. Adam insisted, ignoring Luce's pleas, and the hotel manager angrily told them she could not leave and come back, that there was no time for personal rendezvous for his employees while they were on duty.

Once outside, Luce turned to him, her face stunned as she whispered, "Dr. Adam, it wasn't easy for me to get that job. There aren't all that many decent jobs, you know, and I promised myself I wouldn't do what I did before, no matter what happened." Her eyes were troubled as they met his; then she stared at her feet and said slowly, "After I . . . after me and Jeannie talked some, and I watched her, I got to thinking how she was different. I still don't know exactly how, but I've missed her something fierce. She was good to me, stuck up for me to her mama."

Adam nodded. He'd noticed Jeannie's defense of Luce. He took her arm and they walked in silence down the sidewalk for a block or two, and he had to admit to himself that he had acted rather highhandedly. "I'm sorry about your job, Luce, but I have to ask you some questions." He glanced down at her. With her pearly fairness, she looked anything but dangerous. "Have you at any time during the past year been in contact with or have you yourself had typhoid?"

The look in her eyes gave her away. She nodded slowly. "I'm all over it, though, and I wasn't even very sick, not near as sick as a couple of the other girls." She touched her hair. "One of them lost all her hair."

"How long ago was this?"

"About six months, why?"

He hesitated, then said, "It's possible you may be a typhoid carrier. And as for losing your job at the hotel, you certainly shouldn't be handling food for other people. It presents a grave risk to them."

Suddenly her eyes were filled with a guilty horror. She halted, and stood staring up at him. "You mean even if I'm well, if I never had it very bad, I could give it to someone else?"

"I'm afraid so."

"Danny, and those men at the hotel . . ."

She looked so devastated that Adam felt a deep pity for her. "You didn't know, Luce. But now that you do, there are steps we must take to prevent this from happening again."

Tears were sliding slowly down her cheeks. "Pa always said I would end up no good; he said I was nothing but trouble."

The ever-present mule skinners were shouting and cursing; the crowds milled around them, jostling and ogling Luce, who spoke so softly Adam could barely hear her.

But he'd heard enough to prompt him to say gruffly, "That's nonsense. You were ill; you couldn't help that. And neither could you help what happened in Saratoga. But we must prevent it from happening again. You understand that, don't you?"

She nodded. "I just can't stand to think it was my fault that little Danny suffered so, that it was my fault!" Once again her green eyes brimmed with tears.

"Come on," urged Adam, his hand on her elbow.

"Where are we going?"

"To find a doctor under whose care we can put you, who can advise you."

"Dr. Adam, without a job I can't stay here," Luce said, her voice low and stricken. "And I don't have much money . . . I've only been working a little over a week."

"I'll be glad to help out," Adam found himself saying.

"Pa would never let me take charity—" She stopped, then said, "Guess Pa doesn't care what I do now anyway. He called me a . . . a tramp, and he's right. Oh, I denied it to his face, but he could tell I wasn't decent anymore."

"Luce, you don't have to tell me this," began Adam, but she interrupted him.

"I have to tell somebody! It's on my mind . . . it's all I can think about. Dr. Adam, my pa was right, I am a tramp." A sob caught in her throat. "That first time he threw me out, it was because of some things he'd heard about me. They weren't true—not then."

Adam couldn't keep from responding to the pleading in her eyes. "I believe you."

"It's just that men think I'm . . . I'm pretty, I guess, and he was always afraid I'd get into trouble." She shrugged her shoulders. "He's a good man, but he just goes by the way things look. And I did flirt, I *did* like to look pretty!"

Troubled and uncomfortable, Adam murmured, "Just because you like to look pretty doesn't mean you're bad."

"You still don't understand," she said slowly. "I went to work in a saloon here in Beaumont, serving drinks. It was fun for a while, but then the owner said I had to be 'nice' to the men. I knew what he meant, but I knew I didn't want to do it, either. So I . . . I just didn't. He kept after me, but the men seemed to give me a lot of money anyway, just because . . ."

"Because you're pretty," supplied Adam.

"I guess so. But then I got sick, with typhoid, and my boss, he told me he'd pay for my room and the doctoring if I would . . . oh, I didn't know what else to do! But I hated it, I hated it! And one morning I got up and just left. I went home, believing they'd take me in. Mama would've, but Pa . . . he wouldn't, or couldn't. I don't know which."

"Luce, I'm sorry."

Adam's troubled words seemed to agitate her further. "Oh, I know no decent man will want me now, but I can't stand to think of being a . . . a whore all my life!" The offensive word fell from her lips bitterly, as though it made a bad taste in her mouth.

He drew a deep breath. "You'd best come back to Saratoga with me."

"But my pa won't let me come home—"

"We'll find some place for you," he said, feeling some of her desperation himself. "Perhaps Jeannie would let you stay at her cabin."

"Do you think so?" Her face was suddenly lit with hope. "She's the only woman I know who doesn't make me feel dirty. Do you think she'd have me?"

Although Adam wasn't quite certain what would happen if he took her back to Saratoga, he knew he couldn't abandon Luce to the dangers of the thronging city. "Let's go and get your things together, Luce. We're going home." He didn't even stop to think of what he'd just said.

Because Jeannie had been helping her mother and had not yet gone to her own cabin that evening, she was still at the boardinghouse when, at almost eight o'clock, someone knocked loudly and insistently on the back door.

"I'll get it, Mum," she said as she went to open the door. To her surprise she saw Mr. Barrett, a wild look in his eyes. "Mr. Barrett, what's wrong? Is it Danny?"

"He's took a turn for the worse and the Doc ain't in his office," was the breathless reply. "Where is he? He's gotta come!"

"I'm afraid he's out of town, on an errand." Jeannie was reluctant to tell him about Adam's mission to find Luce; she wasn't at all sure how he'd take it.

"*Errand?*" sputtered Barrett. "My son's bad off, and I need a doctor!"

"I'll come right away, and do what I can for Danny until Dr. Adam gets back." Common sense told her if he was coming back tonight, he would probably have already come, but common sense also told her not to say so.

"You do that, and I'll go on to see if I can get one of the other doctors to come."

Before she could reply he had vanished into the darkness. When she turned back to the kitchen and saw her mother standing nearby, she knew she'd been listening, and didn't need an explanation. "I don't know how long I'll be, Mum. Tell Dr. Adam as soon as he comes."

The situation she found at the Barretts' was far from reassuring. Danny was moaning softly, intensely clutching his little stomach, his legs drawn up tightly. Mrs. Barrett, seated on the side of the small cot, tearfully said, "Oh, Jeannie, he was doing so well. I even went out today to take my eggs to the store—Cy buys them you know, gives me twenty cents a dozen for them. And I thought it was good that John wanted to stay with him, but when I got back . . ." She trailed off, as if she knew she'd been babbling. "Is he going to be all right?" she whispered.

Jeannie squeezed her shoulder instead of answering. "Why don't you make us some tea?" Viona Barrett did as she was bidden, but she watched as Jeannie tried to coax Danny to straighten his legs.

"It hurts," he whimpered; it turned into a little gasp as she gently pressed on the left side of his abdomen.

"I'm sorry, really I am, Danny," murmured Jeannie. "That hurt a lot, didn't it?" He nodded, his eyes wide with pain and fear. "Viona, how long has he been sick?"

"Oh, oh . . ." She looked distractedly at the kettle in her hand, as if she'd forgotten why it was there. "I left four o'clock, right before supper. John, he brought in a mess of squirrels this afternoon, said he knowed how Danny loved squirrel stew." At the quick look of apprehension on Jeannie's face she added, "I told him again what you and Dr. Adam said, no solid foods—"

She was interrupted by a sudden, croaky little noise from the bed. "A pan!" cried Jeannie. "Get a pan . . ." It was too late; the boy had thrown up all over the covers and himself. Jeannie had his clothes off and him cleaned up almost before Mrs. Barrett knew what was happening. "Why don't you change his bed and I'll hold him, Viona, if you have a clean quilt we can wrap him in."

Once again, almost as if she were in a trance, Mrs. Barrett did as Jeannie said. Jeannie held the little boy in her arms, one hand pressed to his forehead. *He's burning up*, she thought frantically; *his temperature must be at least 103*. "Viona, hasn't Danny's temperature been normal for the last couple of days?"

The woman nodded. She'd just seen what Jeannie had on the bed, and drawn the same conclusions. Danny had eaten squirrel stew; the mess confirmed it. "I told John . . . I told him. He don't never think I know nothing . . ."

"Get the thermometer, please. It's in my bag, on the table." A few minutes later she read the thermometer and swallowed— hard. At the pleading, questioning look on the woman's face she whispered, "His temperature is almost 104 again."

Viona's face crumpled now. "Oh, Danny . . ."

"Here, you sit in the rocker and hold Danny and I'll make his bed." Jeannie patted Danny's cheek, hiding her alarm at the heat she felt there, then surrendered him to his mother.

For the next couple of hours they hovered over the child. Then when Jeannie took his temperature she found it had dropped a degree, and in the hour that followed it dropped, slowly, even further.

Though Viona was jubilant, Jeannie had grave reservations. She was not a doctor, but Adam had explained what the consequences would be if a recovering typhoid patient were given solid foods too soon. He had gone into careful detail so that she knew, roughly, what was happening. He was bleeding internally, she was almost certain. She kept surreptitiously feeling Danny's pulse, and saw that the previous pallor of his face was now replaced by a pink, almost healthy color. But his breathing was shallow and rapid, and he was perspiring profusely. She knew enough—enough to be very frightened that if Adam did not come soon, Danny would die.

She closed her eyes, her cheek against his, unaware that her lips moved as she prayed. *Oh, Lord, I don't know how to pray, I don't know what to ask for . . . but I know you love this child. I know you care for these people . . . Dear God, work in this situation, use it for your good . . . your glory—*

The door burst open suddenly, and Mr. Barrett and Adam stood there, the question plain on both their faces.

"Oh, John, he's not good! It was the stew; you shouldn't have given him the squirrel stew! Dr. Adam . . ."

Mrs. Barrett's plea was unspoken as Adam rushed over and lifted the child from Jeannie's arms. He was limp and already turning blue. Tears, silent and slow, were trickling down Jeannie's face as Adam placed the child on the cot and examined him carefully; felt for a pulse, listened for a heartbeat. Finally he looked up at the couple, who stood close to each other but not touching.

"I'm too late." The pain, the sadness of countless other losses was in his voice. He gently closed the boy's eyes, one at a time.

"I'm so sorry, so sorry . . ." Jeannie whispered. If only—"

"If only that whoring sister of his hadn't brought this to him." Mr. Barrett's voice was low, hard. "And if that ain't enough, it was her that kept the doctor. He was looking for *her.*"

"Mr. Barrett, this is no time for accusations," declared Adam. "Your wife needs you—"

"My son needed you, Doc, and where were you? Off gallivanting after Luce like every other man in Beaumont, that's where! It's all her fault!"

"If Danny had not been given solid food too soon, he would most likely have continued to recover." Adam's words were quiet and cold.

A stunned look of uncertainty crept into the man's eyes. "You mean you really did tell Vi the boy wasn't to have . . ." Adam nodded slowly, and as realization dawned on him, John Barrett began to breathe heavily as though he were going to cry. "He was so hungry, and you know how that boy loved squirrel stew . . . and I thought she was carrying it too far to say he couldn't eat nothing at all but stuff for babies . . ." His voice broke. "Viona, you know I wouldn't never do nothing to hurt that boy. I love him!" A stifled moan escaped his lips as he stared at the still, slight form on the bed.

"Oh, John, don't," whispered his wife. "Don't . . ." She took a step and reached out her arms. He didn't touch her with his hands, but let them hang down as if he didn't have the strength to raise them. Then he laid his head on her shoulder, and she gathered him close. "There, there," she soothed.

Adam's stricken eyes met Jeannie's and held them for a long time. The only words spoken before they left were Jeannie's, quietly reassuring the Barretts she'd be back. Then she followed Adam outside.

CHAPTER 17

A friend loveth at all times, and a brother is born for adversity.
Proverbs 17:17

Jeannie could see the outline of Adam's hunched shoulders, his bowed head in the dim glow of the moon. Her heart ached—for the couple inside, for Adam, who had nothing with which to fight the terrible things which came his way. She had watched him from the moment he'd stepped off the train in Beaumont, straight into a challenging situation which he met head-on. And Jeannie Gallagher was convinced that for all his gruffness, his quick temper, Adam Jarrett was one of the most tender men she'd ever known. All of the pain, wretchedness, and sickness—of soul and body—that surrounded him affected him deeply. He was suffering now, not only because of the loss of that little boy, but because of his inability to help.

"Adam . . ." She was only a few steps from him; somehow her feet carried her very close. Her hand seemed of its own accord to touch his neck, to stroke the black hair that she found was as soft as Rob's.

His shoulders had begun to shake when he felt her touch, and his voice was so low it was barely audible. "He shouldn't have died; Danny shouldn't have died."

"I know," Jeannie murmured, leaning against him, wanting desperately to comfort him. "It hurts."

"Yes . . . it hurts . . ." he tearfully agreed. For a long time he stood, feeling the agony of soul that death brings, dimly grateful even in the pain that there was another human being who understood and felt the same.

The night sounds filtered through their consciousness and helped to calm both; the sweet trills of a mockingbird that had

185

begun when the moon sliver rose, and was well into its nightly concert; the hoarse bullfrogs, the occasional hoot of an owl. Gradually the storm within Adam abated, only to be replaced by another.

"Jeannie . . ." He slowly turned and encircled her in his arms, holding her close. His lips touched her hair, her forehead, her cheeks.

Disregarding the still small voice within, her hands went up and clasped the back of his neck, pulling him closer. "Oh, Adam, dear Adam," she murmured.

He held her so tightly that for a moment she couldn't breathe; then he bent his head to kiss her lips. Finally he gently cradled her head on his chest, speaking as he caressed her hair. "Jeannie," he said simply, "I love you."

Jeannie's voice was soft and broken as she said, "Oh, Adam, I love you too, but this is—"

"I know. It's wrong."

"It is. But I feel so . . . so . . ."

"I know exactly how you feel."

"What are we going to do?" The question held all the pain of the precious moments they'd just spent in each other's arms as well as the knowledge that the time was stolen, and dreadfully wrong.

"Nothing."

"Nothing . . ." She echoed the awful word, aware that he was exactly right. There was nothing they could do. He belonged to someone else, could never belong to her. Jeannie was a strong young woman bound by principles of a God she loved and reverenced. But at that moment she felt she could no longer resist the desire to be near him, to kiss him once more.

The kiss was a painful, beautiful moment for them both, because they recognized it for what it was—the last. When she drew away he said nothing, just held her very tenderly.

It was Jeannie who finally spoke, her voice steady, "It won't happen again, Adam. I wish I could say I'm sorry it did this time." She stared up into his black eyes.

"I'm not sorry." Low, intense words—words that managed to convey the longing that was in his heart as surely as it was in hers.

"Please forgive me."

"Forgive you? For loving me?" he asked.

"Yes, for loving you, for betraying Carrie, and . . . you, and myself."

For a very long time he was silent. "One of us has to go back in there and be with them. Perhaps, considering the way Mr. Barrett feels about me, it would be best if it were you."

"Yes," Jeannie said, forcing her thoughts away from herself to the tragedy within those walls. "God is at work even in this hard situation, and He will—"

"Why bring God into it," Adam said painfully.

"He *is* here, and I didn't have anything to do with it."

"Be that as it may, with that innocent child lying dead in there and his family torn apart, I can't see that God has done much for them so far."

"But He can, and He would, if only they'd let Him!"

"I'll talk to you in the morning." Adam turned from her abruptly and strode to where his horse was tethered.

Jeannie watched him go, a sudden flash of intuition illuminating her mind. Adam was glad for the sudden anger she'd heard in his tone, glad to be angry, because it was a safer emotion.

Jeannie thought that perhaps the death of his wife had been the death of a part of him that might never live again. The thought saddened her so deeply that she turned as abruptly as he had to make her way back to the cabin.

Another thought, one which she asked God to take away immediately, had also intruded into her mind; Jude had hinted at it a few weeks ago. Perhaps the love Adam felt for her, that her whole self felt for him, could make that part of him alive again—with God's help.

"No, no, no," she whispered, shaking her head in the darkness. "You must not love him that way, you mustn't. Lord, help me," she prayed. Then she went inside the cabin.

When Adam returned to Saratoga, it was too late for him to see Carrie, and he was shamefully grateful. But the next day he was called to the boardinghouse by one of the typhoid victims who thought he was well enough to leave with his family who had come for him. Adam, Mrs. Gallagher, and Jeannie were in the sitting room discussing it when Carrie came in. None of the three noticed her for a moment as she stood at the door quietly watching them.

Adam had done fairly well at his firm resolve not to show his feelings toward Jeannie, and she'd done the same; at least they both thought so. But occasionally their eyes would meet, and there was no hiding the spark that flared between them, as it did now. They looked quickly away, but Carrie saw it.

She lifted her chin a fraction and said, "Adam, Jeannie told me about the little boy. I'm so sorry." Her words were genuine; Carrie was a woman capable of deep feeling. She came over to where they sat, and nodded as Mrs. Gallagher offered her a mug of coffee. Small hands cupped around it, she said, "I'm grateful to Grannie Annie for keeping Rob, but don't you think the danger is past? I miss him. Couldn't we bring him . . . home?" She hesitated for only a fraction of a second before she said the last word.

Jeannie rose, not looking at Adam. "I think it would be all right. And I was also thinking I should go out to Barretts' again, and try taking Luce with me."

"That hardheaded pa of hers won't let her in the door," warned her mother.

"You may be right, Mum. But I've been praying that God will heal and soften his heart. It's a fact, people are more open when something like this happens. He needs Luce just as bad as she needs him, and what he needs most is the Lord."

"The fact is, he might run you off with his rifle," Reba said drily. "Oh, I don't mean he'd out and out shoot you, but he might make a show."

"The man has a right to his feelings without some do-gooder trying to take advantage of them," Adam murmured.

Hurt flared in Jeannie's eyes, but she responded calmly, "I'm not the one who'll be taking advantage; it'll be the Father himself." Then she left without giving Adam a chance to reply.

"Well," said Mrs. Gallagher as she gathered up the cups, "you two better get a move on if you've a mind to fetch the boy before lunch. I'm cooking his favorite, chicken and dumplings, and he's liable to smell it clear over at Grannie's and start walking home." At the door she glanced back at them both keenly. "Thanksgiving is only a couple of days off, and you haven't been doing much planning on that wedding of yours. You do still plan on a wedding, I take it?"

Carrie said nothing, and Mrs. Gallagher shrugged and went on to the kitchen.

Adam got up and prowled restlessly around the room. He finally came to stand beside her. "Perhaps we should postpone the wedding, Carrie."

"If you think that would be best," she said softly, still watching his face.

"Well, the last few weeks have been hard on you, on all of us. I can't see how you could have done much thinking about a wedding."

"I think about it all the time, Adam." Her eyes, so blue, so intense, looked straight into his.

He found he couldn't break away from their searching gaze. "What I meant was, you've had no time to plan, that it isn't fair to expect you to plan a wedding in the middle of nursing men with typhoid fever."

"I know exactly what you mean."

Adam drew a deep, tortured breath and hoped with all his heart that she did not. "Carrie, if I haven't told you before, I want to now. What you did for those men, total strangers, was beyond anything any of us expected of you."

"They weren't total strangers," she replied with an odd little smile. "I've served them meals, washed their dishes, changed their beds for months now."

"I know, and no woman could have worked harder, under harder circumstances, than you have. I'm . . . I'm very proud of you, and grateful."

"Grateful." That strange little smile curved her pretty mouth again. "Thank you for telling me, Adam. As for postponing the wedding, you may be right."

"It's been a difficult time, and I just thought that maybe Christmas, or after the first of the year might be better . . ." He trailed off; the look in her eyes was one he'd never seen before, one he couldn't fathom. For some reason he felt compelled to take her in his arms. Eyes closed, he held her, hating his treacherous mind that remembered how Jeannie had felt last night. He kissed Carrie's forehead softly. "The new year, Carrie. That would be a better time, a time for new beginnings."

"Yes, Adam, a time for new beginnings." She stood quietly, her arms at her sides; though she leaned against him she couldn't bring herself to put her arms around him. The memory of that look, the look of flaming intensity that had passed between him and Jeannie Gallagher prevented her. "Can we go and get Rob now? I'm really anxious to see him, I've missed him so much." She drew back and looked up at him. "Adam you do know how very much I love Rob, don't you?"

"Of course I know." He released her. "Get a wrap, it's cold out. I'll wait for you outside."

She watched him leave, her mind awhirl with half-formed thoughts, plans, and decisions.

That evening Carrie had quite a time getting Rob to sleep. He had, indeed, been delighted to see them, even more delighted that he was going back with them. They'd been able to persuade him to leave the pup he claimed—with no discouragement from Grannie Annie, who'd calmly said as Jude had that every boy needs a dog. The yaller pup would remain there with its litter mates for a while longer.

Carrie sat in the dark, on the edge of Rob's cot, her fingers caressing his silky hair lightly. She'd missed him so very much, had discovered that life without the child was tasteless, meaningless, not worth living. And he loved her, there was no doubt whatever of that fact in her mind. *After all,* she thought, *I'm the only mother he's ever known.*

She also thought of the conversation she'd had a little earlier with Jeannie. They'd been in the sitting room, and Mrs. Gallagher had asked Rob if he wanted some milk and sugar cookies for a bedtime snack. The boy had shouted yes, but he'd glanced at Carrie to see if it was all right. At her nod he had dragged Mrs. Gallagher off to the kitchen.

Jeannie had said, her mouth curved in a fond smile, "He's a fine little boy. I'm glad Grannie didn't spoil him too much."

"Yes, so am I," Carrie agreed, gazing at Jeannie who was turned slightly away from her. Even when she was a little girl Carrie had always been aware that she was pretty, aware that men thought so, too. And she'd always thought Adam would wake up one day from the slumber of grief over Bethany Jarrett and see her—really see her. She wasn't stupid; she knew he never really had. Until they'd met Jeannie Gallagher that day when they'd stepped off the train in Beaumont, she'd believed, hoped with all her heart, that he would. But now . . ."

That red hair, so untidy and bright . . . even now it straggled down her neck in little coppery, curly strands. And her skin was so pale she even had freckles on her arms . . . which were far too slender. Carrie clasped her own gently rounded arms across herself, thinking Jeannie could almost pass as a young man if she wore loose clothes, boy's clothes. What did Adam *see* in her? And then she turned to face Carrie, those brown, wonderfully alive eyes on her.

"Carrie," she said, "I've been thinking. Mum mentioned it first, and it's surely true. You've been so busy with the nursing and all, you've let the plans for your ... yours and Adam's wedding be set aside. He told me you've postponed it."

"He told you *I* did it?"

Jeannie nodded. "And I feel that even if it was needful, what we need to do now is begin straight away to make new plans. Would you like a Christmas wedding? That might be nice, with the decorations and all. I want to help."

Carrie's eyes searched her face; try as she might, she could see nothing but honest warmth. *Why* she thought in dazed amazement, *she actually means what she's saying ... She's offering again to help plan my wedding to the man she loves!* Her throat felt tight, but she managed to say, "You don't have to. I know how busy you are."

"I want to do it," assured Jeannie. "Please believe me."

There was something in Jeannie's brown eyes that Carrie couldn't quite figure out. Was it duty ... or guilt that motivated her ... or was she simply one of the best people Carrie had ever met? She only knew she did, indeed, believe her, and the knowledge stunned her. Slowly she said, "Maybe Christmas is too soon."

"Could be. How about New Year's Day?"

What had Adam said, *a time for new beginnings ...*" Carrie had nodded and listened as Jeannie made suggestions, and spoke of what they could do to make the boardinghouse more festive, prettier. And she could detect no hidden malice, no reason for Jeannie's interest other than genuine caring. It confounded her; and after a while, bewildered her. When Rob came back in with a milk mustache, Carrie was glad to be able to escape, saying he was tired from all the excitement and she needed to put him to bed.

And now, he slept soundly in the darkened room, his thumb still in his mouth, his little bottom stuck up in the air. Carrie kissed his cheek once, twice, and got up. Knowing she couldn't sleep, she wandered to the window, where she'd stood so often watching for Adam, for the light in his office across the street to go on ... or off.

It was on now. She thought of him there, alone; wondered if he had a patient, or if he was reading by the lamp's glow. In her mind's eye she could see his dark head bent over the pages, studying, always studying, even though he was the smartest man she'd ever known. Carrie knew she was not Adam's intellectual equal, had never thought otherwise. But she had thought her love for him, for his son, was strong enough to overcome any obstacle if she gave him time. But that was before they'd come across Jeannie Gallagher.

How could she fight a woman who was so honestly good, so sacrificial? "I wouldn't give him up if I were her," she whispered. Jeannie had something else on her side, too. It had been so strong, in every look, every word and gesture, when Carrie watched them today, that it made her head ache now to think of it. *Why, Adam . . . why couldn't you have loved me that way?*

Carrie knew he didn't, that he never would, now. She'd lost him, and he belonged to Jeannie Gallagher whether he could admit it to her or not. He was a man of honor, who would honor his commitment to her, Carrie was sure. She could be his wife and never be afraid he would go to Jeannie. Adam Jarrett was that kind of man. *But his heart would never belong to me . . .* She turned and gazed at Rob's sleeping form, listened to the faint baby snore. "He's my son . . . He loves me."

The words were no more than a sigh in the still darkness of the room. And in Carrie's mind a plan began to form, a plan to free them all from the dilemma she'd become convinced that Adam and Jeannie were going to ignore. Only she, Carrie, could do this; only she knew what had to be done. It would take courage, but her love for Adam, and for Rob, would give her that. There was simply nothing else to do, and no one but she could do it.

CHAPTER 18

Whither shall I go from thy spirit? Or whither shall I flee from thy presence?   *Psalm 139:7*

The weather finally turned cold; not bitter cold, but a gray mist often slipped around the derricks, the tall pines and ancient hardwoods. It settled quietly and stealthily and crept into the bones of the men obliged to work in it. Although the temperature seldom fell lower than the mid-thirties, the fog was like chilly fingers that squeezed muscles and hunched shoulders.

The three men who'd had typhoid fever had gone home, and Mrs. Gallagher had been able to pick up a half dozen new boarders. But somehow no one had wanted to make much of Thanksgiving. Perhaps each had had his own reasons—Luce especially. Although she'd been grateful when Jeannie had graciously opened her home to her, she was subdued, and kept to herself whenever she ventured into town, for several very good reasons. She was still grieving over Danny's death and her estrangement from her family. And the knowledge that she must keep her distance from others or run the risk of infecting them sat heavily on her.

Mrs. Gallagher had, with difficulty, checked her tongue from spreading the news that Luce was the carrier of the fever, and Adam was treating her with as much knowledge of the situation as he had. But no one, least of all Luce, wanted to take any chances.

Jeannie wore a bright, happy expression all the time. To the ones who knew her best it was too bright, too happy. Adam simply avoided coming to the boardinghouse if he knew she was there. Everyone excused Carrie's half-hidden agitation. After all, hadn't she had to postpone her wedding? So, the days following Thanksgiving passed uneasily, but without event, and Jeannie often sought out Carrie with yet another offering for the wedding plans.

Carrie wondered if guilt motivated Jeannie, but she was still fascinated by the idea of a woman working so hard to make a wedding a success, when the man she loved was marrying someone else. Try as she might she could never detect anything but honesty in Jeannie—honesty and a genuine desire to help. At times it puzzled and confused her, then again it made her long to be like Jeannie.

At breakfast on Christmas morning Mrs. Gallagher looked around the table, which was gratifyingly almost full again. "Well," she said, "it's Christmas. How many of you want to come to church with us?" Her look was challenging; Luce had already fled back to Jeannie's when Reba had asked her the same question earlier.

Adam's glance rested for a brief moment on Jeannie; then he rose, dropping his napkin on the table. "Count me out. Thank you for breakfast, Mrs. Gallagher."

"Anytime, Doctor." Her eyes had a shrewd, knowing look to them. At least he didn't make excuses about not going to church like some men; he just came right out and said no. She liked that. "But don't forget we're all having Christmas dinner this evening, and you're invited."

"I told Rob I'd be here."

The child flashed a smile at his father. He was still entranced with the toys he'd found under the Christmas tree. Jude had carved a truly marvelous toy, a little monkey that obligingly climbed up his string as many times as Rob wanted, which was plenty.

"Well, if you'll excuse me." Adam didn't allow himself to speak to Jeannie; he went to Carrie and bent to kiss her cheek. She gave him a little smile, that sweet, other-worldly smile that had been on her face often in the past weeks.

When Adam had gone, and with him all but one of the new boarders who'd been making sheep's eyes at Jeannie, Mrs. Gallagher said, "How about you, Carrie, are you going to go with us?"

Carrie hesitated. Jeannie asked her before and she'd always declined. "I don't think—"

But Rob tugged at her sleeve. "Please, Mama, go with us. Please?" He'd gone before and liked it, especially the singing.

She could have said it was because of the child that she found herself nodding yes, but she knew deep in her heart there was another reason, one she wasn't able to fathom completely. "I . . . I suppose so. After all, it is Christmas."

Jeannie rose from the table. She wore a cinnamon brown dress of some soft-looking fabric with a cream-colored crocheted collar and cuffs. On any other woman Carrie would have said it was a dull dress; brown was an uninteresting color to her. But Jeannie Gallagher looked as rich and lovely in it as the trees in their autumn foliage did.

"I'm glad you're coming with us, Carrie," Jeannie said as she gathered up the dishes within her reach. "Brother Teale never had much formal education, I guess, but he preaches the gospel, all right."

"What's the gospel?" piped up Rob.

"Why, it's the good news that Jesus loves you, Robbie. You know, like in the song you sing, that all the boys and girls sang in Sunday school last time you went?" He nodded and grinned at her, sporting his usual milk mustache. "But wipe your face, or the folks at church will think you didn't shave!" The boy giggled as Jeannie rolled her eyes.

Carrie felt a stab of resentment at the tone of easy familiarity. She knew only too well how much Jeannie cared for Rob. It bothered her far more, however, that Rob had come to love Jeannie dearly, and looked to her at times for help instead of herself. "Rob, come here and I'll wipe it off," she said. "You're going to have to learn to drink your milk like a grown-up."

Rob's eyes were mischievous as he said, "Like Uncle Jude does his coffee, in a saucer? Can I blow it, too?"

"Certainly not," Carrie replied crisply. She suddenly regretted saying she would go to church, wishing it was over, vowing never to get herself in that position again.

That afternoon they all sat in the parlor enjoying the savory smells of Christmas dinner, except for Adam, who'd been called out on a case. Jude's contribution—three wild turkeys—had been carefully stuffed with Mrs. Gallagher's cornbread dressing and were roasting; Carrie had worked for hours on the shelly beans that were cooking with plenty of ham; there were both Irish potatoes and sweet potatoes and three kinds of pie.

There were also homemade fudge and divinity, but they'd had to put it beyond the reach of Rob, who'd thrown a little tantrum and then fallen asleep in Jeannie's lap as she soothed him.

Mrs. Gallagher looked around. "Well, if I do say so myself, the old place looks fine as frog's fur."

She was right, it did look festive and pleasant. Adam had raised a Northern eyebrow at Mrs. Gallagher's combination of palm leaves and the gray Spanish moss with holly branches and the red-berried yaupon, but even he'd had to admit it looked like Christmas.

Carrie hadn't said much since they'd returned from church. The truth was, she wasn't even listening to the conversations around her as they all whiled away the afternoon until the turkeys were done and it would be dinnertime. In her mind she kept going over what the earnest, sometimes bombastic, red-faced Brother Teale had said in his sermon. *Where had he said it was in the Bible? John, that was it, the Gospel of John.*

I am the light of the world; he who follows Me shall not walk in the darkness, but shall have the light of life. He had spoken at length about it, but because she'd never gone to church much, she didn't understand all his terminology. "Be saved!" he'd kept thundering. "Come to Jesus and be saved from the everlasting flames of an eternal hell . . . ."

What does "be saved" mean? she wondered. Hell was not real to her; she couldn't imagine a place where a fire burned forever, a place of punishment—

"Carrie? Are you all right?"

Jeannie's quiet question pierced the fog of her confused thoughts. "Oh," said Carrie, "yes, I'm fine."

The smile on Jeannie's face was tempered by concern. "You looked as though you were a million miles away."

Wishing she were, Carrie summoned a smile of her own. "Did I? Sorry. Mrs. Gallagher, is there anything I can do to help with dinner?" The older woman had risen and was on her way to the kitchen.

"No, child, you stay put." She stopped, her eyes pausing on Carrie's face. "You look flushed. Do you feel all right?"

Carrie put a hand to her cheek. "Why . . . yes, I'm fine." Her head did hurt, but she wasn't about to say so. She knew it was because of the strain she'd been under, of trying to seem calm and pretending that nothing was different, when everything had changed. And there were so many plans she'd made, and discarded.

Unconvinced by Carrie's words, Mrs. Gallagher shook her head and left the room.

"Mum is a mother hen," Jeannie confessed quietly. "But the truth is, you do look a mite peaked. Maybe we'd better get Adam to check you when he gets back."

"I'm fine, I tell you." With an effort Carrie stifled the flare of unreasonable irritation that she felt. "It's just that with Christmas and all the wedding preparations, I'm a little tired."

"I'm sure you are," soothed Jeannie. "Wait, I just thought of something that might cheer you up. I'll be right back." Gently she eased Rob's head onto the cushion beside her, then quickly went to her mother's room. She returned in a couple of minutes with a bouquet of wildflowers. Their colors were so pale and delicate they looked like fairy flowers.

As she took it Carrie whispered, "Why, they're de—" She started to say dead, but Jeannie smiled and supplied, "Dried. They will last forever, will always look just as they do now. Grannie Annie taught me how to do it. Smell!" she insisted.

Jeannie's delight with her gift was so obvious that Carrie lifted the bouquet to her nose, assuming it could have no odor. To her surprise its fragrance was delightful; there was lavender, and roses, and sweet woodruff, with its fresh-mown-hay, almost-vanilla scent. "Why . . . thank you, Jeannie," she said faintly.

"You're very welcome. I want you to know that if you'd rather have live flowers for your bridal bouquet you certainly can, because there's something blooming in the Thicket year-round."

"No, this is perfect," murmured Carrie as she watched Jeannie slip back close to Rob, who sleepily snuggled up. She inhaled the faint, sweet fragrance, thinking that this bouquet was a perfect symbol of Adam's love for her. It was only a shadow of what he felt for Jeannie herself, and Carrie was suddenly, painfully made aware of that fact, for just then she saw Adam enter the room.

He stopped at the sight of Jeannie's bright head bent to his son's dark one; though it was quickly gone, that look flared briefly in his eyes.

"Isn't it time to eat *yet?*" Rob said croakily.

Jeannie's soft, delightful laugh was a lovely thing, even to the desperately unhappy Carrie. "Yes, as a matter-of-fact, it is, sleepy head. Do you like drumsticks?"

When Adam saw that Carrie was watching him, he came straight to her, not looking at Jeannie again, not even speaking to her. He would have kissed Carrie's mouth, but she turned her face slightly and his lips touched her cheek instead. "You feel warm, Carrie. You aren't coming down with something, are you?"

"I . . . it's the fire. We've had it very warm in here, haven't we, Jeannie?"

"Yes, we certainly have." Jeannie hugged Rob, whose arms had found their way around her neck. "Robbie boy, let's go out and check on those wild tom turkeys." She didn't say, *and give your father and Carrie some time together,* but she implied it. "How's that?"

"Yea! I like Christmas!" He waved at his father gaily, as Jeannie took him out without speaking, or hardly looking at Adam.

It was quiet in the big room for a moment. Then Adam said, "Have you got all the arrangements for the wedding made yet?"

"Jeannie has done most of it. Look," she said as she lifted the bouquet, "she made this for me. There's not a day goes by that she doesn't bring something that she's made, or tell me another idea." Her words had a curious, flat quality, and the expression in her eyes was difficult to read.

Adam put his hand on her arm. "Carrie, what's wrong?"

"Wrong? What could possibly be wrong? Rob escaped the fever; it's Christmas; your practice is doing well; and my . . . our wedding is next week . . ." She trailed off, then sighed. "Nothing is wrong, Adam."

"But you seem so . . . oh, I can't put my finger on it," groaned Adam, scowling.

She smiled; a tiny smile, but a smile nonetheless. "Do you know that when you frown like that you look just like Rob?"

"Well, you worry me."

"You mustn't worry about me, ever. No matter what happens, remember that." She was staring straight into his eyes now, and he couldn't have looked away if he'd wanted to.

"Carrie, I—"

Just then he was interrupted by Mrs. Gallagher's bell, and her jolly words, "Dinner, everybody!"

"We'll talk about this tomorrow, Carrie."

"Yes, Adam, tomorrow." She let him take her arm, but she kept at a slight distance from him as they walked to the dining room, as though she wanted to avoid any real closeness.

Mrs. Gallagher wasn't unduly alarmed the next afternoon when Carrie didn't come down right away after she'd said she was going to put Rob down for a nap. But a couple of hours later when Jeannie dropped by, she remarked that it was odd, because Carrie usually made it a point to help her set up for supper.

Jeannie, volunteering to fill in for Carrie, admitted she'd come by specifically to check up on her. "I was concerned for her yesterday, Mum. She didn't look at all well. Maybe Rob was overtired after the big day. Could be she was, too, and decided to nap with him."

Her mother nodded. "Could be. Come along to the kitchen." Jeannie followed as Mrs. Gallagher added, "You're right, though, she didn't look well. Did you mention it to Dr. Adam?"

"No, I didn't. We . . . Adam and I . . . we haven't talked much lately."

"And why not, Jeannie girl? You needn't try and avoid my question. I've got eyes in my head, I can see something's going on between you two."

"No, Mum," said Jeannie, her voice low and firm. "Nothing is going on between Dr. Adam and me."

"But there could be if it wasn't for Carrie."

The simple, calm statement shocked Jeannie, regardless of the truth in it. "Please don't say that; they're going to be married in less than a week!"

The pain in her daughter's voice wasn't lost on Reba Gallagher. She washed her hands at the sink, dried them off, and placed them on Jeannie's shoulders. "I'm real sorry that things are the way they are. You know that, don't you?"

Quietly Jeannie nodded, determined to hold back the threatening tears. Finally she managed, "You're right about one thing. Adam should check on her. She may be sick." Her eyes pled with her mother not to say anything further, knowing there were many things that could be said.

Reba was obviously struggling with the desire to ask questions, but all she said was, "If she doesn't come down by suppertime, we'll go get him. To tell the truth—"

She stopped and Jeannie prompted, "What, Mum?"

"Well, that girl baffles me sometimes. She'll go along and fit right in, make me think she's just regular folk, and I start treating her the same I would you. Then, she'll act different."

"Different? How?"

"Oh, I can't put my finger on it exactly. Maybe like she's saying one thing and thinking another. Not in a nasty way, you understand, like she just wants to hide her true feelings."

"I think I understand," said Jeannie slowly. "And it's gotten worse in the past few weeks, hasn't it?" At her mother's nod she thought, *Since Adam told me he loved me, and I told him. How silly we were to think we could hide those feelings and pretend there was nothing between us. Carrie probably knew even before we did.* The guilt rose in her, bitter as bile. "Oh, I do hope she isn't sick. Maybe I'd better go and find Adam now—"

Mrs. Gallagher held up her hand. "Give her until suppertime, then we'll see. Although . . . Robbie wouldn't sleep this long, even if she might, would he?"

Her brow creased in a frown, Jeannie said, "I'm going to get Adam. I have the feeling we shouldn't wait." Reba shrugged in agreement.

It took almost an hour to track Adam down, another half hour for them to get back to the boardinghouse. Having filled him in on why she'd come to get him, both were silent as they rode in the late afternoon stillness. The days were considerably shorter now, and the sodden gray sky showed that this one was almost over.

Just outside Saratoga, Adam's breath puffed white as he asked, "How did she seem this morning?"

Head bowed, Jeannie had to admit, "I didn't see her; I don't know."

An explosive little oath escaped his lips. "Neither did I. Because I'm a coward!" He didn't speak again until they reined up in front of the hotel. "Thanks for coming to get me." He vaulted down, leaving her to follow.

Reba was outside Carrie's door, and her face was grave as she said, "It's locked, Dr. Adam."

"Do you have another key?" She shook her head and frowned. "I suppose you've knocked and called her?"

"Yes, I did, but she never answered."

He knocked loudly several times, but there was still no response. Though he was oblivious to them, quite a few boomers came out of their rooms to stare, the complaints on their lips fading as they saw it was the doctor. "Carrie," he called, "it's Adam. Are you all right?"

There was a hush, as if everyone was listening, but no sound came from within the room. Adam spoke, his voice low and tense, "Mrs. Gallagher, I'll take full responsibility for any damage—" Without finishing his statement he took a short step backward, then lunged at the door, his shoulder striking it solidly.

It flew open, and he almost fell. But he caught himself, took a few steps inside. "Carrie?"

She was not there, nor was Rob. The room was very neat; the kind of neatness you associate with a room no one lives in. They found her trunk in the closet, with some of her things in it. But the things she and Rob used most were gone—as were Carrie and Rob.

"She's gone." Adam's unnecessary words echoed in the still room. "*But where?*" His last two words were only a whisper.

It was Jeannie who spotted the letter on the bureau, propped in front of the dried flower bridal bouquet. She picked it up. "It's for you, Adam."

He took it from her as though he were in a daze. It was sealed tightly, and he had a difficult time getting it open. Though he couldn't have said why, he began to read aloud.

Dear Adam,

By the time you read this we will be gone, Rob and I. Please believe me when I say I am deeply sorry for the pain it will cause you for me to take Rob, and I know you will probably never be able to forgive me. But I can't imagine life without him; he is my life. I love you, but it is Rob, since you laid him in my arms as a newborn babe, who has owned my heart.

I can't say there isn't any bitterness in my heart, for before you saw Jeannie Gallagher there was hope that you would come to care for me enough to make a marriage work. I know now as well as you do that your feelings for her are what I wanted for myself but will never have. There is a difference between us, Adam, and that difference is that I saw it, and fought it, then gave in to the fact that there is no future for the two of us. You would, in your sense of honor, have gone ahead with the marriage, and I would have had nothing but the shell of a man. I could fight Bethany's ghost, for I know I could have, if you had let me, been a good wife to you. But I can't fight Jeannie Gallagher. She is too good, too fine, too alive.

You and Jeannie can have other sons, but I will never love another man, will never have another son but Rob.

Please try to forgive me. I will give him everything there is in me to give, the best of me. I love him with all my heart. We are taking one of Jude's horses and saddles, and will leave it with someone who will make certain it is returned to him. I hope he understands. This letter is too long as it is, but I wanted so much for you to know what was in my breaking heart. I promise you I will give my life to Rob, to see that he grows up to be as fine a man as his father is.

Goodbye, dear Adam,

and forgive me.

The silence when he finished was profound, though Jeannie and Mrs. Gallagher were both in the room with him, and men crowded at the door and outside in the hall.

"We'll help, Doc," promised one of the drillers. "Don't you worry about that; we'll find her *and* the little boy!" They started to talk excitedly among themselves.

Jeannie was close enough so that she could touch Adam; she put her hand on his arm. "Oh, Adam, I'm sorry, I feel so responsible," she whispered.

"It's my fault, not yours," he replied harshly. "I should have seen the signs, but I didn't want to. I wanted to believe everything would be fine, that she wouldn't know—" He broke off. "We're wasting time. It'll be dark soon, and she's had a head start of several hours already." As they all knew, the Big Thicket at night was no place for a man alone, much less a woman and a small boy.

"We can hope she made it to Beaumont, or Liberty, before now, Dr. Adam," put in Mrs. Gallagher. "If only we knew what direction she headed."

"But we don't," said Adam grimly. Even as he spoke he was moving from the room. "We'll have to ask around, see if anyone saw them leave town."

They set off a short time later, Jude leading one party and Adam the other; a strange but gratifying mix of boomers and Thicket natives united to a man in the task at hand. They had all, at one time or another, been helped by Dr. Adam, and they set aside any animosity they might have felt for each other. Jude's face was grave with worry—for he loved Rob like the son, the grandson he'd never had, and he cared for the woman who loved that little boy so much.

Jeannie watched them go, her mind and head in a painful jumble of prayers. She felt an almost overwhelming guilt, and had had no time to ask God to take it away. She did so now as she watched the men disappear into the Thicket.

"Oh, Father, take it from me," she whispered. "Rid me of it, so I can get on with what's really important . . . asking that you guide them to Carrie and Rob . . . that you watch over them. Oh, dear Lord, it's so wild out there, and she's not used to such. And Robbie . . ." Her control slipped then, and the tears flowed freely down her face.

CHAPTER 19

For thou wilt light my candle; the Lord my God will enlighten
my darkness.   *Psalm 18:28*

For a long time Carrie had thought about leaving Saratoga.
Like a person who contemplates suicide seriously, she left no
telltale clues so that no one would discover her plan and stop
her. She didn't want to be caught, to be stopped and persuaded
to stay. She was convinced that the only reasonable way for her
and Rob, for Adam, was the way she'd chosen. Her plan had
been to slip away from the boardinghouse and make her way
back to Beaumont, and from there to catch a train. To where,
she'd not decided.

The man in the stable knew Rob and Carrie, knew how Jude
doted on the boy, so it had been easy to borrow Jude's horse.
"I'll make sure to get him back," Carrie had promised him with
a pretty smile. "Rob wants to see that puppy of Grannie Annie's
he's so fond of."

Later, that stable hand confessed he'd thought it queer that
she'd headed in the opposite direction of Grannie's, but someone
else had come in just then and distracted him. He hadn't taken
time since to ponder it.

With a few carefully chosen possessions in a sack, some
water and snacks to pacify Rob, Carrie had set off at a decorous
pace, with Rob in front of her, clutching the pommel of the large
western style saddle. Mercifully he hadn't noticed, nor remarked on the fact that, as the stable hand noted too late, they
were going the wrong way.

They'd gone only two or three miles from Saratoga on the
corduroy road toward Kountze when Carrie heard Jude's familiar voice, raised in command to a team somewhere not far

204

ahead of them. He hadn't come into view yet, but she could tell it was him. Knowing he'd probably taken a temporary job driving a team, she also knew he'd ask more questions than she wanted to answer. She reined the horse sharply to the left and moved into the trackless woods.

Rob piped up, "Mama, did you hear Uncle Jude?"

"Shhh. Rob, we're going to play a game of hide and seek with Uncle Jude. Now you be real quiet." She held him tightly and the horse, an old one who was even tempered most of the time, did as she bade him and plodded his way into the bush. Carrie halted him, and, hardly breathing, hoping desperately she'd gone far enough to keep them from being seen, listened as Jude encouraged his team.

"Giddy up thar, fellers, it's not far now. You can make it!" There was the snap of a whip, but Carrie knew Jude never hit an animal; he just made the whip sing in the air above them. Somehow, it always worked.

He began to sing in that rough, pleasant growl he had. "Oh, ol' Dan Tucker was a fine old man, washed his face in a fryin' pan. Combed his hair with a wagon wheel, died with a toothache in his heel!"

Rob quivered with excitement; Carrie quivered with fear they'd be discovered. It wasn't long before the woods were silent again, silent in a different way. There was still the chirrup of birds and crickets, the occasional croaking of the frogs, but those were not threatening sounds. Rob's little body shook with excitement, and he giggled out loud. "We fooled him!"

"Yes, Robbie, we fooled him. He didn't even know we were here." Carrie knew she had to get moving, because the daylight was fading fast. There'd been no real sunshine all day, only a heavy, low, gray sky. She couldn't see the sky now, except in tiny patches through the leafy canopy above them.

Just then a rabbit exploded through the bush to the side of them, followed closely by a fox. The horse, normally quite docile and gentle, shied and wheeled in a circle twice, three times. Startled, Carrie still managed to hang on to the saddle and to Rob.

Rob, thinking the whole thing was a lark, laughed. "Do it again, Mama!"

Her fear made her say more sharply than she intended, "Hush, Rob, and be still!" She nudged the horse with her heels and urged him in the direction she believed they'd come. They weren't more than twenty yards from the road, she was sure. If they didn't meet any more people who knew them, Carrie hoped to be in Beaumont before nightfall.

A half hour later she knew what must have happened when the horse had shied. They'd gotten turned around, and she'd somehow gone the wrong way. Her throat tight, her mouth dry with the fear that they were lost, she was grateful when Rob sagged against her, his thumb in his mouth. He usually took a nap long before now, and habit was strong. Carrie had no watch with her, but she could tell the afternoon was sliding into early evening. She pulled the reins up, for more reasons than one. She hadn't the least idea which way the road was now, and the thick tangle of growth prohibited moving much further.

The labyrinth of vines and swamp had deceived her. She peered into the hidden, murky depths of the woods, but was unable to see her way out. She knew that the muttering she heard was probably owls, knew it in her head. And still her heart pounded in her breast, her arms tightened involuntarily around the sleeping child.

Her head had not stopped aching since the day before yesterday, and now there was a peculiar ringing in her ears. Suddenly she wanted nothing more than to lie down, to sleep as the child was sleeping.

She managed to dismount without waking Rob, to slip off the saddlebags which held the small store of food and water she'd thought Rob might need. She'd only drink a little, to calm the raging thirst. Only a little. In her haste to find the water, she neglected to tether the horse securely, but he was an obedient old animal and stood patiently, head down, as she lay Rob on the ground and took a frantic swallow of the water.

I won't drink any more. I'll save the rest for Rob. One last swallow, then no more . . . not a single drop more . . .

She lay down beside Rob, curving her body close to his, her arm protectively around him. Something in the farthest recesses of her mind told her that at all costs she must see that Rob had what he needed.

The woods' silence was almost comforting—the churring of insects, the frogs' chorus, the dry rattle of palmetto leaves when the wind moved. She stared at the close-woven arch over their heads, through which very little of the gray afternoon light seeped. At least it wasn't dark. If only her head didn't hurt so badly, if only she weren't so warm.

Warm. She struggled sleepily with the idea, knowing something was wrong with it. Like a child, like Rob did sometimes, she puffed her breath out, and it made a little while cloud for an instant. The air wasn't warm. The woods weren't warm. Everything was cold. But she felt the heat within her body, felt it on her face. Maybe if she slept for a while, she'd feel better. Brain fuzzy, eyes hurting. Close them for a while. Sleep.

"Mama, wake up. Mama?"

Carrie felt Rob's hands patting her face, but her head hurt too bad to open her eyes. "Go . . . go back to sleep, Rob . . ."

"But I'm hungry, and I want a drink."

Something in his tone forced Carrie to open her eyes. To her horror, she saw that it was very dark, and that they were not in their room at the boarding house. *Where were they?* She struggled to sit up, felt the chill dampness beneath her hand. She was outside, somewhere outside . . . dimly she remembered leaving Saratoga. But why? And why was she here, with Rob? It was very dark . . .

"I want a drink," whimpered Rob. "I'm thirsty."

Carrie tried very hard to think, but her mind refused to cooperate. She couldn't remember, couldn't piece together what was happening to them, but somehow she forced herself to respond to the child. "There, Rob, it's all right." *My throat hurts* . . . "Here, here's some water," she said, finally remembering the flask. She fumbled with its cap and managed to get it open without spilling the contents.

My fingers feel funny.

"Don't drink it too fast, Rob." *I'm so thirsty* . . .

Rob carefully tipped it up and drank greedily. "Want some, Mama?"

She took the slim metal flask. "I . . . no, I'm not thirsty."

"Well. I'm hungry."

Carrie rubbed her eyes, trying to think. Then she said, "The bag, Mrs. Gallagher's oatmeal cookies." It took a while for her to find them, and when she did, she felt exhausted, as though she'd been working in the kitchen all day. *My brain hurts.*

Satisfied, Rob quietly ate his way through three cookies, and as children will, he accepted the situation and didn't question the fact that it was nighttime and they were out-of-doors. "Are we still hiding from Uncle Jude?" he asked.

Squeezing her eyes shut against the pain, against the horrible knowledge that Jude couldn't find them now even if he was looking, Carrie murmured, "Yes, Rob."

"But it's dark."

Carrie heard the beginning of fear in his voice. "There's nothing to be afraid of, Rob—"

Just then a cry, a long terrifying scream rang out and echoed through the inky blackness; then came the sound of many scurrying feet. "Ohhhh!" Carrie's wail was involuntary; Rob flung himself at her, crying.

"What was that? What is it, Mama?"

She held him tight. It had sounded like a woman screaming in mortal pain. She could hear the awful sound echoing round and round in her throbbing head. It was so dark, so dark. "Hush, hush, Rob. It will be all right . . . all right." His face was buried in her midsection, and Carrie's head, so heavy a moment before, suddenly felt weightless. And though she thought it would have been easier to hold it up now, she found she couldn't. It sank to Rob's own, and the two of them huddled together beneath her wool cape. It was so dark. "Sing to me, Rob. Please sing to me."

There was a little silence as the child tried to fathom their circumstances, and could not. Finally he began, his voice quavering. "Ol' Dan Tucker was a fine ol' man . . ." He stopped, having forgotten the rest of the words. Then he began again. "Jesus loves me, this I know . . . for the Bible tells me so . . ." But that was all he could remember of that one, too. "Mama—"

"It's all right, Rob. He will take care of you, of us. Jesus does love you." It was so dark. Carrie struggled to clear her mind. What had that man said, that preacher, Brother Teale? "I am the light of the world, he who follows me shall not walk in darkness, but shall have the light of life."

"Oh, Jesus," she whispered, "it's so dark . . . I need you. Help me, help me and Rob, please. I believe you can . . . I believe you will . . . I would follow you if I could see you . . ."

The black of the Thicket all around them was deep and unyielding. Rob finally drifted into sleep, comforted by Carrie's warmth, her arms close around him. Carrie's eyes were shut tightly, but in her head, her mind, her heart, it was not dark. She was not asleep, not unconscious, but somewhere in between, or beyond. And the lovely, clear, pure light that flooded her soul calmed her, made her smile. The sound of the scream did not come again, though two yellow eyes gleamed in the brush nearby.

Owls winged slowly, forbiddingly overhead, making their sure, deadly way to little scurrying creatures who would not be alive when dawn came again. All around the two, the woman and the child she sheltered with fevered body, were sounds of nocturnal animals large and small, prowling through the tangled brush, whirring through the air above them.

CHAPTER 20

*Heal me, O Lord, and I shall be healed; save me, and I shall be
saved; for thou art my praise.*   *Jeremiah 17:14*

The two search parties met in Saratoga the next morning,
and greeted each other with the same report. Jude said heavily,
"We could look 'til doomsday and not find 'em."

"Don't say that," was Adam's sharp command. "You men,
get some breakfast, and those of you who can and are still willing, we'll continue the search in half an hour."

"Half an hour," groaned one man. "It'd take a half day to
get the kinks outta my poor body."

"I'll say, and we didn't see hide nor hair of 'em," another
grizzled searcher chimed in.

"All the more reason to set off again immediately," said
Adam grimly. "I'm very much afraid Carrie . . . Miss Chaumont
may be ill."

"Typhoid?" asked Jude, scowling.

Adam nodded and was about to say something further when
he saw Jeannie come out of the boardinghouse, then hasten
over to where the men stood at the hitching rail. "Jeannie," he
said tensely, "do you have any news?"

"In a way. Uncle Jude's horse came back to the stable."

The sudden bleak look on Adam's face was the same he saw
on Jeannie's and on Jude's. "That means they're on foot. Not
good."

"No, but there's a man inside who says he was traveling on
the road to Kountze, and he saw the horse come out of the
woods, riderless."

Jude shook his head. "Purty slim chance, Dr. Adam, that
we can trace 'em that way. What we need is some good dogs.

210

No telling how far the horse wandered after he got loose."

"We have to try, Jude," Adam insisted, "and we certainly don't have any other leads." Jude nodded glumly and started to follow Jeannie and Adam into the boardinghouse when a straggle-bearded man came over to Adam just as they were about to enter.

He spoke in a careful, low drawl as he said, "My name's Wilson, Dr. Jarrett, and I heerd Jude mention as how you needed dawgs. Wal, I got a pack of good 'uns you fellers're welcome to use. I'll come along, too, a'course." At Adam's gratified expression he muttered, "Cain't see why y'all didn't think of it in the first place."

Hope rose strong in Adam. "Will you need something that belonged—*belongs* to them?" he asked, cursing inwardly at his slip.

"Shore enough, that ought to be of some help." He nodded, and spat carefully away from Adam's black boots.

"Is it far to your home?" asked Adam, eager to be out looking again. He was relieved when the man shrugged, pulled up his drooping britches and mentioned that he "never went nowhere without his dawgs, that they was over at the stables waitin'."

Jeannie, who'd been listening silently, volunteered to get something of Carrie's and Rob's, biting her lip at the spasm of pain that crossed Adam's face.

Less than the promised half an hour later, Adam and several of the men he'd persuaded to accompany them—plus Wilson and his dogs—set out for the spot described by the man who'd seen Jude's horse. Knowing how vital it was that they find Carrie soon, Adam pushed them all unmercifully. At least there were a few weak but welcome rays of sunlight as they spread out ten feet apart and scoured the woods for any sign of the young woman and boy.

They stamped over the forest floor of fallen trees, hindered by briar and brush, paying little attention to the wild beauty of holly and dogwood, oak and maple, hawthorne, trailing vines and draped Spanish moss. Overhead there was little evidence of the sky, and very little sense of direction had it not been for the mournfully excited baying of Wilson's dogs.

Stumbling over fallen logs, circling sloughs, they cursed the dew-wet webs that softly smacked their faces, the disturbed spiders that scurried down their shirt collars. There was never a word about giving up, only a grim intent to find the lost pair, the unspoken hope that they'd find them before it was too late.

None of the weary searchers could have said how much time had elapsed since they'd begun to search, but it was close to three o'clock that afternoon when the timbre of the dogs' cries changed.

Wilson called out, "They've found something!"

Adam, near enough to hear the words, found he couldn't speak as he followed the man toward the sound. His heart thudded painfully in his chest in dread of what they might find.

The dogs were fixed in a semi-circle, their whip-thin tails wagging furiously, their wrinkle-folded eyes alight with interest. Rob, wide-eyed, sat staring back at them, with no fear, nothing but delight at being awakened by a whole pack of hound dogs that looked like his beloved pup at Grannie Annie's.

Adam rushed up and dropped to his knees, his arms outstretched. Rob flung himself at his father.

They'd all agreed—Adam, Jeannie, and Mrs. Gallagher—that the best place for Carrie would be at Jeannie's cabin. It would have been foolish to take her back to the boardinghouse and run the risk of infecting the men there. Mrs. Gallagher had taken Rob, saying she and Jude would watch him closely for signs of fever. And Luce Barrett welcomed, almost begged, the opportunity to help with Carrie's nursing. She obviously looked upon the situation as means of making up for what she'd done.

She helped Jeannie bathe Carrie's hot, restless body with tepid water countless times during the following days and nights in a futile attempt to lower the damaging fever. Carrie was often delirious now, and cried out in terror when the nightmares assailed her.

Through it all, Luce had been a rock. Saying only that it was "fitting" that she should help, she had done her share, and more, of the distasteful chores. Scrubbing Carrie's soiled nightclothes with lye soap and washing the endless amount of dirty linens again and again were, more often than not, what Luce insisted on doing, leaving Jeannie free to nurse Carrie.

In spite of the hard work, Luce loved the peace, the calm that seemed to be in the air at Jeannie's cabin; the wonderful jumble of mysterious jars, of appealing smells—except for here, in Jeannie's bedroom, with that terrible odor she'd come to dread, to hate. It was the odor of typhoid fever. A kind of revolting, dead mouse smell; perhaps it was the smell of death itself. To combat it, Jeannie had a bayberry candle burning all the time, and a pretty little nosegay of wildflowers by the bedside. Luce suspected the flowers were often there, sickness or not. She'd been around Jeannie Gallagher long enough to see her love for flowers. She'd also been around her enough to want to imitate her in as many ways as possible.

Yes, she thought as she watched Jeannie carefully wipe Carrie's flushed face with a damp cloth, *I want to be like her . . . to know how to help, to heal people, not be sick and make them sick, too.* This desire to help, in any way that Jeannie needed, manifested itself in the timid question, "Is there something I can do?" Repeated frequently but earnestly, it almost always resulted in Jeannie responding, as she did now, with a useful task for Luce.

"Why, yes, why don't you mix up some more juice. She might like the plum this time, Luce."

Luce hesitated a moment. Her expression as she gazed at Carrie's face was much the same as it had been when Adam confronted her in Beaumont with the horrifying fact that she had brought the typhoid to the men at the hotel, to her own dear Danny. Carrie cried out in delirium just then, and Luce bit her lip. "I'll get the juice," she said, and moved from the room, though she lingered at the door even yet.

Jeannie looked up; she'd forgotten Luce was there. "Thank you. Luce, you've been a big help. I can't begin to think what I'd have done without you." She saw the look of gratitude the girl flashed her as she left. Her words were true enough; it had been five days since they'd found Carrie and Rob in the woods, and Luce had quietly and unfailingly been Jeannie's right hand. Rob showed no signs of being any the worse from their ordeal, nor any signs of typhoid fever, but Carrie was another story altogether. Her fever had reached 104 the night they'd brought her in and although it climbed higher at times, it never dropped lower, to Jeannie's consternation.

She had vowed to make absolutely certain that Carrie received the most careful, the most dedicated nursing possible. She well knew that such nursing could mean the difference between life and death, and was determined at all costs to pull Carrie through.

Jeannie sat down quietly in the chair beside the bed. Even with the flush of fever on her cheeks, the long black hair a bit tangled, the deep blue eyes closed in restless sleep, Carrie was so lovely that Jeannie had to chastise herself for her envy of the woman's beauty. Why Adam hadn't fallen in love with her was a mystery. And Carrie loved him so. Often in her delirium she would cry out for him, or moan his name softly over and over. And when he was there, which was several times a day, Carrie would visibly relax when he took her hands, whose palms were yellow now from the horrid fever, and spoke gently, quietly to her.

"There, there, Carrie," he would soothe, "try to rest. You're safe now, and I'll never let anything harm you again. I'll keep you safe, I'll take care of you." The promises fell from his lips, but his black eyes were full of the bitter fear that he couldn't keep them, that the fever would claim her. Very rarely would he allow himself to meet Jeannie's eyes, and never did he speak to her of anything but Carrie's treatment.

What had he said this noon? "I'll be back this evening. There's been a serious accident over at the Hooks well."

Jeannie had assured him, for the hundredth time, it seemed, that she and Luce would take care of Carrie.

"She mustn't die." He'd said it in a low, almost inaudible tone just before he left her bedside, his face hard and set.

Jeannie gently swabbed out Carrie's mouth to rid her of the awful phlegm that collected there, and applied a thin layer of glycerine to her parched lips, then sat down again to wait.

For what? she asked herself. She knew very well that the twenty-four hours Carrie had spent in the woods had weakened her considerably, that the stress of the previous weeks had taken its toll—stress brought about not only by her selfless nursing of the men at the boardinghouse, but by the situation between the three of them. It was certainly the knowledge that Adam would never love her as he had Bethany Jarrett, as he now loved Jeannie herself, that had weakened Carrie the most.

I never wanted him to love me, never wanted to love a man like Adam, never thought I could, or would. But I do. I do, and right now I'm waiting for the sound of his footsteps, the sound of his voice . . . "Oh, Father, forgive me, please . . ." She spoke the last words aloud, and was startled to hear them.

The late afternoon light that slanted in the west window was too weak to be warm, but Jeannie's pain-filled heart saw it as evidence of the Spirit in the room, of His presence that had been sent to warm her, to offer her the peace that eluded her . . . to comfort her. The Comforter. And suddenly she knew that God had forgiven her yet again, and she did feel His peace. Holding both of Carrie's hands in hers, Jeannie laid her head on the coverlet, her lips moving silently, the prayer in her heart asking only that His will be done.

That was how Adam found her. The light of day had gone, and no lamp had been lit. He stood in the doorway, the scene before him filling his senses. Instinct told him Carrie wouldn't make it, but his stubborn will kept saying, *We must pull her through; we cannot let her die.* And though he couldn't bring himself to pray to Jeannie's God, or even to believe there was a God, he still clung to the faint hope that her prayers would be heard. For he knew that she was praying for Carrie.

"Jeannie."

At the quiet, intense sound of her name being spoken, she raised her head to see his tall, broad outline in the doorway. "Adam, I'm so glad you're here."

"She's worse?"

"I'm afraid so," she admitted, her voice no more than a whisper.

"Luce, would you bring a light, please?" he said as he came into the room. "What makes you think she's worse?"

Jeannie moved aside and watched as he took out his stethoscope, put the thing to the thin, white muslin nightgown covering Carrie's body and listened to her heart. "I . . . it's just a feeling, mostly. But then, I—" She halted as Luce, lighted lamp in hand, walked softly in and placed it on the chest beside the bed.

Luce didn't speak, but neither did she leave. Jeannie gave her as much of a smile as she could muster. "Luce has been more of a help than I could ever tell you. But we both agree the delirium is deeper, somehow."

Adam took Carrie's hands in his own, and for an unmeasurable space of time they were all silent, their attention focused on the small figure on the bed.

Suddenly Carrie awoke, her blue eyes looking wildly around the room—at Adam, at Luce, finally at Jeannie. "Jeannie!" she gasped, the painful panic in the word making them hold their breath in fear.

In an instant Jeannie was at the other side of the bed on her knees, her hand smoothing Carrie's knotted brow. "I'm here, Carrie, I'm here."

"It was so dark, and someone was screaming . . . I'm afraid, it was so dark in the woods." She pulled her hands from Adam's grasp; they fluttered like wounded birds for a moment, then dropped to the coverlet where they picked nervously at nothing.

"Bring the lamp closer, Luce." Jeannie leaned nearer. "Carrie, dear, you're here in my room, you're safe. Adam is here, and so am I. You're safe."

But Carrie did not look at Adam again. It was Jeannie's anxious white face she was staring at as she slowly recognized her, as she came awake more fully. "I'm safe," she repeated. "Yes, I am, you know. He's here."

"Yes, Carrie, Adam's here—"

"No, no, not Adam. *He's* here. He is the light, like Brother Teale said." For a moment her eyes shut wearily. Then they opened again, and the look on her face was no longer one of fear or pain. It was one of excitement . . . of joy.

"Carrie," said Jeannie, her voice hushed, "tell me what you see."

"Light. Beautiful light. It's not dark anymore. He loves me, you know. And I love Him. I love Him. And He's waiting for me in the light . . ."

"Oh, my dear Carrie," whispered Jeannie. "You're right, He *is* the light, and He *does* love you, He does!"

"Yes." There was only a faint whisper. The restless fingers quieted slowly, and Carrie's face, radiant now, grew still.

A gasp from Luce was lost in the explosive word that burst from Adam's lips. *"No!"*

But Jeannie knew that Carrie had slipped away, was now a part of the Light in a far better way. "Adam, she's gone."

"No." His shoulders hunched, he bowed his head lower and lower until his black hair touched Carrie's still form. "Carrie . . . forgive me. I'm so sorry. I failed you; I failed you from the beginning." He didn't cry, but his body was full of pain and shocked anger.

Jeannie reached over the bed to place a hand softly on his shoulder. "Adam, she's at peace now; she's not in pain anymore."

His head jerked up. "How do you know that? How does anyone know what's out there?"

She withdrew her hand, shocked in spite of herself at his vehemence. "I know what the Scripture tells me, and I have faith that it's true."

"Faith? Don't make me laugh! What did your faith do for

Carrie? For Danny? Or any of the poor wretched souls you mouth these useless platitudes to?"

"Adam, don't do this—" Jeannie began, but he cut her off.

"Me? Don't do what? I'm not the one who brought typhoid to these people. I've done my best to help them!"

Stricken, Luce put a hand to her mouth, and the tears that had been threatening a few moments before flooded her eyes, poured down her face. "But I didn't mean to, I didn't mean to!" Before Jeannie could stop her, she'd run from the room.

His face stony, Adam muttered, "I didn't mean to hurt her. I wasn't thinking."

"No, you sure weren't!" Jeannie's retort was sharper by far than she'd intended, but the look on Luce's face had been terrible. She felt torn; she wanted to go after the girl, but her instinct told her she must stay with Adam, that he was very close to the edge of absolute despair. His next words proved it.

"You're right, of course. Everything that has happened is because of me. I'm a miserable excuse for a man." If he had not said the words with such calm, detached certainty, they would have been melodramatic, even comic. But there was a deadly seriousness about them that was chilling.

Jeannie shivered. "Adam, you're looking at the whole situation from the wrong angle."

"From my own," he replied, quietly now. "What other angle is there than one's own?"

She longed with all her heart to say, *From God's*. But something kept her from it. "Let me help you—"

His smile was cold. "Like you helped Carrie? And Danny? And that poor girl at the saloon who thought she could solve her problem with a knitting needle? No thank you. I can manage without your help—or your God's help, either."

"But you can't," she whispered. "No one can."

"I can, and I will." He stood, and without looking at the still form on the bed, he added, "Poor Carrie. All she wanted was for me to love her, to let her love me and Rob. But I denied her everything. Poor Carrie."

Jeannie thought her heart would break as she watched him walk slowly out, his footsteps sounding very loud in the deathly quiet of the room. She wanted to go to him, to hold him until her healing tears cleansed him, until he would allow God to heal his mortally wounded spirit. But she knew that he would only push her away, even as he'd pushed Carrie away, as he was pushing God away at this very moment.

She heard the outside door close, knew he was gone. Then, and only then, did she begin to pray again: that God would not cease speaking to Adam's heart, that He wouldn't cease calling Adam to himself. And she prayed, more fervently than she'd ever prayed any prayer, that God would choose her to bring Adam Jarrett to a full knowledge of the Lord he now denied. Somehow she knew that Carrie would understand, would have prayed together with Jeannie if she had not slipped away to be with God, her new Father.

CHAPTER 21

Trouble and anguish shall make him afraid; they shall prevail against him, as a king ready to the battle. For he stretcheth out his hand against God, and strengtheneth himself against the Almighty.   *Job 15:24–25*

The winter that followed Carrie's death was not a severe one to a man born and raised in upper New York state, as Adam had been. But throughout the long, foggy, bone-chilling weeks, he swore he'd never been colder in his life. The miasma that hung over the bayous of the Big Thicket was the same that lurked in Adam Jarrett's soul—lurked and mocked, whenever he was still enough to hear. It wasn't often that he was, however.

If he had been a man driven when he'd first come to the Thicket, it was doubly true now. And although the thrust of his practice had shifted—the bulk of it consisted of Thicket folk now—he still was called when certain boomers got themselves in trouble. It was a well-known fact that he could stitch up a cut neater and faster than most around and dig out a bullet with no more pain than was absolutely necessary. Folks even called him to deliver babies when Jeannie Gallagher was not available.

Too frequently Adam worked almost around the clock, ignoring the warning signals his body had begun to send: the occasional lapse of memory, his increasingly short temper. A couple of times he'd found himself riding on some lonely road or trail and realized he had no idea where he'd been or where he was supposed to be going. Often people would say something to him and then laughingly accuse him of wool-gathering. He'd blink, and apologize with, "I'm sorry ... What did you say?"

219

Not even the letter from Landra and Hollis, announcing their new baby boy, lifted his spirits.

He seldom saw Jeannie. She tactfully refrained from coming to her mother's boardinghouse at mealtimes, aware that Adam ate there, that it was about the only time he saw Rob. Almost apathetically Adam had given over the care of his son to the willing Mrs. Gallagher and Jude, both of whom loved the child dearly. Adam persuaded himself Rob was none the worse for it, and perhaps this was mostly true. For since he'd stopped grieving openly for Carrie, Rob seemed to be thriving. After a few anxious weeks they'd all breathed more easily when it became obvious that he was going to escape the fever and there were no new cases in the area.

One day in late February Adam met Luce Barrett on the street, surprised when she smiled and spoke to him. He'd been rude, even brutal to her that last time he'd seen her. Aware of that, he said gruffly, "Luce, I never apologized to you for my behavior that day . . . the last time I saw you." Having spent the weeks since avoiding even thinking of that day, the next words came hard. "I'm sorry."

"Oh, Dr. Adam, you don't have to apologize. I know how hard Carrie's death was for you. It's all right, really it is."

He nodded, thinking she looked different, somehow. Her hair was curled prettily in a loose, shining knot high on her head; her eyes were clear and looked directly into his. She wore a demure, becoming green calico dress, and her face seemed almost to shine. *Was it health*, he mused, *or was it something else?* "Luce, you're looking well."

"Thank you, Dr. Adam, I am well."

Her smile was sweet, so different from the first time he'd seen her. He felt prompted to ask, though it wasn't like him at all, "Could it be that you're in love?"

She laughed, delighted. "I guess you could say that! I've certainly found someone who loves me. I've always admired Jeannie Gallagher, wanted to be like her. And since I've been living with her—"

"You're still there?" interrupted Adam, chiding himself for the quick stir of interest he felt.

"Yes, I am, though I hope for not too much longer. She's given me so much more than a place to stay . . ." Luce trailed off, then began again, tears shining her eyes slightly, "She told me about the Lord, how He loved me no matter what I'd done, how He'll love me forever and can make me into a different person. And one day it just didn't make sense to say no anymore to someone who loved me that much. I gave my heart to Him, and that's why I'm so happy."

He stared at Luce, suddenly angry, thinking how wrong it was for Jeannie to force her beliefs on this poor girl, who depended on Jeannie for the very roof over her head. He started to say so aloud, then decided she wasn't the one who should hear it. Knowing she wasn't really to blame, he said politely, "That's nice, Luce."

"Dr. Adam, I've been talking to my ma, and she says she thinks my pa might be willing to talk about my coming home. And if I do, I can tell them what I've found, and how happy it's made me, and they'll believe, too! Jeannie says that's how it's supposed to work. She tells me; I tell them."

Adam suppressed the sharp retort that rose to his lips. "Yes. Well, take care, Luce, and don't forget to observe all the precautions we discussed."

She assured him she would, and he hastened down the street to his office, still very angry. By the time he reached the general store, he'd made a decision; he would go to Jeannie's and tell her how wrong he thought she was to take advantage of Luce when she was so terribly vulnerable. There were patients waiting in his office, and though he didn't want to admit it to himself, for once he wished the office were empty, that he could go inside and lie down and sleep forever. For a few moments he leaned against the upright post of the hitching rail, thinking, as he had several times during the day and the night before, that his chest hurt when he breathed. He assured himself it was nothing, that he'd only been working too hard. However, it didn't dissuade him from his decision to ride to Jeannie Gallaghers'. He straightened and stepped inside.

It was early evening before he was free to go, and as he approached Jeannie's cabin, the windows on either side of the sturdy Z-door glowed with welcoming light. Unreasonably aggravated at the sight, he passed a hand over his eyes, shutting out the cabin for a moment; his head hurt slightly.

She met him at the door as though she'd seen him coming. The light in her eyes was no less welcoming than that in the windows. "Why, Dr. Adam! It's so good to see you! Come in." She stood aside as he stepped in. Seeing the set, grim look on his face, she added, "Is something wrong?"

Adam looked around the cozy room with that same unreasonable resentment he'd felt earlier. There were two chairs drawn up to the fireplace, with a graceful-homely bent twig table between them. The fire had burned to the rosy, glowing, just-right-stage that offered optimum warmth. An earthenware teapot and two cups waited on the table. "Is Luce here?"

"No, not yet. I'm expecting her in a bit, though." She stood quietly, expectantly, her arms at her sides.

He stared at her for a long moment. She was wearing the cinnamon-brown dress, the one that made her look like the best of autumn days, and she looked so marvelously alive, as Luce had, that he was angry all over again. He cursed himself inwardly for his illogical reaction, for the fact that he seemed unable to think clearly. "It's about Luce that I've come."

"Oh, is she all right?" Her brows knit in sudden concern. "Sit down, Adam, and tell me—"

"No thank you. I don't intend to stay that long. I saw Luce today, talked with her."

"And?" Those brown eyes were watchful, unwavering as she waited for him to speak.

"She seemed well, but almost dangerously euphoric, and it worried me."

Jeannie's laugh was quick and low, a musical sound. "Sure, and you'll have to tell me what euphoric means!"

"It means she showed an extreme, excited happiness." As soon as the words were out he realized he should have phrased them differently.

Her gaze on him was speculative now. "Do you mean to stand there and tell me that being happy is medically dangerous?"

"I didn't mean to say that at all." He frowned. "What I mean to say is, that I find it highly improper for you to force your beliefs on a young woman as vulnerable as Luce obviously is. Just because you are allowing her to stay in your home doesn't give you the right to take advantage of her."

"Force her . . . take advantage of her?" echoed Jeannie. "She told you I did that?"

Adam saw that the surprise in her wide brown eyes was genuine. He couldn't think; the room suddenly seemed very hot. "Perhaps the word *forced* is too strong."

"It sure is! And you don't have any right to come here and say such things to me. I don't mind telling you, it makes me angry." The lights in her eyes were not just reflections from the fire; anger augmented them.

"Obviously we look at the matter differently."

"Obviously." She took a deep breath. "I'd like to know if you said these things to Luce."

"No, what do you take me for?"

"An interfering man who needs the very thing he's upset about poor Luce having, the love of God," she said with spirit. "And if you weren't so stubborn, you'd admit it!"

"I've seen no evidence that God can help with any of my troubles," he defended himself, knowing as soon as the words were out he shouldn't have said them, that she wouldn't allow them to go unchallenged.

"But Adam," she said softly now, "He can."

"As I've said before, there's no evidence that He's done anything. People still suffer, they die."

"Everyone suffers, and as a doctor you should realize better than any of us that everyone has to die. But to suffer knowing He's there, to die knowing He's waiting for you, don't you see, it makes it all bearable."

"I don't see it at all. What you're saying is ridiculous."

She stared at him. For a long moment the only sounds were the merry snap of the fire and the faint, sad call of one mourning dove to its mate that pierced the gloom outside. "It's because your eyes are blinded, Adam. You won't let yourself believe—"

"No, I won't! And from now on, it might be best if we stayed clear of each other, believing as we do."

"I've been trying," she replied quietly, the anger she'd felt a moment before ebbing away in the face of his awesome pain. She looked at him closely, seeing for the first time the unnatural flush of his face. "Do you feel all right?"

"Of course I do! I'm not one of your poor, vulnerable, broken birds. I came to—" He broke off, putting a hand to his forehead. If only his head didn't hurt, he could think better.

"Why did you come, Adam?" she asked, guessing why, knowing he probably couldn't admit that he was searching, and in desperate need, that the business about Luce was just a pretense.

"You know why, because I saw Luce and was concerned about her. But don't worry, I won't come again. This is the last time." The warmth of the room, which had seemed so welcome before, felt suddenly oppressive. Adam struggled to breathe, and felt as though all the air had been sucked from the little cabin, from his body. He had to get outside where he could breathe. He dragged his black hat on and turned to go.

"It doesn't have to be the last time, I don't want it to be," she said just before he opened the door. "I'm praying that you'll come to—"

"Save your prayers," he grunted over his shoulder. "I'm past God's help anyway." He stumbled a little as he went out the door, then walked unsteadily to where his horse was tethered. Each step was frighteningly difficult, as though his feet were encased in lead. The effort of putting one before the other made his breathing harsh and labored. For a long time he stood at the side of his horse, a curious detachment plaguing him.

It seemed as though he were outside his body, watching himself as his head slumped down, touching the horse's neck; watching as he tried to mount the horse, only to slide slowly, inexorably to the ground. Then there was nothing but blackness.

"Adam!" cried Jeannie. She'd stood rooted in the doorway, a bewildering set of emotions assailing her as she watched. Anger at his stubbornness, pain at his great need and refusal, and finally, horror as she saw him slump to the ground. "Adam!"

She was at his side in a moment, deeply shocked to find that his face was burning hot, his pulse racing, and he was barely conscious. "Are you in pain?"

The groan that escaped his lips was faintly audible; his hands clutching at his chest told the story. There was something far worse wrong with Adam Jarrett than anger or fatigue.

The chill evening air swirled around them and Jeannie knew she must get him back inside. She knelt on the damp ground beside him and cradled his head on her lap, anxiety coursing through her as she felt the heat in his body. "Adam, can you hear me?"

"Of . . . course. I must have fallen . . ."

In the dim light she could see the glaze of fever in his black eyes. "You mustn't lie here, you have to help me get you inside. Can you stand?"

"Of course," he repeated. But when he thrust her aside and tried to alone, he could not.

Jeannie got one arm around his body, and with her other hand lifted his arm over her shoulders. Slowly they rose together. Though his feet stumbled, and twice they almost fell, she managed to get him into the cabin and onto her bed.

"Have to get back to the office; there'll be people waiting," he mumbled. Looking around the room and finding it unfamiliar brought a scowl of confusion to his flushed face.

"Oh no, you don't," Jeannie stated firmly. "You must lie down and do as I tell you."

"But—"

"No buts, Doctor. You're a very sick man." Jeannie knew it would be best to get him out of his clothes and into a clean nightshirt, but she hesitated, something she wouldn't have done had she not felt the way she did about Adam Jarrett. Instead, she took off his boots and jacket, and pressed him back against the pillow when he tried to rise. Then she lifted his feet onto the bed and covered him with a quilt.

"Now, stay put until I fetch your bag." She bent over him, her hands on her hips, her eyes flashing a warning until he nodded in agreement.

A short time later Jeannie sat on the edge of the bed, after listening to his chest carefully. "Adam, we both know that I'm not a doctor, but I'll tell you straight off that I know you're a very sick man." She was clasping the stethoscope in both hands, and her troubled eyes held his. "Grannie Annie would say your lungs are consolidated. I'm sure you also feel a great deal of pressure, as well as pain, when you try to breathe deeply. Don't try to fib to me," she added at the expression on his face.

But Adam couldn't deny her words. His exhaustion was so deep he could barely force himself to nod. "I feel as though I can't get enough air..." His breathing was shallow and rapid now, and his pulse had begun to race alarmingly.

She nodded. "I know. Try not to panic. Are you thirsty?" Once again he nodded weakly, and she went to get a cup of water. She lifted his head and held the cup at just the right angle, biting the inside of her mouth as she saw how hard he worked to breathe. "Adam, tell me what you want me to do. Is there something in your bag that would help?"

"Look . . . look for the elixir of veratrum." He stopped, his eyes closed.

Jeannie rummaged in the large black bag, fighting an unaccustomed panic. She knew her lack of objectivity was caused by her feelings for Adam. She despised the weakness it showed and fought it. It could keep her from correctly assessing the situation. She found the little cork-stoppered brown bottle labled Veratrum Viride. "Here it is!" she exclaimed. "How much should I give you?"

"Not much." He didn't speak for a moment; his eyes were closed as he added with effort, "Large dose can be dangerous."

"A half teaspoon?" Seeing that barely perceptible nod, Jeannie hurried to the kitchen to get a spoon.

Within a short time she was relieved to see that his pulse had slowed, and a faint sheen of perspiration appeared on his face. His fever dropped a degree or two, as well. But when she listened to his chest again her expression was grave. "Adam, I fear you have pneumonia. Have you been coughing at all?"

He shook his head. "No. Most likely . . . you're right."

She stared at him for what seemed like an endless moment, knowing that for all practical purposes, his treatment was up to her. She could not bring herself to leave him in order to seek help, and her years of nursing told her she needed desperately to help him cough, to rid himself of the deadly fluid collecting in his lungs.

"Adam, I'm going to try a poultice. Is that all right?"

There was no answer this time, not even a nod. His eyes were closed, and Jeannie stood looking down at his laboring body for a few moments. Then, the decision made, she whirled and went to the little trapdoor beneath her kitchen floor where she stored her root vegetables and dragged up a basket of onions. By the time she'd peeled and sliced a double bowlful, the tears were streaming down her cheeks. They were not only from the aromatic onions; the prayers that winged their way from her heart to the Father were partly the cause.

Oh, God, he doesn't know you yet. Please show me how to keep him alive so he won't die without you. He's known such heartaches. I can feel it in my own heart even though he's not spoken it. I know it's your will that not one of us perish without coming to know you, to know your love. Oh, Father, he's so alone, so desperate, so miserable!

Just as she had the first batch of onions softening in the black iron skillet and was measuring a length of worn sheeting to tear it into squares, Luce came in the back door, shedding her bonnet and dropping a parcel in the chair.

"I could smell those onions clear outside!" She laughed. "What are you cooking, anyway, and whose horse is that outside?" A quick shake of Jeannie's head and a closer look at her face made Luce's expression turn grave. "What's wrong, Jeannie?"

With her head Jeannie indicated the bedroom. "It's Dr. Adam. He came to . . . to visit and collapsed at his horse."

"He collapsed?" cried Luce, her green eyes wide. "I just saw him in town."

"I know, he told me." Without explaining further, Jeannie continued, "I believe he has pneumonia, and if we don't get him coughing and help him get rid of some of the congestion in his lungs, he could get far worse," she finished, not wanting to say he could die, but knowing it was a very real, frightening possibility. "He's been driving himself so hard these past weeks he has no reserves of strength left, I'm afraid."

"What can I do?" asked Luce simply.

Jeannie's little smile was apologetic. "Do you mind spending the next few hours peeling onions?"

"Of course I don't." She went directly to the table and sat down, beginning at once. Halfway through peeling the first, she smiled through her tears. "I've heard of this, but never saw anybody do it. You're sure it works?"

"It has to," said Jeannie, her eyes dark with resolve. She spooned the hot, cooked onions onto the square of sheeting, folded it carefully, and carried it quickly into the adjoining bedroom. With a lot of tenderness and a few tugs, she removed his shirt. Placing the poultice on Adam's broad chest gave her a pang. He *was* a doctor, and this seemed such a homely remedy . . . but she'd seen it work often enough, knew it could if she was diligent enough.

Throughout the long hours of early night she and Luce took turns peeling the onions, cooking them, and making squares of the fragrant, steaming things. Jeannie placed them one time on Adam's chest, the next on his back. She had to change the quilts that covered him a couple of times, for he was soon sweating profusely and they were quite wet.

Jeannie knew this was a good sign, and redoubled her efforts with the poultices until her small hands were red and blistered. Once, when Luce timidly suggested she should relieve her, Jeannie shook her head. "No, Luce, I have to do it."

Luce, awed by Jeannie's intense devotion to the task at hand, to the man himself, nodded. She'd been living with Jeannie Gallagher long enough to divine the feeling her friend tried so carefully to hide; she realized Jeannie loved the tormented Dr. Jarrett even though she'd never said so in words. With tears in her eyes that had nothing to do with the onion poultices, she acknowledged softly, "I understand."

"Yes, I believe you do." Jeannie accepted the hand Luce extended, accepted the love she felt in its tender squeeze. "Luce—"

She was interrupted as Adam struggled to sit up, as he began to cough. It was a deep, rattling cough that came from the depths of his infected lungs. She rushed back to his side, supporting him, praying that the poultices had, indeed, done their intended work. "The basin, Luce, hand me the basin!"

Luce ran to do Jeannie's bidding and barely managed to reach them in time with the basin. She was appalled at the horrible-looking fluid that spewed from the doctor's mouth.

Jeannie murmured, "It must have been an abcess . . ." She held the basin with one hand, her other arm clutching his heaving shoulders.

When it was finally over and he lay spent on the pillow, Luce whispered, "Is he going to be all right, or was that a sign he's going to die?"

"Oh, no," assured Jeannie; the relief in her voice almost painful. "I think he'll be all right now, Luce, though it will still be a long, hard fight." Then, in a lower, troubled tone she added, "At least I believe his body will heal. As for his soul and heart, only God can tell."

CHAPTER 22

Therefore if any man be in Christ, he is a new creature: old things are passed away; behold, all things are become new.   *2 Corinthians 5:17*

Jeannie was right, it was the turning point for Adam. Throughout the rest of that interminable night, his body fought the infection that raged within him. At Jeannie's insistence Luce fell asleep some time after midnight, but she kept her vigil at the sick man's bedside all night. By the time morning crept into the room, her head was nodding. She had placed her chair against the wall and was able to rest a bit, listening for the familiar, insolent sound of her favorite rooster as he announced the new day.

Adam was calm and still now. He had fallen into a deep, exhausted sleep after the onion poultices had done their work. She well knew there was nothing more she could do except make certain he continued to rest and that he drank plenty of fluids. She gazed at him, grateful for the chance to look at his face. Her eyes wandered from the broad brow beneath his dark, damp hair to his Indian-straight nose, his fine mouth, his chin—a face that showed such strength even in sleep that it made her shiver.

Oh, Lord, he is strong in so many ways, and I love him for that strength. But I know he needs your strength more than ever. Please, speak to his heart especially now, make him open . . .

"Jeannie."

The sound of her name, spoken clearly but in such a low tone, brought her close to him. "Adam, what is it? Can I get you something?"

"No." His eyes closed again, then fluttered open. "This is your cabin."

She heard the question in his quiet, confused statement. Wanting to reach for his hand, she dared not as she explained, "You came last night to talk to me about Luce, but you collapsed as you were about to get on your horse."

"But what—"

"Pneumonia. Last night Luce and I put enough onions on your poor fevered body to feed all the boomers in Saratoga for a week!" She managed a shaky little laugh.

"Onion poultices?" One of his fine dark brows quirked slightly. "Not very scientific."

"But still effective. Doctor," she chided gently, "you coughed up enough bloody phlegm to make me believe you surely had an abcess in one, or maybe even both of your poor lungs."

"I . . . I'm sorry about the mess, the inconvenience," he muttered, his eyes struggling to focus. "It's morning. You've . . . have you been up all night?"

"That I have. You've been a very sick man."

He tried to sit up, but she rose immediately and gently pushed him back. "Stay put. You're not the doctor on this case; you're the patient. Hold on for a couple of minutes and I'll have some tea made in two shakes of a lamb's tail."

"But—"

She shook her head, the dishevelled red curls flying. "You're to rest and get better. I'm bound to see that you don't leave this room for however long it takes to get you well." She paused at the door to make sure he didn't try to get up again.

"But your reputation—"

"My reputation is good, Adam," she answered calmly. "People hereabouts know me. Besides," she added and her mouth curved in a smile for the first time in many hours, "as weak as you are, you're no threat a'tall, even to a little bitty woman like me."

Adam stared at the doorway long after she was gone. His mind was a jumble of impressions. Jeannie half pulling him inside last night, the nightmare of simmering onions and hot sweating hours, the blessed relief of the fever abating some time in the early morning, the fragrance of the bed in which he lay. Lavender, and another scent that was extremely pleasant, reminded him of the precious few times he'd been near her.

A feeling that he'd had before and repressed almost violently suddenly assailed him, a feeling that was almost overwhelming now in the aftermath of his ordeal. Something in his heart, at the very core of his being was, in some way he couldn't explain, urging him to . . . *to what?*

His head hurt with the effort of trying to figure it out. When Jeannie returned it was to find him with his eyes squeezed shut, his fingers rubbing his forehead over and over.

"Adam, what's wrong? Does your head hurt?" She put the tray, with its teapot and two cups, on the small table by the bed. Before she thought better of it, she sat close beside him, clasping his restless fingers with one hand, her other smoothing his forehead.

"Not just my head," he whispered. "It's deeper. It's . . ."

"It's your soul, Dr. Adam. The pain is in your soul, and only God can take it away. He longs to, you know." She held tightly to his hand. "But you must want Him to, you must allow Him to . . . He'll not force you."

He shook his head from side to side, over and over. "So much has happened, so much."

"Tell me, Adam; say it out loud." Jeannie's quiet words fell into the stillness of the little room.

"I loved my wife . . . I loved Bethany. Perhaps I loved her too much."

"Ah, no, we can never love too much." Her words were very, very soft.

His eyes were closed, as though he were living it all again. "After we married she wanted to go back to her home, in Louisiana. Away from her parents, from the new home her family had made in New York. We met in New York, you know."

Jeannie smoothed his fingers with her own. "Did you, now."

"Yes, and she told me from the beginning that she wanted to return to Greenlea, her childhood home across the river from New Orleans. I was willing. But then, I'd have done anything . . . anything for her. I would never have hurt her. You believe me, don't you?"

She felt the convulsive tightening of his hand. "Of course I believe you."

"And when she persuaded me that she had to have a child, even though she was . . . she had—" He chopped off his sentence, the look on his face full of such agony it made Jeannie's stomach twist.

"Go on," she encouraged quietly.

"She had leprosy."

In spite of her firm resolve to listen impassively no matter what Adam said, Jeannie felt almost faint. "She had . . ."

"Leprosy." He said it again, that harsh, ugly word. "And because of *my* weakness, she became pregnant with Rob. When I took him away to prevent his contracting the disease from her, it was the final straw, more than she could bear no matter what she'd sworn." His mouth quirked in a faint imitation, a terrible parody of a smile. "It's ironic, isn't it, that pneumonia was what killed her, not the leprosy itself. Maybe I'll die of it, too—"

"Hush, Adam, don't even say that!"

He ignored her passionate words. "She suffered more than any woman should have to. And when she could no longer bear the loss of her child, she deliberately went out and lay in the rain, knowing that in her weakened condition she would most likely contract it. And she never fought it at all, she just . . . died."

"Maybe you'd better rest now," said Jeannie, her voice full of pity.

"No, I've begun. I want to say it all." His black eyes sought hers. "There hasn't been anyone I could talk to since Landra."

"Landra?"

"Bethany's sister. She loved Bethany, too—everyone did. We grieved together, she and I. But it wasn't her fault that Bethany died; it was mine."

"I don't believe that," began Jeannie, but he cut her off.

"It's true. No matter how she begged, I should have been strong. I should have seen to it that she never had a child. I should have known what it would do to her to take her baby from her . . ." His face twisted in remembered pain.

"It's done, Adam. What's done is done," said Jeannie, feeling more helpless than she ever had in her life.

"Yes, that's true, isn't it?" he sighed with terrible bitterness. "And then things went from bad to worse. We kept it a secret for many months after she died; that she had suffered from leprosy, I mean. There were three others living at Greenlea, who were also victims of the disease. I was trying to help them, to treat them. But the villagers found out that we were 'harboring,' as they put it, those poor unfortunate souls. They were so terrified, so *prejudiced*, that they burned Greenlea, our home. As if that weren't bad enough, they also burned the plantation down the road where we'd hoped to establish a hospital for the treatment of people who have Hansen's disease. They burned them both to the ground, and with that insane action went our hopes, all our hopes." His voice had sunk to a whisper, from the awful memories as well as exhaustion.

"Adam," asked Jeannie almost against her will, "what is Hansen's disease?"

"Leprosy." Again, that tragic, bitter word. "I was trying . . . *we* were trying to find a treatment; we'd hoped even to find a cure for it. But because of the hateful, blind prejudice we were driven out. The mob even killed Anson—" Adam choked a sob and continued, "one of my patients that we'd fought so hard to keep alive."

Jeannie was unable to bear the pain in his voice any longer. "Here, drink this," she said as she lifted the cup of tea to his lips.

He obeyed almost like a child; he carefully drank the warm liquid, trying to calm himself. "We had no choice but to take the two remaining patients and go to the hospital at Indian Camp, upriver from New Orleans. The facilities there were so lacking, so barbaric, that to call it a hospital was a farce." His expression was bitterly dark. "At any rate, they dismissed me last July for . . . for insubordination."

With an understanding nod her eyes met his as she confessed, "I can believe that. But I can't believe you didn't have cause."

"I thought so at the time." His eyes closed again and for a long while he was silent. When he finally spoke he stated, "I don't know why I'm telling you all this."

"I do," she assured softly. "You've been carrying it around far too long, and you need to share your burdens. And . . . and I've wanted you to tell me."

"Why?" The word was no more than a sigh.

"You know why. Because I care about you, because when you hurt, I hurt, and I know how bad you've been hurting."

"You're an extraordinary woman, Jeannie."

"I am only what God has made of me."

"God." Adam took a deep, shuddering breath. "I never

thought much about God before Bethany became ill. And then when she died with so little left to her—" He paused and added carefully, "She was the finest person I've ever known, and she loved God, went to Mass even more than was required, said her prayers, did everything she was supposed to. Only it wasn't because she was supposed to; it was because she wanted to. She had given her whole heart and life to God. And when she died, I became convinced that God didn't exist except in the minds of people like Bethany who want to believe, who . . . who need a crutch."

"A crutch? Is that how you see God?" Her brown eyes were filled with compassion for the hurting, misguided man before her.

"What did He do for Bethany . . . or Carrie, for that matter?" he asked angrily. "It took everything I had to keep from telling you to stop filling Carrie's mind with those useless hopes. And when I talked with Luce yesterday, it was the final straw. Useless," he murmured again.

"It isn't useless. Carrie died happy in the knowledge of God's love." She stared directly into his eyes. "You need that love, that forgiveness that only God can give, before you can begin to forgive yourself, to love yourself."

"Love myself?" He groaned. "I hate myself! I'm a failure. I failed Bethany, and all those who depended on me at Indian Camp, and Carrie. Poor Carrie . . . I'm nothing, nothing." He turned his head away from her, but she could see the terrible shaking of his body as it was wracked by silent sobs.

Jeannie waited until he quieted, knowing that this was as crucial a time as Adam Jarrett had ever faced in his life. She could see, now, that he had suffered many terrible things. Finally she spoke in a low, intense voice, "Adam, because you may have failed in the past doesn't mean your entire life is a complete failure." She paused now as though she were searching for the right words. "Give me your hand." She reached for it when he made no move. "I'm going to pray aloud, Adam. Is that all right?" Still no response, but he didn't say no.

As she closed her eyes, his right hand clasped hers tightly. "Dear Father, I come before you with an open heart, needing your wisdom and guidance now more than ever before. I know you've been calling Adam, and that you know all about his hurts, wounds, failures, and defeats. He has a deep need for you, Lord, and I pray that you will come now and fill it. Oh, Father God, I thank you that you care! I thank you that you never give up on us, that you sent Jesus, your own Son, to die for us . . ."

The hush that fell over them both when she ceased to speak aloud was like nothing Adam had ever experienced. It was as though someone other than Jeannie was waiting for him to decide something. *Someone?* He frowned slightly. *But who?* There were only himself and Jeannie Gallagher, her bright head bowed low, in the room . . . weren't there?

He knew suddenly that it was not so, that God was with them, and His Holy Spirit, and His own Son.

The question burned within him. "Jeannie, what did you mean when you said He sent His Son to die for us?"

Joy stirred within her as she replied, "For God so loved the world . . . that he gave his only begotten Son, that whosoever believeth in him should not perish, but have everlasting life . . ."

"Is there more?"

"Oh, yes, Adam, there's much more!" Jeannie said. Her breath caught in her throat, however, for she knew what was happening. Adam's heart was opening, his soul was reaching toward God. "For God sent not his Son into the world to condemn the world, but that the world through him might be saved."

"Saved . . . what does that mean? Saved from what?"

"From yourself, from all the doubts and fears and guilt and sins, and horrible memories, from the pain and misery they cause. From the world and anything that would make slaves of us." She held his eyes with hers. "Do you want to be free from all that?"

He didn't hesitate. "I do."

"Then you must tell the Father right now, and ask His Son, His Spirit to come live within you."

"But I don't know how."

Closing her eyes again for a brief moment, Jeannie tenderly continued. "Within your heart, dear Adam, invite the Lord to come into your life. Tell him you're sorry for running from Him. Ask Him to forgive you and to take away all the hurts and sins and then thank Him for doing it."

When Jeannie slowly lifted her head and saw his face, she

knew it had happened, for Adam's expression was alight with relief and peace. She saw such joy in his eyes, it made the warm tears slide down her own face just as they were glistening on his. The room filled with an overwhelming presence of peace.

Afterword

A merry heart doeth good like a medicine. . . . Proverbs 17:22

Adam Jarrett accepted another gift from God a couple months later as he and Jeannie stood before a beaming Brother Teale and were united in marriage. As she had wanted—and Adam had been in complete agreement—the wedding was celebrated outside.

The first whispers of spring had become a lovely chorus. Wild azaleas and redbud spangled the abundant, new green of the April grass; the ferns offered a lacy background for the heady fragrance of the honeysuckle and magnolia blossoms. There were coral-root orchids and forget-me-nots tucked in Jeannie's bridal bouquet, twined in her hair. That bright hair shone like fire in the sunlight, dazzling the already bemused groom. The bridal party made a striking sight. Grizzled Jude stood next to the tall, broad-shouldered Adam. Landra, Adam's sister-in-law, stood next to the bride.

There was a large crowd of both Thicket dwellers and boomers gathered to watch—all wishing nothing but good to the pair that meant something special to each of them.

As the minister spoke the familiar words of the marriage ceremony in his strong, homely voice, Mrs. Gallagher sniffed and Jude tried not to. Rob and Luce sat on either side of Grannie Annie, who obviously thought of herself as grandmother of the bride. Hollis, holding his and Landra's hefty baby boy, beamed joyously as he watched the couple take their vows.

"Do you, Adam, take this woman to be your lawfully wedded wife, to love her, honor her, cherish her, as long as you both shall live?"

Adam looked down into the endless depths of Jeannie's alive

237

brown eyes; he saw the shining, everlasting love and peace in them. "I do," he declared, his voice low, but clear and firm.

With this woman at his side, with her courage, her love, with the love of God he himself had come to know, he was certain they could face whatever came. The depth of richness God had brought into his life overwhelmed him. He almost felt light-headed.

He heard her reply, in answer to the question he had missed, "Yes, I do."

She gazed up at him, her eyes filled with the same certainty he felt.

Having completed the ceremony, the minister said happily, "You may kiss your bride."

Brother Teale's words echoed in the hush, and as Adam lowered his head to touch the lips of his bride with his own, he knew that his heart was free now to love her, to enjoy her sweetness, the steadfastness of her heart and life. And, together, they were free to serve and love the One who had made it all possible.